A Glorious Christmas

Christmas Town Book 5

by

Ginny Baird

A GLORIOUS CHRISTMAS
Christmas Town Book 5

Published by
Winter Wedding Press

Copyright © 2018
Ginny Baird
Trade Paperback
ISBN 978-1-942058-34-2

Edited by Sally Knapp
Cover by Dar Albert

About the Author

From the time she could talk, romance author Ginny Baird was making up stories, much to the delight—and consternation—of her family and friends. By grade school, she'd turned that inclination into a talent, whereby her teacher allowed her to write and produce plays rather than write boring book reports. Ginny continued writing throughout college, where she contributed articles to her literary campus weekly, then later pursued a career managing international projects with the U.S. State Department.

Ginny has held an assortment of jobs, including schoolteacher, freelance fashion model, and greeting card writer, and has published more than twenty works of fiction and optioned ten screenplays. She has also published short stories, nonfiction, and poetry, and admits to being a true romantic at heart.

Ginny is a *New York Times* and *USA Today* bestselling author of several books, including novellas in her Holiday Brides Series. She's a member of Romance Writers of America (RWA) and Novelists, Inc. (NINC).

When she's not writing, Ginny enjoys cooking, biking, and spending time with her family in Tidewater, Virginia. She loves hearing from her readers and welcomes visitors to her website at http://www.ginnybairdromance.com.

Books by Ginny Baird

Christmas Town Series
The Christmas Cookie Shop
A Mommy for Christmas
Only You at Christmas
The Doctor Orders Christmas
A Glorious Christmas

Holiday Brides Series
The Christmas Catch
The Holiday Bride
Mistletoe in Maine
Beach Blanket Santa
Baby, Be Mine
Jingle Bell Babies

Summer Grooms Series
Must-Have Husband
My Lucky Groom
The Wedding Wish
The Getaway Groom

Romantic Ghost Stories
The Ghost Next Door (A Love Story)
The Light at the End of the Road
The House at Homecoming Cove

Romantic Comedy
Real Romance
The Sometime Bride
Santa Fe Fortune
How to Marry a Matador
Counterfeit Cowboy
The Calendar Brides
My Best Friend's Bride
The Borrowed Boyfriend
Tara (Beach Brides Book 2)
Crazy for You

Bundles
Christmas Magic:
The Complete Holiday Brides Series (Books 1 – 5)
The Holiday Brides Collection (Books 1–4)
A Summer Grooms Selection (Books 1–3)
Romantic Ghost Stories (Books 1 – 3)
Real Romance and The Sometime Bride
(Gemini Editions 1)
Santa Fe Fortune and How to Marry a Matador
(Gemini Editions 2)
My Best Friend's Bride and
The Borrowed Boyfriend
(Gemini Editions 3)
Wedding Bells Bundle

Short Story
Special Delivery
(A Valentine's Short Story)

Ginny Baird's

A GLORIOUS CHRISTMAS

Chapter One

Gloria Chavez stared out her passenger-side window at the gorgeous Christmas Inn, as fast-falling snowflakes cascaded around it. The house looked like something out of the movies, its structure combining small-town charm with old-world grandeur. The large two-story home was painted white, with black shutters. Its dark green front door held an enormous Christmas wreath brimming with fresh pinecones and red holly berries. The covered wraparound porch sheltered a collection of big white rockers. Two whimsical reindeer sculptures bedecked with twinkling Christmas lights flanked the entrance, welcoming travelers from afar. Fresh greenery draped from the porch railings and the worn flagstone path leading up to the stoop had been shoveled nearly clean, showcasing snowdrifts more than a foot deep on either side.

Gloria pulled into the vacant parking spot by the curb and cut off her ignition. The moment her SUV's wiper blades quit swishing, the front windshield became coated in snow. Dusk was settling in, the limited daylight fading quickly. A little ways ahead of her, Gloria spied the blinking taillights of a mail truck, evidently making a late afternoon delivery to the mailbox on the street in front of the Christmas Inn. As long as Gloria was headed indoors, she could be a thoughtful guest and bring in the mail. She only had one small suitcase anyway. Unlike her friend, Savannah, Gloria didn't pack her entire wardrobe for one short getaway. Gloria wasn't planning to stay in Christmas Town for more than a brief while. Just long enough to help Savannah through her ongoing panic attacks about the baby Savannah was sure was coming any minute now.

Gloria intended to assist Savannah with making preparations for the baby, and had also volunteered to assume some of Savannah's duties in running the local children's theater during the transition. The theater had a Christmas puppet show programmed for mid-month, and Savannah was in a tizzy about pulling everything together in time. Gloria would lend her theatrical expertise in coordinating the production, and therefore ease some of the pursuant worries stressing her friend. Gloria loved Savannah dearly. She was the closest thing to a sister that Gloria had. So, Gloria was happy to take the extra time off from her job as a high school drama teacher in Miami to come to Savannah's aid.

Her big musical of the semester was done, and her students were scheduled for end-of-term projects and exams. Gloria made arrangements to grade the term papers and enter her grades remotely from Tennessee, while a substitute would administer the final exams, which could be graded electronically. Gloria was only missing ten full days of school anyway, since this was just before the holiday break. She hadn't taken one day's leave in nearly five years, and—fortunately for

Gloria—her new principal was a new mother herself, and therefore very understanding of Gloria's desire to support her best friend in her time of prenatal need.

After the baby's arrival, Savannah's mother Janet would come from Virginia to help. Plus, Kurt had tons of family in town, including his parents and two brothers. One of them, Walt Christmas, ran the Christmas Inn. He was a single dad to college-age twins and purported to be very handsome. Particularly when Savannah was doing the reporting. She'd been hinting at getting Gloria and Walt together for months now. Not that this made any sense to Gloria, since her life was in Florida. Apart from her teaching job, Gloria had several ties to her community, not the least of which was her baby brother, David. Although he was a grown man with his own career and personal life, Gloria couldn't help her mother-hen instincts to still look after him. She certainly wasn't moving several states away to some magical winter wonderland to...

Gloria drew in a deep breath, stopping herself. *Moving! Ha! Here I go, getting carried away again.* With Gloria's imagination, that was an easy task. She was always thinking one step ahead! Imagining a bigger picture! A large beautiful canvas of broad color strokes! Because that's how Gloria was: optimistic and forward-thinking. Always seeing the good in life, and imagining its greatest possibilities. And, in this picturesque East Tennessee town, almost anything seemed possible. Savannah had been accurate in her description of the place. It was every bit as charming as she had said.

After exiting the highway, Gloria had spent a brief bit on a bypass before entering the town via a roundabout housing a large courthouse building and a library. A high flagpole stood in its center, towering above a snow-dusted sign: *Welcome to Christmas Town, Tennessee... Where everyday dreams come true!* Gloria sighed happily, realizing they'd certainly come true for Savannah. Her life had also once been in Miami. But that was before she'd reconnected with her long-lost love, and Christmas Town native, Kurt Christmas.

As she'd driven down South Main Street, which became North Main Street at the T-intersection with the Grand Hotel, Gloria had passed all the fun shops Savannah had told her about. Savannah's sister, Olivia, ran the business All Things Christmas, and Savannah's favored coffee shop, Jolly Bean Java, was right across the way. The one grocery store in town, the Merry Market, was on the corner beside that, and a quaint eatery, Santa's Sandwich Shop, stood on the other side of Jolly Bean Java. Then there was the string of cool places lining Santa Claus Lane, which began at the T-intersection facing the Grand Hotel and ended at the old train depot abutting forested and snow-capped mountains. Since trains had stopped coming to Christmas Town some time ago, the former station now served as the North Pole Nursery, run by Kurt's other brother, Ray, whose wife Meredith helped Ray run that business and also their Christmas tree farm.

Savannah had spoken glowingly of the Snow Globe Gallery, on the other corner across from the Grand Hotel, and the delectable candy store, Nutcracker Sweets, beside it. The Elf Shelf Bookshop was great for coffee and browsing, too. But no business in town had a reputation to match that of Hannah Livingston's Christmas Cookie Shop. People came from miles around to purchase Hannah's special holiday cookies, which were supposedly imbued with all sorts of magical properties. Gloria had found Savannah's stories about Hannah's cookies cute, but she hardly believed that baked goods could inspire good works, forgiveness, or true love! In Gloria's experience, the way to a man's heart was through a hearty roast beef, served with garlic mashed potatoes and greens. Not that Gloria was planning on cooking for any men here in Christmas Town. And, she certainly wasn't after capturing anyone's heart!

Gloria adjusted her white faux-fur hat on her head and flipped down her driver's side mirror, briefly examining her reflection. Long brown hair tumbled past the shoulders of her matching faux-fur coat, which extended all the way to her calves, meeting the hilts of the knee-high white pleather boots complementing her itchy white gloves. Gloria's fingers were growing sweaty inside them. Surely, she wasn't nervous about being in Christmas Town. She was more likely overheated because she wasn't used to dressing this warmly in Miami.

Gloria hadn't even owned a winter coat prior to this trip. She'd had to go on an enormous shopping spree before packing. Well, the spree had seemed enormous to her, anyway. For clotheshorse Savannah, the pair of white jeans, couple of sweaters, and sparkly red ball gown Gloria purchased would have seemed like nothing. The ball gown had been bought at Savannah's insistence that Gloria come prepared. In the event her stay ran over, Gloria might get to attend the annual Christmas Town Ball on Christmas Eve! Savannah had even sneakily suggested that Gloria might go as Walt's date.

Just the thought of finally meeting him made Gloria's blood pump harder. It wasn't like it was a big deal. Really. With the current restoration of Sisters' Row, which housed the only rental close by, alternate accommodations were basically nonexistent in Christmas Town, which didn't even have one meager hotel. Savannah's house was small, and she was too overwrought to host a visitor. Even a visitor she thought of as family and adored.

Gloria didn't take offense. Savannah was the sweetest woman on earth, but a little high-strung that way. So Walt had generously offered Gloria a place at the Christmas Inn. He typically didn't rent out rooms during this time of year, since he reserved the house for his family. As his sister-in-law Savannah's best friend, Gloria was close enough to "family" to qualify. At least, that's what Walt had stated amicably in his e-mail when he'd invited Gloria to stay at the inn for free. Although Gloria was pretty sure Savannah had put him up to it.

She met her own dark eyes in the mirror and addressed herself seriously.

"Walt Christmas," she said with a nod. "So nice to meet you."

No, that's too stuffy.

Gloria adjusted the tilt of the fluffy pillbox hat. "Walt, hey!" Her mouth broadened in a grin, then Gloria quickly pressed her lips together. *Seriously. I shouldn't have gone with the tooth whitening so close to this trip. Even if my dentist did say it would perk up my smile for the holidays!*

Gloria's gleaming pearly whites made her look like she was trying too hard. And, for what? It wasn't like she had anyone to impress! Gloria self-consciously licked her lips, thinking nobody would probably notice her teeth anyway. They weren't supposed to be this shockingly white. It had been one of those fluke things that typically seemed to happen to Gloria. While she'd waited in the dental chair with the whitening trays clenched between her teeth, her dentist had been presented with a last-minute dental emergency. Unfortunately, this emergency kept the dentist in another patient bay for longer than intended. Hence, Gloria's extra bright smile—at no extra charge! Great. Right.

She coughed lightly and blinked at her reflection, trying again. "Walt Christmas!" There was just the right amount of sugar and politeness in her tone, as she kept her grin close-lipped and tight. "I've heard so much about you."

Gloria's cheeks flushed brightly, and she realized she should omit that last part. What Gloria had and hadn't heard about the eligible bachelor was absolutely nobody's business but her own! And Gloria fully intended to keep it that way.

She inhaled deeply and gathered her resolve, as she grabbed her purse and exited her SUV. Next, she popped open the back door and nabbed her sole piece of luggage off the floor behind the driver's seat. Wintry winds blasted her in the face when she stood upright, and Gloria gave a startled gasp. This was a far cry from the balmy warmth of Miami, and Gloria wasn't one hundred percent sure her thin Florida blood was up to it. She'd better hustle toward that mailbox then make her way inside, posthaste.

Walt Christmas lowered the newspaper he was reading in the library, thinking he'd heard something outdoors. It sounded distinctly like wind chimes, a loud cacophony of musical sound coming from somewhere near the street. He folded the newspaper over and placed it on the coffee table before the low-burning hearth. Three Christmas stockings hung from the mantel in the cozy room that contained facing wing chairs by the fireplace.

Walt cocked his ear and listened again to the crazy wind chimes outdoors. Their sound seemed to echo back through the house, resonating down the front hall and bouncing off the walls of his lushly decorated library. Queen Anne–style tables accompanied each of the wing chairs, holding ornate gold lamps, fashioned like winged angels and supporting broad bell-shaped shades. The table by the chair directly across from Walt held a red crystal candy dish, which was kept stocked with treats of the season. At the moment, it was loaded with one of Walt's favorite sweets: peppermint bark.

The antique gold chenille sofa facing the hearth had carved mahogany details, and a large assortment of patterned throw cushions across its back, some in paisley print and others with stripes, all complementing the warm colors of the room. Plush Persian carpets crowned polished hardwood floors, and Walt's roll-top desk was in one corner while a nicely decorated Christmas tree stood in another.

Built-in bookshelves, lining the dark-paneled walls, brimmed with tomes on numerous topics: domestic and international travel, regional history, art, literature, geography, psychology, and science. An entire section was dedicated to holiday lore, most particularly Christmas, and another part of the collection featured classic and contemporary fiction. Young adult novels were included as well, in addition to a smattering of picture books for children. The sturdy wooden toy box, painted with a turquoise hobby horse design, sat near Walt's desk. Walt had built it for his girls when they were young, and it was filled with handcrafted toys made by Walt's dad, the girls' grandpa, Buddy Christmas.

A separate seating group by a south-facing window included a brown leather recliner beside a reading lamp and a red-and-green plaid loveseat with a sturdy matching armchair. The shorter coffee table in front of them contained an ongoing jigsaw puzzle, which generally portrayed a Christmas scene. An old dictionary stood on a metal stand on one side of the door leading into the long downstairs hall, and a century-old globe angled proudly to the right of the opening adjoining the living room at the front of the house. The globe stood three feet tall and the upper portion of the earth-toned orb was tilted to exhibit Canada's Maritime Provinces, highlighted by the muted glow of the tasteful track lighting that also illuminated portions of the bookshelves.

The wind chimes sounded again—more fiercely this time—and Walt leapt to his feet, hustling into the hall and toward the front door. Walt kept three sets of wind chimes of various sizes on the covered front porch of the Christmas Inn, and each was tuned to a different key. The stoutly made Gregorian chimes could generally tolerate winter weather. Even in Christmas Town, where winter weather persisted from early November through late March. Normally, the wind chimes' gentle timbre played a soothing symphony on Walt's front porch, their various tones blending harmoniously like ancient monks' chants. Yet, at the moment, those faithful chimes were howling sharply, their ferocious *gong*s, *ping*s, and *tinkle*s clanking back into the house like percussion instruments gone haywire.

Walt quickened his pace, beholding a strange sight through the sidelight window to the left of the front door. Gusty winds blew snow sideways as huge white flakes sailed up onto the stoop and slammed against the glass. *Wait! Huh?* Walt fixed his gaze out the window, sharpening his focus. There was something fluttering through the air above Walt's front lawn! Lots of somethings!

For the life of him, the floating and soaring rectangles looked like—envelopes?

Walt jerked open the front door, his heart pounding. He could scarcely believe his eyes. It seemed his daily mail delivery had somehow broken free from his mailbox, like a stampede of galloping horses wild-hoofing it out of a burning barn. Letters danced up toward the sky, then spun toward the ground, before fluttering their way toward the clouds again. Something that appeared to be a real estate flyer hovered above the walkway, and a postcard stood on its end twirling around and around and around, just out of reach of a woman's white gloves.

She had long brown hair and wore an unusual-looking boxy white hat that matched her knee-length white coat and boots, as she bounded after the evasive object. "Oh! Whoa! No! Come back here!" She reached up high and snagged the dancing postcard, pinning it to her chest with a clutch of mail she already held there. Then, she cagily sprang to the right and caught an errant letter. The pretty brunette spied the vibrating real estate flyer over the walk and she grabbed that next. She finally looked up in a panic and stared straight at Walt.

He viewed her, dumbstruck, as heavy white snowflakes coated her shoulders and hat, and dusted her ebony locks. Her hair fell in long, loose coils past her shoulders as her cheeks burned bright pink. And, her big dark eyes were the loveliest shade of chocolate brown Walt had ever seen.

"Walt Christmas?" she asked, her brow furrowing sweetly.

When he nodded, she grimaced and raised her shoulders, still gripping his mail. "Hi," she said, appearing the slightest bit abashed. Though Walt was the one who should be embarrassed by the wacky correspondence display. While Gloria couldn't know this, he was quite sure he had caused it. Which could only mean one thing.

Walt's heart stuttered and the mysteriously floating mail abruptly tumbled to the ground.

The woman blinked, glancing around in awe, then she settled her eyes back on Walt. She spoke trance-like, carefully surveying Walt's eyes. "I'm—"

"Gloria Chavez," Walt said, utterly dazed. "I know."

His perusal swept over her and Gloria's face burned hot. Savannah's glowing assessment of Walt's stellar looks had not been understated. He had wavy dark hair and a neatly trimmed mustache and beard, and was over six feet tall. Lean, well built...with a dash of he-man sexiness about him, Walt Christmas stood there on his front porch wearing faded jeans and a gray wool sweater. Beneath it Gloria spied the collar of a red-checkered flannel shirt. Though he was probably over forty, Walt could have passed for a man in his late thirties, due to his fit, athletic form and that youthful spark in his sky blue eyes. Small lines formed around them when he smiled and Gloria's heart skipped a beat. "How was your trip?"

"Uneventful." Gloria swallowed hard. "Until now!"

She couldn't believe she'd made such a mess of this introduction. Not only that, she'd nearly lost all of Walt's mail! Gloria had no clue where those ultra brisk winds had come from. One second, she was opening Walt's mailbox, then the next thing she knew, envelopes were flying all over the place! And, the music! Wow! It had been astounding! Like a heavenly host of angels singing all at once! Only these voices had sounded like bells. No...wind chimes, she thought, spotting them still dancing on Walt's front porch, though they were playing a lot more daintily now that the wind had died down.

Walt bounded off the stoop and headed in her direction. Gloria thought he was coming to greet her, or maybe shake her hand. Suddenly her hands felt sweaty in her gloves again. Then, to her dismay, Walt walked right past her. "Where are you…?" Gloria pivoted around to see him striding toward the carry-on bag she'd left on the sidewalk.

He lifted it easily and queried, "This all you got? Or is there more in your car?" She was surprised he wasn't freezing, since he hadn't bothered to put on a coat. Then again, Walt was probably used to the weather up here. According to Savannah, he'd lived in Christmas Town his entire life—apart from a stint to attend college in Virginia.

"Nope! That's it!" Gloria nervously stooped low to gather the rest of the mail that was scattered about on the walkway and resting on the snowy lawn. Though they'd only been on the ground a few minutes, the edges of the envelopes were already moist. She shook them out and added them to the collection of correspondence she held. "I'm really sorry about your mail," she said, as Walt drew nearer. "The wind! It just—"

"Totally not your fault!" His perusal was warm and friendly. "How about we get inside?" he asked, motioning toward the house, where he'd left the front door partially ajar. "It's a bit warmer in there, and lot less windy." His smile sparkled. "Plus, we've got cocoa on the stove."

"Hot cocoa?" Gloria grinned eagerly, then she quickly pursed her lips, self-conscious about her smile.

Walt shot her a curious look. "My daughter Noelle's just made a full pot."

Gloria nodded and trailed after him as Walt led her inside. When he shut the door behind them, he set down her suitcase, and held out his hand. "Thanks for grabbing the mail."

She passed it to him with an embarrassed flush. "Next time, I'll try to hold onto it."

"No worries." His mouth tipped up in a grin and Gloria's pulse raced. Yep. He was definitely handsome. There was no point in denying that. "Happens to the best of us."

"Well, it's never happened to me!" Gloria exclaimed, speaking the truth. The way those letters had escaped from her was uncanny. They'd bolted right out of her hands! What's more, each piece of mail seemed to be evading her grasp, like it had developed a mind of its own! *Though that's crazy, right? Surely all in my head.*

She viewed Walt perplexedly. "Wait a minute… Are you saying this weird flying mail thing has happened to you before?"

"No!" he answered quickly. He swallowed hard. "Not in a…really, really long while. The wind around here can sometimes be…" With his free hand, Walt rubbed the back of his neck. "Unpredictable."

Gloria blinked, wondering if she'd packed enough in the way of warm clothing. "Gosh."

"It doesn't happen often," Walt rushed to assure her. He searched her eyes and for a fleeting instant Gloria felt seriously faint. Probably because she was overdressed in this silly coat and hat now that they were inside. It clearly wasn't due to the way Walt looked at her, almost like he could see straight through her. Or right into her heart and head.

Color swept his temples as he held her gaze. He voice sounded rough when he added, "Almost never, to tell you the truth."

Gloria got the distinct impression that Walt was hinting at something, but she was having difficulty deciphering *what.* All she knew was that, try as she might, she couldn't look away. It was like Walt had entranced her somehow with his rugged, manly frame and those deep blue eyes. He smelled good, too. Deliciously yummy...of warm citrus and spice, with the slightest hint of—toasted coconut. *Huh?*

Gloria's heart thumped harder as the seconds ticked by and Walt seemed to try to read something in her eyes. She tried reading his right back. But that only made her feel more lightheaded, like she was getting swept away by large ocean waves. In a weird sort of way, she could almost hear them crashing—*ker-splash, ker-splash, ker-splash*—and tumbling against the craggy shore. Seagulls soared and warm breezes blew, transporting Gloria somewhere far away. Somewhere with sun and sand, and happiness. Somewhere with Walt Christmas.

Gloria's cell jangled loudly, breaking the spell between them with its Christmas ringtone, "Frosty the Snowman," and Gloria jumped. The jolt back to reality hit her like an icy blast of air. Gloria wasn't sure what had just happened to her, but it had felt strange, transformative, and...lovely. She resisted a sigh and mentally pulled herself together.

Walt scrutinized her oddly, appearing taken aback himself. Whatever had gone on just then, he must have felt it, too. He didn't look shocked in a bad way. More like pleasantly surprised. Pleasantly surprised, and more than a bit befuddled. Which made this grown man in a full beard look pretty adorable, actually.

Gloria ducked her chin to hide her blush and removed her cell from her purse. The caller was Savannah. "I should probably take this," she apologetically told Walt.

He nodded in understanding and laid the mail on the foyer table. Next, he motioned toward the back of the hall. "I'll just go and…" He paused to clear his throat, which had clogged up on him all of a sudden. "Set your suitcase in your room," he finished with some degree of difficulty, as his neck flushed red. "When you're done with your call, you can meet Noelle and me in the kitchen." He pointed to an elegantly decorated parlor to Gloria's left and through it she spied the end of a large dining room table. "It's right through…there."

Chapter Two

Walt slipped from the foyer and Gloria accepted the call, pressing her cell to her ear. "Savannah, hi!"

"Where on earth *are* you?" Savannah sounded breathless and more than mildly panicked.

"I'm here!"

"Where *here*? In Christmas Town, here?"

"At the Christmas Inn, here!"

"*Squeeee!*" Seconds later, Savannah sounded more serious. "Then why haven't you come on over?"

"Because, *chica*. I've only just arrived." Gloria was still kind of catching her breath, too. Though she decided not to mention her earlier eye-lock with Walt to Savannah, as Savannah would surely have a field day with it.

Gloria stepped into the parlor and got a clear view of the dining room with its impressive mahogany table, which had seating for twelve. A tall vase of stargazer lilies stood in the center, dark pink speckled blooms opening on some of the flowers, while others were still closed buds. Sweet fragrance wafted toward her, filling this section of the downstairs, where heavy green velvet green curtains hung in swags, pulled back by rich gold cords. "Boy, this place is fancy!"

Everywhere she looked, expensive Persian carpets lined the floors, polished walnut gleaming beneath them. The furnishings were old-world, but stylish, with an ornate gold-framed mirror hanging over the fireplace in the parlor, and a wintry landscape painted in oils hanging above another fireplace in the dining room. "*Whoa*," she whispered into the receiver. "How many fireplaces does this house have?"

"Seven or eig— You know," Savannah said, stopping herself. "You can get Walt to give you the full tour later. But for now... *Ow! Ow! Ow! Ohhhhhh!*" Her cries rose on an alarming crescendo.

"Savannah? Are you—?"

"It's coming! Oh my goodness, the baby! It's—"

"Savannah," Gloria commanded steadily. "Take a deep breath. It's too ear—"

"*Yeooowwww!* It hurts, Gloria! It *hurts!*"

"Did you call Kurt?"

"Of course I called Kurt!"

"Well? What did he—?"

"Braxton..." Savannah puffed out a breath then she started panting—hard. "Hicks... He said to call him back in fifteen minutes, if it doesn't get better. But, what am I supposed to do in the meantime?"

"Just calm down, and I'll be there as soon as I—"

"Don't wait too long! I don't want to have this baby aloooo—*oh, oh, oh—own!*"

Gloria massaged her steaming forehead beneath the brim of her fluffy white hat then yanked the accessory off. What if Savannah truly was in labor? And, all by herself and desperate? "Okay, all right. Sit tight. Let me—"

"I can't sit!" Savannah whimpered. "It's like someone has hitched a strap around my middle and cinched it *innnnn*! Ohhhh!" She let out another convincing moan, and Gloria's temperature spiked. While Savannah had complained about contractions before, she'd never seemed to suffer this badly. Maybe this actually was for real!

"I won't even take off my coat," Gloria replied in a rush. "I'll be right there."

Walt stepped into the downstairs guest suite, completely unnerved by the episode with the flying mail. Not to mention that connective moment with Gloria. When she'd looked at him with those big, dark eyes, Walt had experienced an incredible urge to take her away—to someplace utterly fantastic and beautiful. Not that he would have done that. Of course not... Even if he still could! And, Walt was quite unsure about the current state of his abilities. They were far beyond rusty. The fact was he hadn't used them in years! And yet, something mighty strange seemed to be happening here.

Though he'd attempted to play it cool in front of pretty Gloria, his blood had pumped harder and he'd felt all jittery inside—almost nauseated, honestly—at the realization that certain things were beyond his control. Walt had been controlling his life just fine for the past, oh...decade. Why had Gloria's arrival suddenly set things on end? He'd known she was coming ever since Savannah had arranged it near the beginning of her pregnancy.

Savannah and Kurt's cottage was a cute one-and-a-half-story affair with one bedroom and a tiny office that was scarcely big enough for a nursery. If Gloria had stayed there she would have needed to sleep on the sofa, and share the single bathroom with the newlyweds. Walt's younger brother, Kurt, had married Savannah in early February, and it hadn't taken long for the young couple to get started on their family. It also hadn't taken Savannah long to start dropping hints about her gorgeous Latina friend in Miami, with not-so-veiled insinuations about how fabulously Walt and Gloria would get on.

You're quiet; Gloria's outgoing! She's smart, and so are you! Plus, neither of you is "married, married, married." Walt had gaped at Savannah when she'd said this last part. Walt had been married. One time, and his union with Rose had been excellent. He wasn't planning on sullying that memory by trying to start over unsuccessfully with someone else. And it would be unsuccessful, too. No relationship survived when a man's heart wasn't in it. And Walt's heart most certainly would not be into this one. No matter how remarkably gorgeous and talented Gloria Chavez was.

He'd tried to tell this to Savannah, but she'd become rather pigheaded about it, insisting that, since she knew them both, she was the perfect one to tell they'd make an ideal match. Before moving back to Christmas Town, Savannah hadn't struck Walt as the matchmaking sort. Now, it seemed she couldn't stop herself. She was nearly as bad as Kurt, or—worse yet—Walt's mom, Louise. As Christmas Town's mayor, Lou prided herself on knowing everybody's business, and making sure those "businesses" ran just as smoothly as she imagined they should.

Walt loved his family; he really did. But, at times, certain members of it could be really big buttinskies. Yet, Walt was okay with that. He'd been deflecting his mother's attempts to pair him up with someone for the past few years, and he could withstand Savannah's meddling, too.

But, it was no longer Savannah's meddling that concerned Walt the most. It was the other crazy stuff that had happened today! There had to be a reasonable explanation for that. Nerves, more than likely. Savannah had been hounding him so hard about Gloria's upcoming visit that Walt had somehow manage to freak himself out about it.

Not that Savannah wasn't right about Gloria. She clearly was a gorgeous woman. Gloria was apparently smart and agile, too. She'd exhibited a great deal of dexterity while trying to pin down Walt's flying mail. Walt was sure there was a simple explanation for the fluttering correspondence incident. Just as he knew there was a decent reason for him experiencing that mental lapse while gazing into Gloria's dark brown eyes.

Hopefully, these episodes were merely minor blips on Walt's lifeline. Things that had occurred on the fly, as it were, and that would simply go away... Once Walt put his mind to ignoring them hard enough, that was.

If the issues continued, however, Walt might need to see his brother, Kurt, about them. Apart from being a fine physician, Kurt was truly talented in managing certain "maladies" common to the Claus and Christmas families. In the meantime, Walt would do well to play things as normally as possible between him and Gloria, and hopefully his system would reboot itself, putting Walt back on track. He'd been a single dad forever now, and the lifestyle suited him fine. No need to go stirring up trouble, just because his girls would be graduating from college soon, and likely moving away.

Walt tried hard not to contemplate that as he placed Gloria's suitcase on the luggage rack to the left of the four-poster bed. A nightstand was beside the bed, with a comfortable reading chair on the other side of it. The blue glass lamp on the nightstand had been crafted from an old-fashioned oil lamp. Its cream-colored lampshade matched the others in the room and picked up the lighter hues of the colorful patchwork quilt on the bed that had been handmade by Walt's late great-grandmother Christmas. The Christmas Inn was once the home she shared with Walt's great-grandpa, and their family of seven children. Their third son, Stephen, was Walt's grandfather, and his father's—Buddy Christmas's—dad.

This was a grand old house, which Walt and his late wife Rose had restored to its original beauty. For a time, it had passed out of the Christmas family and had eventually become abandoned. When Walt moved back to Christmas Town with Rose, he did so with the singular ambition of repurposing this historic family property as the Christmas Inn. Rose, who was a genius at interior design, was delighted to help him. They were already expecting their twins, Noelle and Joy, and couldn't imagine a more pleasant spot than Christmas Town for raising their family. It was ten years ago this

Christmas that their sweet family had been broken apart.

Each year, as a part of their family tradition, three Christmas stockings hung from the mantel in the library. One for each of Walt's twins, and the other in memory of their mother. Walt felt a melancholy tug on his heartstrings, when he realized only Noelle would be here to open her stocking this year. Joy, an art major in college, was spending her junior year abroad in Florence, Italy, and Walt knew that he and Noelle would miss her badly. In fact, he already did, and had…every single moment since he'd put his precious baby girl—who was now a gifted and beautiful young woman—on that plane. Yet, she was having the time of her life. Walt was grateful Joy could have that enriching experience.

Walt turned toward the hall, thinking he'd better make his way into the kitchen. He'd tarried long enough, and Gloria was likely done with her call and presently conversing with Noelle over hot cocoa. As Gloria's host and the owner of the Christmas Inn, Walt needed to make sure she got comfortably settled in. He'd also need to provide her with directions to Savannah's house, which wouldn't be difficult since Savannah and Kurt lived right down the street.

Gloria peeked into the kitchen and a pretty young woman with long blond hair and big blue eyes looked up. She wore glasses with heavy, cranberry-colored frames and sat on a stool, flipping through a women's magazine on the counter that extended from the center island. "Hi!" Her pleasant features lit up in a grin. "You must be Gloria!"

"You must be Noelle." Gloria smiled warmly. "Savannah's told me so many great things about you! You're a writer, I hear?"

"Hope to be." Color warmed Noelle's cheeks. "Someday!" She scooted off her stool and hustled over to the gas-stove cooktop on the other side of the center island, where a mid-size saucepan had been set to simmer. A gleaming, and very sleek-looking, stainless steel hood hovered above the impressive array of eight burners, and an elegant assortment of pots and pans hung from a dangling fixture above the midsection of the island. Gloria noted a double wall oven behind Noelle, and the built-in bookshelves surrounding a kitchen desk that were stuffed with cookbooks, some which appeared to be decades old.

The kitchen cabinets were painted white with brushed chrome drawer pulls, and the countertops, including the one on the center island, were a rich onyx. The black and white checkerboard tile floor complemented the inviting color scheme, which meshed hominess with the industrial strength required to outfit an inn. The deep-set, ivory porcelain farm sink sat below a large window with a view to the snowy backyard, where white-coated pines quivered in the wind.

Noelle stirred a wooden spoon in the pot and the heavenly aroma of rich dark chocolate filled the kitchen. "Cocoa?" the coed inquired. Savannah had told Gloria that both Noelle and her sister were juniors in college, but that the other twin—Joy—was away in Italy. "I just made it a few minutes ago."

"I'd love some, but I'm afraid I can't stay." Gloria dropped her cell back into her shoulder bag and began slipping on her gloves, as she held her hat under the crook of her arm.

"Leaving already?" a man's voice boomed. "I hope our company wasn't that bad."

Gloria stared toward the doorway connecting the breakfast area to what she assumed was the end of the front hall. Walt stood on the threshold, his blue eyes twinkling, and Gloria struggled with her composure. *What is it about that man! He's completely...unnerving.* "No, no. Not at all. The company here is terrific!" She drew in a quick breath and gave the glove portion covering her pinky finger a final tug. "It's just that I'm needed at Savannah's. That was her on the phone ... she sounded pretty panicked."

Noelle beamed with surprise. "The baby, already?"

"Could be Braxton Hicks." Walt astutely observed Gloria. "That's what's been going on all week, anyhow. According to Kurt."

"He said it's pretty common," Noelle concurred.

"Yeah, well...just in case!" Gloria nodded pleasantly at them both.

Walt met her gaze and Gloria's heart skipped a beat. "How about if you take a traveler?"

"A traveler?" Gloria asked weakly. "What's that?"

Noelle was one step ahead of her dad, and already pulling an insulated travel mug from a cabinet by the sink. "One of these!" she proclaimed, holding it up in full view. "If it's Braxton Hicks, you could be there a while. And, if it's not—"

"You might need your energy," Walt added with a wink and Gloria's cheeks warmed. What was it with her today? Oh yeah, she was overdressed. That's right. The sooner she got back out in the snow, the better. And she really *did* need to hightail it down to Savannah's. Although, that cocoa Noelle was ladling into the travel mug did look awfully good…

"I'd send some to Savannah," Noelle said, handing Gloria the travel mug. "But she's not supposed to have tons of chocolate these days."

Walt stared past Gloria's shoulder and blanched.

Noelle saw him looking that way, and raised her eyebrows in wonder. "But cookies and milk will do!" the young woman said. "There's some right there on the counter."

Gloria spun on her heel to find a cute, glass milk bottle sitting on the counter beside the sink. It looked like the old-fashioned kind that used to get delivered by a milk man, only it appeared to be a one-person serving. A festive red-and-green bow wound around the neck of the bottle, which contained a clamp-down cap. Beside it, a sweetly decorated cache of Christmas cookies nestled in a light green plastic baggie, secured with a glittery red ribbon in lieu of a twist tie.

"Milk and cookies, right!" Walt coughed loudly, seeming to have something stuck in his throat. "How about that?" He hacked again, and Noelle hustled over, soundly patting his back.

He waved his daughter away with an embarrassed look.

Gloria glanced at Noelle. "Water?"

"Sure!" Noelle opened a cabinet and quickly filled a glass from the water filter on the kitchen sink spigot. She handed Walt the glass and he took several long swallows before taking a breath.

"Thanks. I..." He glanced around, seeming out of sorts. "I'm...sorry about that!"

"No need to apologize. Gosh!" Gloria eyed him worriedly. "Are you all right?"

Walt shook his head and blinked. Then he shook his head again, harder this time.

Noelle's forehead creased with worry. "Dad?"

"Huh, yeah?" He seemed to snap out of it. "I'm fine! And, Noelle's absolutely right. Cookies and milk will be great for Savannah. Assuming she's not *really* in labor."

Gloria grinned then tamped her smile down a bit. "If she *is*, maybe *I'll* eat the cookies."

The others laughed at this as Noelle grabbed a small paper sack from a slide-out drawer beside the kitchen desk. Gloria saw it was embossed with a logo from the Christmas Inn.

After Noelle packaged the milk and cookies, she passed the sack to Gloria. Gloria was surprised to note that the milk was still ice cold. While she hadn't seen it initially, it couldn't have been sitting on the counter for very long as its chill even permeated the bag and her gloves.

"Why, thanks!" Gloria said. "I know Savannah will appreciate the gesture."

"Please give her our best," Walt said.

"And, let us know about the baby!" Noelle chimed in. "If it's really coming, we'll want to know."

"Yes. Yes, of course!"

Walt gave Gloria directions to Savannah's house and she departed quickly, once again offering her thanks for their treats. The moment the front door clanked shut in the foyer, Noelle turned to her dad.

"Want to tell me what's going on with the milk and cookies?"

Walt rubbed the side of his neck, observing his daughter. The truth was, that was something he was still trying to figure out himself. Things were much worse than Walt had thought! He was seriously coming down with something. "I must have left them there earlier?" he began in a lame attempt to veil the truth.

Noelle folded her arms in front of her. "Nope. Sorry. Won't work."

"Your old man can be quite absentmind—"

"You would never forget Christmas cookies! They wouldn't even last ten minutes in your sight! You'd eat them all yourself."

"Now, that's a bit unfair." Walt slowly cocked his chin. "I never touch the ones you and Joy bake each year before the holidays."

Noelle rolled her eyes. "That's because we stash them in our hidey-holes."

"Where are those hidey-holes, exactly?"

Walt stared into Noelle's astute blue eyes, which only grew bigger. "No. No way!" She giggled excitedly and reached for Walt's arm. "Is this…? Oh my merry Christmas!" Noelle grinned and squealed with glee. "One of the Christmas *gifts* you and Mom told us about?"

"Gifts?" Walt asked, as Noelle pinched his arm, clamping down tight.

"Yeah." She lowered her voice even though no one was listening. "Those special *talents* that run through our blood. The ones that date back to where the Christmas and Claus family lines first divided? Joy's hinted to me about her painting. But you...?" She perused him with wonder. "Wow!" Noelle said, appearing delighted. She mercifully let go of his arm. "Wow, wow, wow!"

"Now, Noelle—"

"Dad! It must be true!"

"You're *overreaching*, sweetheart." But even as he said it, Walt felt his face color beneath his full beard.

"Cool," she persisted, undaunted. "What else can you do?"

Walt shifted on his feet, his gaze skirting the pile of mail on the entryway table. "Nothing! Nothing at all."

"O-*kay*," Noelle replied, acting as if she didn't believe him. "Whatever you say."

Walt froze in place as one of the letters on the table started to flutter behind Noelle's back. He leapt toward it, and snatched up the mail, gripping it tightly in both hands.

Noelle craftily narrowed her eyes. "Dad?"

"I'm just going to sort through these letters before Gloria returns," he said, striding away. "Might be some bills I need to pay!" he added as an afterthought, proud of himself for sounding convincing.

"What about your hot cocoa? I thought you wanted some?"

"Would you be a lamb and bring it to me in the library?"

Chapter Three

Gloria hustled down the snowy sidewalk headed east, away from Main Street and the Corner Church. According to Walt, Kurt and Savannah's house was only six doors down Church Street and the second one on the right after passing Mistletoe Lane. When she arrived at that street crossing, Gloria paused in alarm. Something seriously weird was going on at the house on the corner. The cute white stucco bungalow had a black slate roof and crimson-colored shutters. It was outfitted cheerily for Christmas with a large door wreath and greenery draped from the porch railings, which served as the backdrop to dripping icicle lights. More twinkling lights wound their way around the sturdy columns supporting the low-hanging roof. But the house's outdoor decorations weren't the remarkable part. That lay in the stunning wildlife display dotting its lawn!

Every kind of woodland animal imaginable crowded the front yard and loitered near the tall privacy fence hedging the side and backyards. There were neighborhood cats and dogs…various squirrels and chipmunks…a formidable stand of deer—*whoa!*—a few of them sporting enormous antlers…a passel of raccoons…a possum…and even a pair of skunks!

Numerous colorful birds perched on the waving branches of trees lining the yard, calling out in melodious song. Most amazing of all, none of the beasts seemed intent on fighting the others. The creatures appeared amicably gathered together, almost like a group of patrons anticipating entrance to a theater. *Or, perhaps…?* Gloria found herself thinking curiously. *A band of subjects awaiting their audience with a king?*

Gloria held her breath, her heart hammering. While they looked tame enough from a distance, she wasn't sure how the animals might react if they noticed her approaching. The last thing Gloria wanted to do was call attention to herself and unwittingly cause a stampede! And, Savannah's house was so close! Gloria could see Savannah's SUV parked in the drive of the next house over, which was slightly larger than this one, with a single second-story window situated above its front door.

Savannah's place was a cheery red brick charmer with a high-pitched tin roof and sleek dark shutters. It was decorated for Christmas as well, but in a much more understated manner. Gloria reasoned that was perhaps because Savannah had been spending her time preparing for the baby, rather than decking the halls. Savannah *had* taken pains to handcraft the gorgeous fabric door wreath, though. She'd fashioned it from colorful red and green bandanas she'd twisted together, and had recently sent Gloria a photo of her masterpiece by text.

Gloria gripped the cookie bag she held in one hand tighter and steadied her travel mug of cocoa in her other hand as she tiptoed across the street. The fading daylight made the lights adorning the small stucco house seem to glow all the more. As she approached the animal-laden yard, a multitude of heads turned in her direction, some of them fixing on Gloria with penetrating dark eyes. Gloria hurried past them, deferentially dipping her chin. "Hi! Hello," she said as pleasantly as she could muster. Then, she scampered down the sidewalk and gratefully up Savannah's front walk and toward her covered porch.

On the way, Gloria couldn't help but note that the house to the left of Savannah's was decorated even more outlandishly for Christmas than the one on the corner. While it lacked the live-animal display, the smart two-story Tudor was all decked out for Christmas. Evergreen garlands and Christmas lights shaped like snowflakes draped from the porch railings. A pretty wreath with a red-and-green checkered bow hung on the front door, and smaller wreaths of the same design dotted every street-facing window. The windows further housed glowing Christmas candles, lending the home extra cheer, while a big, bouncy blow-up display of Santa riding in his sleigh behind a team of reindeer bobbed back and forth on the snowy lawn.

Towering, red-and-white-striped plastic candy canes lined the path to the front door. And, the covered front porch held a tall wooden snowman that was circled from his base to the tip of his black top hat in multicolored Christmas lights. An old-timey-looking, dark green and gold child's sleigh stood beside the snowman. It was the kind with a deep bucket seat and real steel runners. *There's no doubt that people love Christmas around here*, Gloria thought to herself, as she rang Savannah's bell. *No doubt at all.*

Walt set the heavy paperweight down on the stack of letters, hoping it would keep them in place. The paperweight was actually the vessel Walt used to hold pens and pencils on his desk. The solid brass item stood six inches tall at its highest point and was shaped like a holiday Christmas stocking, gaping open at the top. A personal message to him had been emblazoned on the turned cuff of the stocking, which was also made of brass: *To Walt from Rose, Merry Christmas!* It had been something whimsical and precious his late wife had given to him during their first Christmas together as a couple. The gaudy item was almost ugly in a way. But the fact that Rose had picked it out and had it engraved made it beautiful in Walt's eyes.

His gaze fixed on the pile of the envelopes that seemed to twitch around their edges. Walt had counted five Christmas cards, three bills, a real estate flyer, and a postcard advertising a holiday brunch next Sunday at the Grand Hotel. Ten pieces of mail that only minutes ago had been flitting around Walt's front yard, coincidentally at the time his latest guest had arrived. The one with the long brown hair and gorgeous dark eyes… Not that Walt had particularly noticed anything much about Gloria's appearance, other than the fact that she'd been dressed from head to toe in winter white.

In reaction to his lie, the mail flipped up at one end, as if lifted by an invisible hand. Then—*clank!*—the brass paperweight tumbled over, and—*clank! clunk!*—spilled off Walt's desk! Luckily, it landed on the carpet, rather than denting the hardwood floor. Walt reached for it then recalled the mail on his desk. But it was already too late! The obstinate correspondence had fluttered up into the air, fanning out in a crazy arc above his desk.

"*Hey! Wait! Stop that.*" Walt's words were a hushed whisper, but the mail paid him no mind. The postcard to the left seemed to take the lead, pivoting toward the door to the living room, as the other pieces of correspondence obediently turned to follow.

Sweat beaded Walt's forehead as he tried to reason this through. As misguided as it was, Walt suspected he knew where this cache of mail thought it was destined. Not here, to the Christmas Inn—but somewhere much farther north. Walt's gaze snagged on the globe by the bookshelves, then he leapt to his feet, grabbing for the mail. But it darted out of reach, scampering along on the air in a merry little jig like some kind of airborne Slinky: rising and falling, then collapsing in on itself, before rising and falling again in springy waves.

"Stop! Come back here!" Walt called hoarsely, chasing after it. But the dance troupe of mail had already swept through the living room and was pirouetting into the front hall.

Walt scuttled into the foyer, hands outstretched, as the postcard flattened itself sideways then zoomed against the front door, hitting hard then falling to the carpet. The rest of the mail followed suit. *Whack, whack, whack, whack, whack, whack, whack, whack, whack*—before tumbling lifelessly to the floor. Walt ran both hands through his hair, his heart pounding. This couldn't mean what he thought it did. It just couldn't.

"Da-ad?" Noelle's voice warbled, and Walt looked up to see her standing on the threshold to the parlor. She held a mug of hot cocoa in one hand, and her big blue eyes were opened wide behind her glasses. "Want to explain what just happened here?"

"Here," Gloria told Savannah. "Walt and Noelle sent these for you." After their initial moments of hugs and squeals, during which Savannah had relieved Gloria of her travel mug by setting it on the entrance table, Gloria recalled the gift she'd brought along. It was hard to believe Savannah was in labor. She seemed to have calmed down quite a bit since their phone call, and didn't appear physically or emotionally distressed. She'd certainly grown a lot larger around the middle, though. It was exciting to think Savannah's big round belly meant that her child was on the way. Although Gloria gathered that the baby's arrival was no longer extremely imminent.

"Oh, how sweet!" Savannah smiled cheerfully, taking the bag and peeking inside it. "Mmm. Milk and cookies! My favorite treat." Savannah gave a shy giggle. "Lately, anyway."

Gloria admired her best friend, thinking Savannah looked lovelier than ever. While Savannah was normally a striking woman, with her long red hair and emerald-colored eyes, she appeared even more beautiful now with a soft blush across her cheeks and the bridge of her nose. "Look at you!" Gloria chirped gently. "You're glowing."

Savannah's blush deepened as she demurred. "Am not."

"Are, too!" Gloria insisted. "And honestly? It looks great on you. I've never seen you looking so happy, Savannah."

"And I've never seen you looking so…" Savannah's gaze swept over her outfit, then her lips twisted in mirth. "…white!"

"Ha-ha! Yeah! I guess I went a little overboard with the ward—"

Savannah sucked in a gasp. "*Whoa.*"

Gloria tightly pursed her lips, then mumbled cautiously, "Whoa, what?"

"You *whitened* them, didn't you?"

"Nmm-nmm."

"Then why are you speaking like an old lady who's missing her dentures?"

Gloria play-swatted her. "That is *so* not nice." She cupped a hand over her mouth before adding, "And, what if I did, anyway?"

Savannah eyed her astutely then broke into a grin. "This is about Walt, isn't it?"

"No!"

Savannah nodded knowingly. "You wanted to impress him."

"Did *not*." Gloria dropped her hand in indignation then quickly shielded her mouth again. "The dentist was running a BOGO holiday special," she uttered between stretched lips. "Two whitening sessions for the price of one."

Savannah laughed good-naturedly. "Oh, Gloria!
You're too much!"

Gloria removed her hat and narrowed her eyes. "I
thought you were in labor?"

"I thought I was, too!" Savannah set the bag from
the Christmas Inn down on the entry table and took
Gloria's hat, and then her coat when she removed it. "I
was dying. I mean, *dying* in pain. But then, you know!"
She hung Gloria's damp things on a coatrack beside the
door. "It stopped."

"Warm-up contractions?"

"That's what Kurt says," Savannah replied with a
shrug. "But, let me tell you this. It sure feels like the
real deal when it happens."

"Well, I'm glad you're feeling better now. I'd
barely set down my suitcase and I thought we'd be
dashing off to the hospital tonight."

"At least you would have made it in time."
Savannah's eyes glimmered warmly and she pulled
Gloria into a hug, her big baby bulge between them.
"Thank you, Gloria. I'm so glad you're here."

Gloria tightly hugged her back, reflecting on how
much she missed having Savannah close by in Miami.
"I'm glad, too."

Gloria glanced around Savannah's nicely furnished
home. The dining room was to the left and a cozy living
room with burgundy-colored Cordovan leather
furnishings and a fireplace to the right. A decorated
Christmas tree stood at the front end of the living room,
centered before the window facing the street. Its lights
twinkled merrily and a single Christmas stocking hung
from the mantel of the hearth.

"Oh, how sweet!" Gloria said, staring that way. "Is that for the baby?"

Savannah smiled wistfully. "She—or he—will be here by Christmas."

Savannah had told Gloria she didn't want to know the child's sex, as she hoped to be surprised. She'd seen the sonograms, of course, but even as detailed as they were, Savannah couldn't trust herself to definitively decipher any anatomical differences. Kurt's more trained eye had known for months whether their baby-to-be was going to be little Julia or Jacob, though he'd honored Savannah's wishes in keeping this secret from her. In the meantime, Savannah had stocked her layette with cute neutral onesies in sunny yellows and teals, with a few dark red and green items tucked in to add holiday color. She'd also already received several gifts of darling baby clothing, and had sent Gloria enthusiastic electronic updates with each new acquisition.

Savannah stepped into the living room and started toward the door on its far end that appeared to join a back hall. "Come on." She smiled happily. "Let me show you the nursery!"

Walt stared at his daughter and the pretty blonde stared back. Thanks to the Christmas family genes, both of Walt's girls were on the taller side. Each stood about five foot ten, and Noelle had to be more than five eleven in her smart black ankle boots. This still left her several inches shorter than her father. At six foot four, Walt was the tallest of the Christmas boys, which included the eldest, Ray, and Kurt, who was their younger brother.

Noelle gaped in disbelief at her father. "Were you *throwing* our mail at the front door?"

"*Throwing?*" Walt asked, completely flummoxed. "Don't be silly, Noelle. The mail simply got away from me!"

"I've heard of feisty correspondence, Dad, but that's kind of ridiculous."

"Ha-ha. Yes." Walt bent low and gathered the errant letters into his hands. "The truth is, I was actually…in fact, umm…*picking up* the mail."

Noelle's right eyebrow arched sharply. "I thought Gloria brought it in a while ago."

"She did!" Walt stewed over some potential explanations, deciding on an accurate one. "I was just bringing it back."

"Back?"

"Inside."

"We are inside."

"Inside of the library, I mean."

"How on earth did it get *out*?"

Walt weighed how much to tell his daughter. There were certain things about their family that Noelle wasn't supposed to discover until the time was right. That time being from the first moment she fell madly and deeply in love. As the fates had it, her sister Joy had been an early bloomer. Not that Joy understood all the talents she was capable of. Some of those had been cut short due to her breakup with Devon Slade. Devon and Joy had started dating in high school, then amicably agreed to take a break when Joy went off to Italy. Though they both were creative people, they'd been drifting apart ever since Joy had gone to college and Devon had stayed in Christmas Town to focus on his art, which was woodworking.

Noelle viewed Walt with concern when he failed to answer.

He glanced pointedly out the sidelight window to the left of the front door. "A big gust of wind hit when Gloria was carrying the mail in earlier, and it sort of got scattered all over the place. I want to be sure we didn't leave anything behind on the lawn."

"You're going outside *now*?"

When Walt nodded, Noelle eyed the mail in his hands. "Here, give that to me and I'll set it on the foyer tab—"

"No!" he spouted, a tad too emphatically.

"O-kay, then. In the library with your cocoa?"

"I think I'd better just—hang onto these letters for now."

By the way she looked at him, Walt worried that Noelle feared he was becoming mentally unhinged. "Why's that?"

"Because I need them. To assist me!" Walt swallowed hard. Even to himself that sounded absurd.

"Like…'little helpers'?" Noelle asked gently, as if she were speaking to someone on the verge of cracking up. Walt seriously hoped that he wasn't. But he couldn't totally be sure.

"Nope! Not those! Little Helpers are—"

"*Elves*. Right. I know." She surveyed him judiciously. "I've heard the stories."

"Legends, Noelle. *Legends*."

"Oh, sure! Because legends are based on fact."

"Or, oral history!"

Noelle waited patiently. "Anything else?"

Walt decided not to mention that DNA might be involved. "Nope. I think that about covers our bases." He paused briefly. "For now."

The mail started vibrating in his hands, sending tiny tingling sensations to his fingertips. Walt clutched the stash of mail to his chest with one hand and grabbed the front doorknob with the other, thinking he could really use some fresh air. He also needed a break from Noelle's relentless questioning. She had a way of getting things out of Walt, when he wasn't very, very careful.

"This wouldn't have anything to do with those cookies and milk, would it?"

"Cookies? Ha-ha!" Walt forced his most serious fatherly expression. "Nope."

"You're going to have to tell me what's going on, you know." Noelle was an incredibly persistent young woman when she wanted to be. "Someday."

"Someday!" Walt said, his voice cracking unnervingly. "Yeah!"

Gloria sat with Savannah at the small table, which was situated against a wall and facing the stylish galley kitchen. The window over the sink had a view to the side yard, where heavy snow continued to fall. Quarters in the quaint, modernized kitchen were cramped, with the table only large enough to accommodate two chairs. While Savannah drank from the swanky milk bottle and nibbled on her pretty Christmas cookies, Gloria sipped from her travel mug of cocoa, which was still piping hot and tasted chocolaty smooth and delicious.

Savannah had shown her the rest of the house, which included a master bedroom behind the living room, a single hall bath, and the much tinier bedroom located behind the kitchen, which was to be the baby's room. A door across from the bathroom concealed a staircase leading to the modest second floor, which housed a slanted-ceiling attic. Savannah shared that Kurt was refurbishing the space so it could be used as a playroom for the baby.

And what a well-pampered infant little Julia or Jacob was going to be! The nursery was decorated in happy springtime colors, with a yellow-and-white-checkered gingham comforter on the crib and a matching cushion on the seat of the rocker nearby. The shelves of the changing table had been stocked with small baby undershirts, burp cloths, and disposable diapers. A new box of baby wipes and other supplies were stashed there, as well. The theme seemed to indicate a warm-weather country landscape, with a precious barnyard animal mobile dangling over the crib. Savannah had turned its crank to play its sweet tune: "Old MacDonald Had a Farm."

Gloria wasn't sure why Savannah had claimed to need her help in preparing for the baby, because—from the looks of things—Savannah was all set! As the director of the Christmas Town Children's Theater, Savannah was not merely extremely organized; she was also artistically inclined. And, nowhere were her talents more evident than in the outcome of her beautiful nursery.

She'd painted the upper portion of the walls pale blue with white puffy clouds hovering near the ceiling and the golden globe of the sun peering out from behind one of them. The area below the chair rail was verdant green and reminiscent of freshly mowed grass in summertime. Portraits of cute barn animals were located around the perimeter of the room, completing the scene. There were chickens, cows, and piglets, even horses and a couple of goats!

Her reflections on the nursery design made Gloria think of the house on the corner that she'd passed by.

"You've got a really great house. I love what you and Kurt have done with it, especially the nursery."

Savannah smiled proudly. "Thanks! It feels like home."

"Speaking of houses," Gloria began cautiously. "How well do you know your neighbors?"

"Neighbors?" Savannah's brow knitted. "Which ones?"

"The ones on both sides," Gloria quipped in low tones. "Particularly that house with the menagerie in the front yard. It was so freaky, Savannah—"

"Watch it. My sister lives there!"

"What? Who?" Gloria blanched momentarily. "Olivia?"

"Yes, with Nick."

Savannah had mentioned something to Gloria about her brother-in-law Nick being good with animals, but it had been so long ago Gloria had forgotten the details. "How nice that you have your sister so close."

"Yeah, I know!" Savannah's face brightened. "It is kind of crazy, but after a while you get used to it."

"Used to what?"

"Just about everything here."

"Isn't having all those animals around a hazard?"

"Hazard?" Savannah queried innocently. "In what way?"

"For pedestrians. Drivers!"

"Oh, they never go into the street. Nick told them not to."

"Nick told them..." Now, Gloria recalled what Savannah had said. It was something about Nick talking to animals. Savannah's brother-in-law sure sounded eccentric.

"Besides," Savannah continued breezily. "Olivia bakes them tons of treats. Organic stuff made from all-natural ingredients the animals can eat. It's super nice of her!" Savannah paused, then whispered conspiratorially, "But, the truth is this helps out Olivia, too. Ever since meeting Nick, Olivia's been baking up a storm. It's almost like she can't stop! Can you believe they have two double ovens in their house? Two of them! Olivia keeps whining that's not enough and hankering for a third, but Nick says she'll have to wait until they get a bigger house."

Gloria would never tell Savannah this, but her sister Olivia sounded pretty eccentric, as well. "And your neighbors on the other side?"

"Sandy and Ben Winchester. They've got three kids. Lily, who's eleven now, and two-year-old twins: Holly and Rose. Ben is Hannah's big brother—Hannah, who owns the Christmas Cookie Shop and is married to my brother, Carter, our local sheriff."

"And Sandy?"

"She's the artist who runs the Snow Globe Gallery. Plus, she's Nick's little sister."

"What a very small world!"

Savannah munched happily on a cookie. "Yeah, but in a good way. That's Christmas Town for you.

"You sure you don't want one of these?" Savannah asked her for about the billionth time, trying to share a darling snowman cookie wearing a black top hat and a cobalt scarf. Those cookies from the Christmas Inn were some of the most amazing ones Gloria had ever seen! They looked homemade, but not. Way too fancy to have been produced in a regular kitchen. Then again, the Christmas Inn's kitchen was far from "regular." It was extra-large and incredibly well equipped.

"These really are the world's best!" Savannah said, taking another chomp of the snowman cookie she was halfway done with. "Who made them? Noelle?"

"I'm not sure," Gloria said, remembering that Noelle seemed surprised by them. "Maybe Walt?"

Savannah sputtered a laugh then covered her mouth with a napkin. "Walt Christmas did not make these cookies."

"How can you be sure?"

"Because! He'd have eaten every single one!" Savannah's eyes twinkled merrily as she took a gulp of milk. "I mean it," she said, when Gloria viewed her doubtfully. "Probably right off the cookie sheet before they'd even cooled! The man has no self-control around Christmas cookies. None. Kind of runs in the Christmas family." She grinned then shrugged happily. "At least, among the men."

Walt quietly closed one kitchen cabinet and then peeked in another. He was scouting the area in which those cookies and milk had appeared, seemingly by magic and right out of thin air! Perhaps there were more of them somewhere. Walt briefly peered inside the refrigerator, then began scouring through the shelves holding the cookbooks, by running his hands along the tops of the tomes and dipping his fingers behind them where they stood slightly tilted sideways.

"Dad! What are you doing?"

Walt turned on his heel, his face steaming. "Looking for cookies."

"Cookies? Well, you won't find any over there. Or in the refrigerator, either."

Walt wondered how long his daughter had been standing there observing him. The last he knew, she'd gone into the parlor to work on job applications for her spring semester at college on her laptop. Noelle currently had a non-paying internship during her holiday break at the county courthouse, and also worked part-time at the Elf Shelf Bookshop.

Walt tried a hopeful tact. "You know those hidey-holes you mentioned earlier?"

"Yeah, what about them?"

Noelle strode to the coffeepot and poured herself a cup. Even though she'd prepared the cocoa for Walt and Gloria previously, she hadn't partaken of that herself.

"I was wondering if you could tell me where they are?"

Noelle's eyebrows shot up. "Nice try, but I don't think so," she said with a laugh.

Walt cleared his throat and tried to sound convincing. "This is serious, Noelle."

The girl set one hand on her hip. "First off, you don't need any cookies. You're trying to cut back, remember? Uncle Kurt says they're bad for your health."

"Well now, I can't see what harm just one or two—?"

"Secondly, the hidey-holes are empty. I haven't done any Christmas baking this year, and—since Joy's not here—she obviously hasn't either."

"But, what if...?"

"Ohhhh." Noelle's blue eyes sparkled. "You think they might have somehow refilled themselves?"

"Ha-ha! Don't be silly, Noelle." After a beat, he pressed ahead. "But do you think you could at least check and see?"

"Sure, all right. I'll take a look." She appraised Walt warily. "But, not while you're still in the kitchen."

"Of course. Right! Wouldn't expect anything less of you, daughter."

A few minutes later, Walt heard cabinets slamming open and shut in the kitchen, as he tried to visualize in his mind's eye which particular ones they were. "Well?" he called over his shoulder as he stood in the dining room facing the parlor. "Any luck?"

"Nope, no cookies! Not a one!" Noelle appeared on the threshold to the kitchen and Walt turned to face her. "The coast is clear."

Gloria giggled at Savannah's stories about the Christmas men. Walt sounded totally hopeless. The oldest brother, Ray, was evidently nearly as bad. Kurt apparently had such a weakness for desserts that he'd sworn off sweets completely, while his dad, Buddy, was the biggest Christmas cookie fan of all, and he had the rotund physique to show for it. "Well, I haven't met the other brother, Ray, but neither Walt nor Kurt appear to have suffered any ill effects so far. Walt seems very fit and—"

"So, you noticed, huh?" Savannah asked with a teasing lilt.

"Stop that!"

"You can't deny he's hot, Gloria."

"I never said that he wasn't."

Savannah's eyes danced merrily. "I bet Walt thinks you're hot, too."

Gloria's mouth dropped open. "How did we get on to me and Walt? We were talking about the Christmas men and cookies!"

"Yeah," Savannah said smugly. "But, you're the one who mentioned Walt's body."

"I was about to mention Kurt's, too."

"Hey!"

"Not in the wrong way, silly. Only to say he stays in great shape."

"Yeah." Savannah sighed dreamily. "Buff, blond, and beautiful. I know." Next, she gave a mischievous grin and patted her tummy. "Precisely what got me into this predicament!"

"What?" Gloria asked jokingly. "Kurt being a heartthrob? Or, does this have something to do with cookies?"

"Both things, maybe," Savannah answered a bit mysteriously. "Which reminds me! I have a present for you." Savannah shuffled to her feet and toddled over to the refrigerator on wobbly strides.

"How sweet! Savannah, you didn't have to get me anything."

"Just think of it as a welcome gift." Savannah returned to the table and handed a small paper bag to Gloria. "This is for you to enjoy later." Savannah sat back in her chair and lowered her voice. "But only under one condition."

"Oh? What's that?" Gloria's pulse pounded. Savannah was up to something and she knew it.

"That you share it with Walt." She had that sneaky expression on her face and that little twinkle in her eyes. "But you'd better be quick about it, or else Walt might just gobble the whole thing up himself."

Gloria remembered Savannah telling her about the supposedly magical cookies produced each season at Hannah Livingston's Christmas Cookie Shop. "Hang on one Miami minute!" Gloria scrutinized her friend then stared down at the bag, which she saw contained a shiny gold seal from the Christmas Cookie Shop. "This isn't one of those Virginia Cookies? The ones named for the little girl who wrote to that paper asking if there really was a Santa Claus?"

Savannah shot her a saucy stare. "Might be."

Gloria pried open the paper bag and gazed down at the darling heart-shaped gingerbread cookie. It was decorated with a dark-red-icing heart, and swirly pink letters proclaimed: *Forever Yours*. Gloria pinched closed the bag and gasped. "This is a Commitment Cookie. The sort that's supposed to bring people together… Savannah, honestly!" She was annoyed but laughing all the same. "Don't you ever give up?"

"On you and Walt? Never. Not when you two are so clearly suited to each other, and your falling in love could result in your moving to Christmas Town."

"Well, I'm not interested in moving! Much less in Walt."

"Liar." When Gloria gaped at her, she continued, "Dental special, ha! You whitened those teeth on purpose, because you wanted to look your best. Although, truthfully? It wasn't necessary. You've always been gorgeous, Gloria. And the last time I saw you your smile looked just fine."

"What's more," Gloria sternly went on. "*Walt's* not interested in me."

"Don't be so quick to judge!"

"Savannah—"

"I can't recall who exactly said this," Savannah chirped in a sing-songy tone, "but someone I know is a big fan of people getting *married, married, married*…"

"That's totally different and you know it! When I suggested you marry Kurt, you were already head over heels in love with him. Besides that, you and Kurt were long-lost loves. Former flames!"

"There's no flame like a new flame," Savannah teased. "And the Christmas Inn is a hotbed of flames! Why do you think there's mistletoe hanging above every single threshold?"

"What? Is there really?"

"Don't act like you didn't notice."

"When would I have had time?" Gloria contended. "The moment I got there I raced to your side." She teasingly lowered her eyebrows. "Which might have been unnecessary."

"Oh, come on!" Savannah said with a giggle. "You know you were dying to see me."

"Yes, it's true. But you could at least have let me unpack my suitcase first."

Savannah reached out and took Gloria's hand. "I'm so glad you're here." Her eyes brimmed with sincerity. "Really I am."

"I'm glad too, *chica*." A smile warmed Gloria's face. "I'm also glad you didn't go ahead and have that baby without me."

"She—or he—will be along soon enough," Savannah said happily. "Do you want to come to the hospital?" She seriously surveyed her friend. "I mean, when it's time?"

"Of course I want to be there! Why do you think I drove all the way here from Miami?"

"Maybe to get a good look at Walt?" Savannah teased. "All up close and personal?"

"You've got to stop that, Savannah. It's seriously *not* happening. Me and Walt, I mean." Gloria worked hard to forget that transformative sensation she'd experienced when gazing into Walt's deep blue eyes. That had only been a fluke! Surely! Walt was simply a nice-looking man. It wasn't Gloria's fault that he'd taken her breath away. He clearly hadn't been trying, as Walt had seemed just as thrown by the exchange as Gloria had been. Which was why it was for the best that Gloria put thoughts of a romantic relationship with Walt well out of mind, while squelching Savannah's attempts to not-so-subtly get them together.

"His life is here," Gloria continued reasonably, in an effort to further convince herself as well as Savannah, "and I've got a job that I love in Miami. Everything is different at school now, with the new principal there. So, so much better. And then there's David," Gloria said, mentioning her good-looking younger brother, who was a minister. "He's family and you understand what family means. When you moved to Christmas Town things were different. Your brother and sister were already here."

Savannah's face hung in a frown and Gloria's heart pinged, because in many ways she and Savannah were family, too. She knew Savannah meant well, but it was an impossible situation. One that a simple heart-shaped cookie couldn't fix. From what Savannah had said, Walt hadn't even dated since his late wife died. It was a pretty big stretch to think he'd go from being a committed bachelor dad to wanting to get *married, married, married.* Not that Gloria was interested in marriage herself. With Walt in particular, that was! She was certainly interested in marriage in general. Someday. Way on down the road. Maybe with some nice guy back in Miami, or at the very least in the state of Florida.

"What I mean is," Gloria continued more gently. "How about we give the whole Walt Christmas thing a rest?"

"A rest?" Savannah asked worriedly. "But you're only here for a couple of weeks."

"Then the break should last a month." Gloria winked firmly, and Savannah sat back in her chair, her face clouding over. For a moment, Gloria feared that she might cry.

Savannah blew out a soft breath and slowly shook her head. "Okay, fine." She held up both hands and spoke resignedly, but without sounding bitter. Mostly, Savannah just seemed sad. "If that's honestly how you feel, then I'll stop meddling in your love life. From this day forward... I promise, Gloria." She earnestly met Gloria's eyes. "Really, I'll try."

Though the pronouncement sounded heartfelt, Gloria found herself wondering if Savannah could maintain her resolve in resisting further matchmaking. Getting Walt and Gloria together as a couple had been a "project" of Savannah's for quite some time, and Gloria questioned Savannah's ability to finally let it go. Although she honestly hoped she would. Gloria could only imagine what Savannah might have said to Walt! Hopefully not as much as she'd said to Gloria about him.

"Besides..." Savannah thoughtfully rested her palms on her big, round tummy. "I've got other things to focus on these days. Priorities."

"You certainly do," Gloria concurred in chipper tones. "And, I'm here to help you."

Back at the Christmas Inn, Walt nervously adjusted the flatware at Gloria's place setting at the dining room table. Normally, Walt and the girls didn't eat with their guests. But, normally, they hosted enough guests for their guests to eat together and keep each other company. On the occasions where just one room at the inn was occupied by a couple on a romantic getaway,

Walt would prepare a special candlelight dinner for two.

Having his brother's wife's best friend stay here was more than a little awkward. Gloria was neither a paying guest nor a personal acquaintance of Walt's. The fact was he barely knew her. It was true that Savannah had dropped tidbits here and there. Talking about Gloria's talents as a teacher, and skills as an actress and singer. She also was a very caring person who volunteered with an outreach program in her community for troubled youth. Savannah had further said that Gloria was pretty, and she'd hit that nail fairly squarely on the head. Not that hosting an attractive and accomplished single woman at the inn would personally impact Walt in any way. He'd offered to put Gloria up as a favor to Kurt and Savannah—his family.

The mail taking flight, that mild teletransportation episode, and the appearance of the cookies and milk had simply been systemic flukes, holiday hiccups of some sort that probably meant Walt was coming down with something. They clearly didn't implicate Gloria as the *cause* of these events. *No, no!*

At Walt's vehement inner denial, the edges of Gloria's cloth napkin began to quiver. Walt slammed a sterling silver fork down on top of it. Then he added a dessert fork to its right and a salad fork to its left. Next, he grabbed the knife and spoon and dumped those on the pile, as well.

Noelle looked up at the resulting clatter. She sat cross-legged on the parlor sofa with her laptop balanced on her knees. "Dad! What are you doing?"

"I'm…um…" The napkin started to waver again, and Walt grabbed a silver candlestick holder and pinned it down. "Setting the table."

Noelle viewed him worriedly. "Need my help with that?"

"No, thanks." Walt swallowed hard, darting a wary gaze at the napkin. "I've got it."

Perspiration beaded his brow as Walt fretted over how he was going to handle dinner in beautiful Gloria's presence. Then he remembered the extra special candy dish that he kept in the library and relief flooded through him. *YES! Why didn't I think of it sooner?*

Gloria took Savannah's hands in hers and issued a bright smile. "Now! What can I do? The nursery looks pretty complete. There must be something else—"

"Shopping!" Savannah's green eyes rounded. If there was anything that could snap Savannah out of the doldrums it was thoughts of visiting a totally chic boutique. "Gloria, honestly, you don't know what a nightmare it's been."

"For the baby?"

"For me! The baby's things are pretty much purchased—for now. But, my wardrobe? Yikes! What a disaster!"

"Oh, Savannah. I'm sor—"

"Imagine trying to shop for clothes when I don't even know what size I'll be."

"Postpartum?"

"It could take a while," Savannah confessed in a whisper. "To get my old figure back."

Gloria viewed Savannah's cute maternity outfit, which included a pair of stretch jeans and a colorful Christmas-themed tunic with candy canes on it. Savannah's long red hair was tied back in a dark green ribbon and she wore simple silver hoop earrings, which matched the color of her white gold wedding band and its accompanying engagement ring with a large solitaire diamond.

"Well, you'll still have your maternity clothes—"

Savannah appeared positively horrified. "You can't expect me to wear these same old things after I've had the baby! They make me feel hideous, like I've swallowed an overblown balloon."

"I think you can blame the baby for that, and not your wardrobe."

"Gloria, please!"

"All right. I'm sorry." She reassuringly squeezed Savannah's hands then released them. "Don't worry, I'll help with that, and anything else you need done, too."

Savannah heaved a happy sigh and picked up her milk. "Thank you."

"When shall we begin?"

"How about tomorrow afternoon? I can show you the theater in the morning, then we can do a girls' lunch at the Grand Hotel. Afterwards, we'll go shopping."

"My schedule's clear," Gloria said with a grin.

"I also want you to meet Liz." Savannah paused thoughtfully. "She's working at the daycare tomorrow, but might be able to slip out for coffee, particularly since Jingle Bells Booties has grown, and—"

"Jingle Bells Booties?" Gloria interrupted with a laugh.

"Yeah, I know." Savannah good-naturedly rolled her eyes and took a sip of milk, before setting down the bottle. "The name was Lou's idea."

"Lou Christmas?"

"Kurt's mom, yeah."

"Who's also the town mayor."

"Say, you catch on fast!"

Gloria chuckled and shook her head. "It's not like you haven't been priming me for a year."

"I can't believe it took you so long to come here."

Gloria spoke past the sore spot in her throat. "You know I wouldn't have missed your wedding for the world…"

"I'm so sorry, Gloria." Savannah appeared abashed. "I didn't mean it that way. I know you had your *tia*'s funeral."

"Certain conflicts couldn't be avoided."

"I know," Savannah said kindly. "Really, I do." She shot Gloria a telling look. "I've just missed you, that's all. Skype and phone chatting aren't the same."

"Agreed," Gloria said warmly. "But, I'm here now."

"I wish it wasn't for such a short time."

"Savannah—"

"But I'm happy to take all the time that you can give me." She stopped herself then added happily, "*Us*. Thanks for being here, Gloria, and not just for me. Also for the baby and Kurt."

Gloria had met Kurt briefly during Savannah and Kurt's honeymoon trip to the Florida Keys. As Gloria hadn't been able to make the wedding, Savannah had badly wanted Kurt to meet her special best friend. So the newlyweds had stopped in Miami to have lunch with Gloria on their way south. Kurt Christmas had been every bit as handsome as Savannah had claimed, with a solid, muscled build, dark blond hair, and very dark brown eyes. While Savannah had shared photos of him beforehand, none of the snapshots had done the good-looking doctor justice. Perhaps because part of Kurt's attractiveness lay in his charisma and charm.

"I'm excited about seeing Kurt again. It's been such a while."

"Since our honeymoon, I know!" Savannah shook her head in astonishment. "Can you believe it?"

"Barely," Gloria said, still grateful she and Savannah had been able to do their girls' getaway to Kiawah Island last summer. Kurt had a medical conference on the West Coast and Savannah used the opportunity to meet up with Gloria while he was away. The two women had rented a condo on the beach, and Savannah had shared the news about her pregnancy during their first night there. Gloria, who'd arrived prepared with prosecco, wine, and champagne, had joked she'd have to drink it all herself. She hadn't, though, and had actually saved a special bottle of bubbly to present to Kurt and Savannah upon their baby's arrival.

"Kurt will be happy to see you again, too." Then Savannah added apologetically, "He texted earlier that he had a last-minute emergency, so he'll be late tonight. Otherwise, he'd already be home by now."

"No worries," Gloria said pleasantly. "I'm sure we'll have plenty of time to catch up."

"Yeah."

Gloria's gaze snagged on the clock on the range. "Nearly six-thirty already! Wow! I guess I'd better get back to the Christmas Inn. Walt said something about dinner at seven, and I probably should freshen up first. Maybe even offer to help." She viewed her friend with concern. "Will you be okay here?"

"Of course! I'm perfectly fine now." Savannah giggled with embarrassment. "Now that my 'false alarm' is over with."

"Sounds like it *was* Braxton Hicks."

"I can't stand it when Kurt is right," Savannah said sassily. "Mostly because he's right—often."

Gloria laughed. "Sounds like you're lucky to have a doctor in the house."

"Yeah." Savannah blushed deeply, quite obviously enamored with her husband, and Gloria was so happy to see her like this.

Contented, in love, and very, very pregnant...

At least for the next little while.

Chapter Four

Walt gingerly set the Dutch oven on the cooktop while wearing his oven mitts. He cracked the lid on the pot slightly and the hearty aroma of Irish stew filled the kitchen. Braised lamb, sautéed onions and carrots, and white potatoes—all in a savory broth. He planned to serve it with a sturdy soda bread and a tossed green salad. Chunky mocha chocolate chip ice cream was for dessert, and Walt intended to douse his with a liberal splash of peppermint schnapps. Only seconds ago, he'd nabbed a large piece of peppermint bark from the candy jar in the library and popped it in his mouth, steeling himself for a negative reaction.

Though peppermint was known to subdue certain family abilities, its ingestion could also backfire—like it had with Kurt when he'd reconciled with Savannah. Still, peppermint seemed to work fine for most folks in the Christmas and Claus families who were descended from the same ancestral line. It served as a stellar antidote to DNA-linked talents gone awry. Like those that sent "Christmas mail" winging its way to the North Pole, or miraculously caused cookies and milk to appear on the counter.

"Smells delish!" Noelle said, entering the kitchen.

Walt returned the lid to the pot, satisfied that the stew looked cooked to perfection. "How are the applications going?" he asked with a smile. He had to mumble just a bit around the candy that was melting in his mouth, but his daughter didn't appear to notice.

"Pretty well," she said, picking up a carrot from the veggie and hummus platter Walt had prepared as an appetizer and taking a nibble. "Finished with four! Five more to go." When Noelle started school next semester, she hoped to have a paying internship lined up at a publishing company or perhaps one of the local papers that served the area surrounding her small private college. Her boisterous sister Joy had gone to a much larger state university, but Noelle preferred the intimacy of more limited class sizes and the benefits of truly getting to know her professors. Several had encouraged Noelle to pursue her writing career and she fully intended to do so. Precisely why she was majoring in journalism.

"No doubt they'll all be clamoring to hire you," Walt said. "With competing offers!"

She eyed him oddly a moment before responding. "Let's hope that some of those offers involve *money*." Noelle laughed sweetly, and Walt couldn't help but reflect on how mature she seemed. Walt didn't know exactly when it had happened, but at some point after his daughters had left for college and before the time they returned home for their first winter break, both Joy and Noelle had morphed from spunky teens into confident young woman. It was hard to believe that both girls soon would be seniors, and contemplating their futures post-graduation.

"That would be ideal," Walt replied with a wink, and Noelle nodded in agreement. She drew a bit nearer and curiously studied Walt's mouth. "*Da-ad*," she said in exasperated tones. "You're not snacking before dinner again?"

Walt swallowed the last of the candy, which had nearly dissolved anyway. "Me?"

Noelle lightly sniffed the air beneath his chin. "Is that peppermint?"

"Peppermint? Ha-ha! Ha!" Walt slyly cracked the lid on the Dutch oven and a warm puff of delicious stew scent filled the room. "Why no, hon. It's lamb!" Then a brilliant idea occurred. "Though a nice dollop of *mint* jelly as a condiment is a fine idea—come to think of it."

Noelle scrunched up her face. "Ew, Dad. Not in the stew!"

"Why not?"

"It wouldn't go!"

"How about on the side then? Or...or..." Walt thought quickly. "Some peppermint jelly and cream cheese on crackers ahead of the meal?"

Noelle eyed him suspiciously. "As hors d'oeuvres, you mean?"

"Yes! Those!"

Noelle grabbed a celery stick and dipped it in the hummus. "But you've already made this."

"When Gloria returns, she might be hungry. The bread needs to bake another fifteen minutes, then it has to cool."

"Are you okay?" Noelle adjusted her glasses. "Because you look a little... I don't know. Off somehow."

"Off?"

Noelle cupped her mouth in a giggle. "This is about Gloria, isn't it?"

"No."

"*Walt? Noelle?* I'm back!" Gloria's chipper voice rang out from the foyer, and Walt's whole face burned hot.

Noelle pursed her lips in delighted surprise then grinned her dad. "We're back here!" she called loudly to Gloria. "In the kitchen!"

Gloria glanced toward the parlor and removed her gloves. Next, she set the bag from the Christmas Cookie Shop down on the entryway table, intending to take it back to her bedroom later. Something smelled fantastic! She ambled into the dining room, noting that the table had already been beautifully set with antique china, crystal water and wine goblets, linen napkins, and what appeared to be real silverware.

Gloria walked into the kitchen holding her gloves in one hand and the errant piece of mail she'd found on the sidewalk in the other. She'd almost stepped on the envelope on her way to Walt's house. It had blown so far away, it was nearly at the corner with Mistletoe Lane! But it had the Christmas Inn address on it, all right, and it was addressed to *The Christmas Family*, which Gloria assumed meant Walt, Noelle, and Joy. "I was going to offer to help with the table," she said brightly, "but I see that it's already been set."

"How's Savannah?" Walt inquired. He was diligently spreading cream cheese on crackers and topping them with some kind of red-speckled jelly, while Noelle checked on the bread baking in the oven.

"Really great!" Gloria shared a sunny smile. "It was a false alarm, luckily. She was doing fine when I left her."

"Glad to hear it," Walt replied.

"Thanks for the cocoa, by the way," Gloria told Noelle. "It was delicious!" She addressed Walt next. "And, Savannah completely *demolished* the milk and cookies."

Walt chuckled at this. "Well, good."

Gloria's gaze swept the kitchen, landing on the Dutch oven. "What smells so divine?"

"Irish stew made with lamb. I hope that's all right?" His brow rose uncertainly, and Gloria couldn't help but think how adorable Walt looked standing there in that neatly trimmed beard and dark green apron. Gloria had always appreciated men with culinary skills. "When I checked with Savannah, she said you didn't have any dietary restrictions."

"None whatsoever," Gloria confirmed, holding out the envelope in her hand. "Believe it or not, I found another one outside."

"No kidding?" Walt stared at the letter with trepidation, and Gloria couldn't fathom why. It was merely another Christmas card, for heaven's sakes. At least that's what it looked like in that oversize red envelope sporting a jolly Santa Claus stamp on the front.

"I'll take it," Noelle said, approaching Gloria.

"Don't bother!" Walt suddenly dropped his knife and stepped in between them. He turned his eyes on Gloria. "Why don't you just—give that to me."

Noelle perused her father. "I was just going to put it on your desk in the library."

"No need to trouble yourself, my dear." Walt grinned tightly and snapped the envelope out of Gloria's hand. "Not when I can do that myself!" When he was halfway through the breakfast area, Walt turned suddenly. "Oh, sorry! Thanks, Gloria! Thanks for bringing in the…um…rest of the mail!" Then he quickly turned away to disguise the fact that his face was positively pink as he scuttled out of the room.

"Don't mind my dad," Noelle whispered once Walt had gone. "Lately? He's been acting a little weird."

"Weird?"

At that exact moment, something crashed in another room. It sounded a lot like glass breaking against a hardwood floor. Noelle set her lips in a firm line and held up a finger. "Will you excuse me—for just one sec?"

Walt stared up at Noelle when she appeared in the doorway to the library from the hall. The shattered lid of the candy dish was at his feet and he was crouched low cleaning it up. He employed his latest piece of mail as a pushing broom and swept shards of glass into a wastebasket he'd turned on its side.

"Dad? What? No!" Noelle uttered quietly, scurrying toward him. "What happened?"

The red crystal candy dish was an old piece, something that had been in the Christmas family for years. Walt gazed at his daughter, red-faced. "I was…just walking by this table and…" He stopped short and shook his head in dismay. "The edge of the envelope must have caught it."

"Well, don't do that with your hands!" Noelle grabbed him by the elbow and helped him stand. "I'll run and grab the vacuum. That will be better…" She eyed the wastebasket. "Since you've already gotten the big pieces."

Walt rolled the huge hunk of peppermint bark around on his tongue. "Thanks, Noelle."

She stared at him aghast. "I can't believe it! You're actually eating more candy!"

Walt tried to shake his head, but Noelle reached out and grabbed his chin. "Let me see."

"What?" Walt blinked in disbelief and stealthily chomped apart a few small bits of the candy with his molars.

Noelle huffed and Walt retorted in a whisper, "I'm not your kid, Noelle. I'm your father."

She tried to pry open his jaw but he clamped it shut, pushing the remaining chunk of peppermint bark into his left cheek.

"Ye-es." Noelle patted Walt's cheek, the one that bulged with candy, as he watched her wide-eyed. "And, someone who can't seem to recall the *rule* about no sweets before dinner." She lowered her voice then hissed seriously, "The one you always imposed on me and Joy!"

Walt chewed as fast as he could then swallowed hard. "You don't understand," he said in hushed tones. "This was an *emergency*." His voice was all raspy and his throat itched. He hoped he wasn't having one of those negative reactions after all.

Noelle's eyebrows arched.

"I'll have to explain it later."

"How much later?"

Walt ventured lightly, "Are you dating anyone?"

"Who? Me?" Noelle firmly set her chin. "You know I'm not, and stop trying to change the subject."

"I'm not..." Walt coughed into his hand. "Changing it, exactly."

Noelle's eye-roll said everything. "Fine. Why don't you go back to Gloria in the kitchen, and I'll finish cleaning up here."

"You sure?"

"Sure, I'm sure." She shook her head in a disgruntled fashion and went to get the vacuum. Walt seized the opportunity to slip the newest piece of mail under the heavy Christmas stocking paperweight with the others. Next, he grabbed a nearby stapler and placed that on top of the stack for extra measure. "Now, stay put," he whispered hoarsely to the letters, "and behave."

"Are you talking to your desk?"

Walt's head jerked up. Gloria stood on the threshold to the living room. She was no longer wearing her coat or hat, having obviously put them away.

"I...uh...well..."

"I went to hang my things in the hall closet," Gloria began. "Then, I thought maybe I should come and see if I could help?" Her big dark eyes bored into him and Walt's heart pounded. There was something very alluring about her. Almost magnetic, and Walt was finding it hard to resist her pull. The fact that Gloria wasn't trying to captivate him somehow made it worse. But Walt couldn't stomach any more peppermint. He'd eaten half the jar of candy already, and was beginning to feel mildly queasy because of it. Gloria glanced around the room. "Did something break in here?"

"Just...the lid of the candy dish."

"Oh dear!" She spied the overturned wastebasket and small shards of glass still littering the floor.

"Noelle's gone to get the vacuum," Walt rushed in. "Perhaps you and I should return to the kitchen?"

"All right," she said, though her gaze lingered on his desk.

"Oh, that!" Walt said suddenly. "I was just finishing up a bit of dictation."

"Dictation?"

"There's a recorder down in the drawer."

"That's odd."

"Yes, but it comes in handy."

"For dictation," Gloria said deadpan, and Walt had the sneaking suspicion she didn't believe him.

"Why, sure! I take notes on the inn," Walt said, starting to get creative. "Jot down recipes and the like."

"If you say so."

"I was recording a bit about the lamb I braised!"

"Sounded more like you said...'behave'?"

Walt's heart hammered as the seconds ticked away. Gloria Chavez was a very pretty woman. She was also obviously intuitive. Gloria suspected something was up with Walt. She just didn't know what. Walt kind of wished he knew the answer to that question himself.

"How about some wine?" he interjected suddenly.

Gloria's face was awash with relief. Her arrival in Christmas Town hadn't only taxed Walt. It had apparently been trying for Gloria, too. "Wine sounds great, actually."

It certainly did, and Walt couldn't wait to pour himself a glass.

A big one.

A short time later, Gloria sat at one end of the long dining room table with her back to the parlor and Walt sat at the other end closest to the kitchen. Noelle, who sat to Gloria's right, was in between them and near the festively adorned sideboard, which held a mini Christmas tree with tiny white lights. The blazing hearth was to Gloria's left, crackling softly with a comforting fire. Through the darkened windows on either side of the fireplace, a steady barrage of small white flakes twirled through the air.

Gloria raised her wineglass and took a sip, querying lightly, "Does it ever stop snowing in Christmas Town?"

"Sometimes." Noelle grinned and set down her spoon. "But never for long!"

They'd recently finished dinner and had moved on to dessert, a heavenly chocolate ice cream variety that Gloria hadn't tried before. Walt had offered her peppermint schnapps as a topper, but she'd declined. Peppermint somehow seemed par for the course in Christmas Town. The moment Gloria had stepped into the Christmas Inn after returning from Savannah's, she'd detected its distinct scent. A squat round peppermint-scented candle burned on an end table in the parlor, and another one of equal size stood flickering on the countertop beside the cooktop in the kitchen. Then there was that peppermint bark candy that Walt had spilled onto the library floor!

"Well, I think you're lucky," Gloria said, addressing Noelle and then her dad. "Living in such a beautiful place as Christmas Town. Savannah told me the streets here looked like something straight off of a postcard, and I have to tell you: it's true!"

"I've seen postcards of Miami," Walt said. "Not too shabby looking there, either."

"But with a totally different vibe." Noelle's face grew animated. "Palm trees...ocean breezes, white sandy beaches... I've always wanted to go. Soak in the sun!"

"Well, you'll have to come and visit sometime!" Gloria suggested impulsively. Then, she quickly glanced at Walt. "I mean, you're both welcome..." Gloria felt her face warm, wondering how she'd gotten herself into this. "Naturally." After a thought, she added, "Joy, too!"

Walt met Gloria's eyes then quickly looked away, setting his sights on the liquor bottle. "A splash of schnapps, anyone?"

Noelle cut him a sharp look and tugged the bottle away. "Papa's probably had enough," she whispered sotto voce, and Walt stared at her agape. Next, she turned pleasantly toward Gloria. "That's really sweet of you." She shrugged, long blond hair cascading over her shoulders. "Sometime! Maybe?"

Walt cleared his throat, furthering the conversation. "Speaking of travel, Gloria... Have you done much of it?" He casually reached for the schnapps bottle, but Noelle slid it further away.

"Not as much as I would have liked," Gloria answered, as Walt viewed Noelle with consternation. Gloria almost giggled at the role-reversal. Noelle was very good at looking after her father, and she obviously loved him. It was clear that Walt adored Noelle, too, despite her bossy nature. In a way, their relationship was charming. "I've explored some of the southeastern United States," Gloria continued, finishing her ice cream. "Along the coast, mostly." When Walt turned his attention back on her, she continued. "Christmas Town is as far west as I've been."

"Then, we're honored…" Walt stared at her for a prolonged beat then took a huge bite of peppermint schnapps–topped ice cream. "Honored you could make the trip this season."

"Bet Savannah's happy about it, too," Noelle said. "She talks about you all the time, and about how much fun the two of you had working together in Miami."

Gloria sighed, missing those days. "Yeah. Those were good times."

Walt's brow rose with the question. "You teach drama at the same high school where Savannah was a guidance counselor, right?"

"That's how we got to know each other, yeah. Savannah volunteered to assist with one of my productions and we hit it off immediately. I was glad to have her help! Savannah's incredibly…"

She hedged on the word, so Noelle took a stab at it. "Dramatic?"

Gloria laughed lightly. "I was going to say theatrical, but dramatic fits, too. Savannah's very skilled in the arts. You should see what she's done with her nursery. It's darling!"

"I'll have to pay Kurt a visit, and ask to take a peek," Walt said.

"I'm sure Savannah would be happy to give you the tour, too," Gloria replied. "She's terribly proud of the room, as well she should be."

Noelle finished her ice cream then said, "You mentioned travel before. Is there any place in particular you'd like to go?"

Gloria drew in a breath and then said wistfully, "Venice—absolutely. It looks so lovely. All of Italy does. Your sister's so lucky to get to study there."

"Yeah," Noelle answered. "She's having fun."

"Correction!" Walt lifted his wineglass and took a sip. "Joy's having the time of her life! At least, that's what she told me the last time we talked."

Gloria glowed at the thought of the young woman having such an amazing experience abroad. She would have loved to have done something similar herself in college, but she'd never had the money. "How amazing for her." Then a brilliant idea occurred to Gloria, one that seemed so patently obvious, she couldn't help but mention it. "The two of you should go to see her!"

Walt appeared taken aback. "Well, I'm not exactly sure—"

"Dad!" Noelle cried, turning toward him. "That's a *fantastic* idea."

"I don't know." Walt seemed caught off guard. "This is supposed to be *her* time away. *Her* experience."

"She misses us, Dad."

"How do you know?"

"Because she told me, hey."

"Well, she didn't tell me."

"That's because she didn't want to worry you."

Walt's face clouded over with emotion. "Worry?"

Noelle reached out and touched his arm. "It's not like that. Really. Joy is having fun. The time of her life, as you say. I just think Gloria's right!"

Walt blinked at Gloria and she stared back at him like a deer caught in someone's headlights.

"It would be dynamite for us to go over," Noelle said. "It would mean so much to Joy. Plus..." she said, picking up steam. "I could write about it! An article for the campus paper."

"Noelle is the editor of her college's newspaper," Walt filled in for Gloria's benefit, while Noelle continued in delighted tones.

"'An American Teenager Abroad'!"

"You're hardly a teenager anymore, Noelle. You've just turned twenty-one years old."

"How 'bout..." She beamed sunnily and scrolled her fingers across the air like a tickertape headline. "'New Adult in the Old World,' then?"

Gloria tentatively addressed Walt. "It does have kind of a ring to it."

Walt stared down at his ice cream, which was melting in his bowl, drowning in a liquid pool of peppermint schnapps.

"Well, if I were you, I'd go," Gloria said, and Walt's chin jerked up. "Think about it, Walt. It could be a once in a lifetime opportunity. An adventure!"

"Yeah, that," Noelle enthusiastically agreed. "An adventure!"

"But you're in school," Walt told Noelle. "Precisely why you couldn't study abroad yourself, remember? You said that your schedule's too packed."

"Not during spring break, it's not."

This stopped Walt cold, leaving him flummoxed.

As he sat there silently gazing at the two of them, Gloria leaned toward Noelle and reassuringly whispered, "Well, if *I* were your parent, I'd *definitely* take you."

Walt gaped at Gloria and she instantly feared she'd gone too far. But, honestly? What an opportunity for the two of them. And, Italy—of all places—the country of Gloria's dreams!

Just then, the front door pushed open and an older woman's voice called loudly from the hall. "Hel-looo!"

"Who's that?" Gloria asked, startled.

"My mom," Walt began, before a big voice boomed.

"Anybody *ho-ho-ho*-ome?"

"And Grandpa Christmas," Noelle said with a grin. Next, she scrambled out of her chair and raced to greet them.

Chapter Five

Gloria followed Noelle and Walt into the foyer where Noelle briefly embraced her grandparents, one after the other.

The woman in her sixties with shoulder-length brown hair frosted gold at the tips admired her granddaughter. She wore fitted stretch jeans and knee-high leather boots and a faux fur animal-print coat. Her head was topped with a Santa hat, and the strap of a very large purse was slung over one shoulder. "You're looking smarter every time I see you!"

"Grandma," Noelle said with a laugh. "Nobody *looks* smart."

"Well, you do!"

"Your grandmother's right," the older gentleman said with a twinkle, as he took his turn hugging Noelle. Walt's dad had deep blue eyes, and a full white beard and mustache with a head of snowy white hair visible below the rim of the bright red Santa hat he also wore. In contrast to his slim and apparently fit wife, Walt's dad bulged mightily at his middle. Although he didn't seem the least bit concerned about it. In a way, he almost appeared...*jolly*. Gloria called herself up short, wondering where that thought had come from.

"Buddy Christmas," the older man said, holding out his hand. "It's so nice to meet you."

"Gloria Chavez! Hi!" Gloria shook hands with Buddy as his wife beamed her way.

"We know who you are!" she said with a wave of her hand. "And, heavens, Buddy! Why so formal?" She lunged for Gloria and took her in her arms, clamping her to her damp coat. "Lou Christmas, dear!" she said, with another sharp tug—*oomph!*—that drew the air from Gloria's lungs. "Welcome! Welcome to Christmas Town!"

Gloria meekly patted Lou's back, trying to catch her breath. "Hi...Lou," she said with a wheeze. "It's so nice to meet you!"

"Mom," Walt said sternly. "You're getting Gloria all wet."

Lou screwed up her face and pushed back to examine Gloria, who she now clutched by her upper arms. "Oh, *dear*."

"It's all right," Gloria assured her generously. "Really!"

Lou let her go then viewed her perplexedly. "Noelle," she said, her light brown eyes never leaving Gloria's. "Please run to the kitchen and bring us a dishtowel." When the girl turned away, she added, "A clean one!"

Buddy peered after his departing granddaughter and toward the dining room. "I told you we'd be interrupting their supper," he said, clearly speaking to Lou.

"Not interrupting!" Gloria rushed to assure them.

"It's true," Walt concurred. "We've just finished up."

Buddy strode toward the table, his gaze landing on the bottle of peppermint schnapps. "Celebrating Christmas early?" he asked Walt in a curious way, and for some mysterious reason Walt reddened.

"It was on the menu, Dad."

Buddy and Lou exchanged knowing glances, then Lou glowed sunnily at Gloria. "Well, well, well! Isn't this just *marvelous*."

Lou started to draw Gloria into another impromptu hug, but then stopped and soundly patted Gloria's shoulders. "You must be a very good influence on my son."

Walt sent his mother a silencing look, leaving Gloria befuddled.

"It's true!" Buddy quipped, striding back toward them through the parlor. "Walt very rarely eats desserts."

"Well, that's better, right?" Gloria asked unsurely. "More healthy to limit one's sweets?"

"Bosh!" Lou asserted boisterously. "Desserts and Christmases go together! Like peas in a pod! Or treats in a stocking! Or...or..." she glanced merrily into the parlor and then back over her shoulder into the living room, each of which held a beautifully decorated Christmas tree. "Or...ornaments on a Fraser fir!"

Noelle returned from the kitchen with the dishtowel, then ratted on her father. "Dad's been eating tons of sweet stuff lately. Mostly, candy."

"Oh?" Buddy and Lou inquired together, as their foreheads rose in unison.

Walt folded his arms across his chest. "Why do I feel like I'm being picked on?"

"Peppermint bark is bad for you, Dad. Especially eating that much of it."

Walt held up a finger. "One day! One day only!" he protested, sounding a bit strained. Gloria couldn't blame the guy. His family was being awfully hard on him. Didn't everyone deserve a break from a strict dietary regime now and again?

"Yes," Walt said, though his voice came out hoarsely. "They do." All eyes turned on him.

Noelle shot him a curious look and Walt cleared his throat. "Everyone…" He briefly glanced at Gloria, then he quickly turned away. "Deserves a little treat now and then."

"What?" Gloria drew in a sharp breath, wondering how he'd known what she'd been thinking. "

"Dad?" Noelle asked with concern. "Are you okay?"

Gloria told herself she was being silly. A sheer coincidence was all it was. It wasn't like Walt had somehow read her mind. Ha-ha!

Walt shook his head hard and pulled his gaze away from Gloria. Then, seemingly against his will, his eyes returned to hers again. Walt's azure eyes were more iridescent than his father's, and ultra inviting, Gloria couldn't help but think in spite of herself. She felt a light breeze gently ruffle her hair and the warm glow of sunshine on her face, and—for a moment—Gloria feared she was getting swept away again. To some place wonderful and unfamiliar.

"Peppermint bark?" Lou said, clearly delighted. "Well, well, *well*." Gloria turned toward the older woman to catch Lou observing her and Walt with interest.

"Come along, dear!" Buddy announced. "Let's hang up our coats."

"We won't stay a minute," Lou assured Walt when he ran a hand through his hair.

It was only then that Gloria looked up and realized she and Walt had been standing smack-dab under a sprig of mistletoe hanging above the doorway between the foyer and the parlor. Walt noticed this at the same time, too, and both of their faces burned red.

Walt blinked and took a giant step backward, as Noelle returned with the dishtowel, passing it to Gloria, who used it to dab at her shoulders, arms, and the front of her winter white sweater, all the while sending curious peeks around the rest of the downstairs.

Though Gloria hadn't focused on this before, she could now see Savannah was right. The Christmas Inn was rife with mistletoe, which appeared to be everywhere. Hanging from the drop-down light just inside the front door. Dangling from both doorways leading out of the entry hall, into the parlor and into the living room. There was another sprig taped to the doorframe leading from the living room into the library, and an additional one draped from the doorframe of the opened double glass doors dividing the parlor from the dining room. While Gloria hadn't seen it, she was now relatively sure there'd be mistletoe hanging above the thresholds at both points of entry to the kitchen. Maybe even also draping from the doorway between the kitchen and the laundry room, which led to the outdoors.

When Gloria had freshened up in her beautiful guestroom with its own en suite bath before dinner, she hadn't seen any mistletoe in there. Then again, she hadn't specifically been looking for it.

As Lou and Buddy bounded down the hall, Gloria overheard Buddy whispering to his wife, "Did you notice the *peppermint* candle burning in the parlor?"

"I did, indeed." Lou nodded enthusiastically then spoke in hushed tones. "She's *very* pretty, isn't she? Every bit as pretty as Savannah said she was."

Walt shifted on his feet, addressing Gloria. "Why don't you and Noelle go visit with my folks in the living room," he suggested, "while I clean up in the kitchen?"

"No worries!" Noelle said brightly. "I'll take the kitchen." She gently retrieved the dishtowel from Gloria and glanced at her dad. "You go ahead and visit with Grandma and Grandpa."

Only Walt wasn't so sure he wanted to *visit with Grandma and Grandpa*. Mostly, he felt like he needed a chance to clear his head. This entire day had hit him like a giant torpedo coming at him from outer space. Or, more like Miami. His gaze roved over Gloria again then he quickly looked away. "I'll go…grab the candle from the parlor!"

Gloria's eyebrows shot up, so he explained lamely, "Ambiance."

"Ambiance," Gloria repeated. Though she didn't look convinced.

While Noelle started clearing the table, Walt strode into the parlor, his knees wobbling slightly. This was bad news, very bad news. Shocking. Unnerving. Abysmal. At the same time, a tiny bit electrifying and energizing, too. Something was happening here, something pretty powerful and compelling. And, there was no use denying it. This sudden resurgence of Walt's family abilities had nothing to do with holiday hiccups, and everything to do with Gloria.

Chapter Six

Gloria sat on the loveseat facing the fireplace and nearest the hall and, after some fairly obvious deliberation, Walt sat in an armchair on the other side of the living room, closest to the library. A tall, lovely Christmas tree stood across the way from him, on the far side of the library door, while Buddy and Lou perched like a couple of pleased lovebirds on the sofa, which was kitty-corner from Gloria and situated between two street-facing windows. Both still wore their Santa hats. Gloria supposed they were really into the season, and they sure seemed to be in great spirits. Both watched her, smiling broadly, before turning their gazes on Walt and grinning at him. He shifted uncomfortably in his chair under their perusal.

"Can I offer anyone an after-dinner drink?" Walt glanced around the room, trying to keep his eyes from lingering on Gloria. "A brandy, perhaps?"

"Brandy would be fine!" Buddy boomed, sitting merrily by the fire. He leaned forward and rubbed his sturdy palms together, savoring the warmth of the flames.

It was amazing to Gloria that Walt had managed to keep all four fireplaces in the downstairs going, without tending to them. She'd assumed them to be the natural wood-burning kind, but upon more careful inspection, she now saw that the hearth in here employed an extremely high-end set of gas logs. Gloria guessed that the other fireplaces were the same. Not that it was any wonder. Surely, having several real wood-burning fireplaces in a home as large as this one could prove a fire hazard. Somehow or other, though, this grand old house had managed to stay standing for years.

"This is such an incredible inn," Gloria said to Buddy and Lou, once Walt had gone to fix their drinks. "Savannah told me it's been in your family for generations."

"Quite some time, yes," Buddy replied. "My grandparents built this house. Then, my parents owned it, and my brother and sisters and I grew up here."

"Wow. How cool!"

"It hasn't always been in the family, though," Lou interjected thoughtfully. "There were some mild real estate troubles and the property fell out of the Christmases' hands for a while."

"When my parents died," Buddy explained, "they unfortunately hadn't left a will. Only a handwritten directive that wasn't very clear on which of us children should inherit it. My oldest brother, the eldest of us five, had already moved to Canada to help with a family business."

"My Buddy, here, was the second son," Lou said, continuing the story. "But Buddy believed the house should go to his sister Liza, since she was getting married and could have made this her new family's home."

"But that was not to be." Buddy sadly shook his head. "Liza's husband was from Idaho, and they wound up moving out west. My other two sisters also married and moved far away."

Lou tapped her chin. "It took some wrangling and couple of years for the family to straighten it all out, and secure an official deed for the property."

"And, during that time, the old house fell into a state of disrepair," Buddy added. "I'd married Lou by then and we'd already purchased our own house on North Main Street. With our attorney's help, my siblings and I eventually assumed legal ownership of this house, and we were able to sell it to a younger couple. They had ambitions of refurbishing the place, but ran short of money and never got around to it."

"Well, it's beautiful now," Gloria remarked, beholding the beautiful room and its grandeur. "Really spectacular."

"That's thanks to Walt!" Lou said.

"And his late wife, Rose," Buddy chimed in.

"The two of them completely restored this home, converting it to an inn."

"That was quite a task," Buddy supplied. "This old house had been empty for years."

"When Walt was a little boy," Lou confided happily, "he used to say he was going to get this house back in the family."

"Fix it up!" Buddy said, nodding. "Make it his own!"

Lou's brown eyes sparkled merrily. "And he did!"

Walt returned from the library carrying two brandy snifters. He gave one drink to his mom and handed the other to Gloria. "What have my folks been telling you about me?"

"Only good things," Gloria said with a grin. "About how you bought and restored the inn. Your ears should be burning!"

Walt's ears tinged red. "Yes, well! Just hold that thought, and let me retrieve the other libations."

Gloria giggled to herself at the word "libations." Walt clearly was an educated man, and very old-world in his demeanor. He was gentlemanly in a way that Gloria wasn't accustomed to, and she found it charming.

"Oh, here!" Lou said, setting down her drink on the coffee table. "I brought something for you," she said to Gloria, "and, I want to give it to you before I forget."

Gloria was touched and more than a little surprised. She hadn't anticipated welcome gifts of any kind, nor had she brought gifts in return. Apart from that special bottle of champagne for Kurt and Savannah, and the nice bottle of wine she'd packed in her suitcase and had intended to give Walt as a host gift. In her hurry to get to Savannah's house, she'd forgotten all about it.

Lou reached for her bag on the floor and tugged it onto her lap. Then, she flipped open its flap and dug inside. "This isn't a keeper," she explained. "It's more of a loaner."

"Oh!" Gloria sat up a little straighter on the loveseat, unsure of what that meant. "Okay."

"Something to brighten up your room at the Christmas Inn!" Lou proclaimed. "Make it feel more homey."

"Lou," Gloria said sunnily, "you shouldn't haaaave…" Gloria froze in fright as Lou tugged a ghastly stuffed creature out of her purse. It arrived bottom- and legs-first, a big round blob and two stubby nubs, and seemed stuck, because Lou had to pull extra hard at one point.

"Here we are!"

Gloria blinked as Lou shoved the odd-looking snowman doll in her direction.

"Meet Mr. Noodles!" It had short stubby arms that matched the legs, a large ball for a body, and a smaller ball for a head, with a tightly wound scarf around its narrow neck. The item had apparently once been white, but now leaned toward ivory… A black felt top hat was sewn onto its head, and it had large black button eyes and a nose. But the largest button of all was the russet-colored one that served as its mouth and seemed to be screaming for *help*.

"Wow! He's—"

"Very special, yes," Buddy said. "Lou's pride and joy!"

"Oh!" Gloria tried not to jump when Lou pressed Mr. Noodles toward her. "Oh, how nice!" She gingerly accepted the snowman then smiled at Lou. Though Gloria worried that her smile looked plastered on too tight. And also, that it might be blinding. "Thanks, Lou! This is totally…unexpected."

"Sometimes the best things in life are!" Lou said with a titter.

Gloria turned the stuffed snowman around to face her. "What adorable detail," she said, examining the item more closely. "Did you do all this yourself?"

Lou beamed proudly. "I took a craft course online."

"Here we are!" Walt said, returning with the two remaining brandies. He gave one to his dad, then startled at the snowman in Gloria's hands. "You still have Mr. Noodles?" he asked Lou, astounded.

"Well, of course, dear," she answered resolutely. "He's an emblem of the holiday!"

"Sooo…" Walt took his seat again and sipped from his brandy. "What's he doing here?"

Gloria turned her gaze on Walt. "He's on loan. To cheer up my room at the Christmas Inn. Isn't that great?"

Walt tried to conceal a grin behind his glass. "Fantastic, yes."

"Well, thank you," Gloria told Lou. "Thanks so much for thinking of me. Mr. Noodles will keep me from getting lonely." She gave the toy a small hug and set it on her lap. "I left my dog behind."

"I'm glad you didn't say cat," Lou confided quietly. "Cats and I have a terrible history." Then, as if to prove it, she sneezed twice.

"Bless you!" Gloria and Walt said almost at once.

While Lou searched her bag for a tissue, Buddy asked Gloria, "What kind of dog do you have?"

"She's an English-style yellow Lab. Very friendly."

Buddy nodded with interest. "Have you had her long?"

"Only since last year. She belonged to my aunt, who passed in February. I brought her to live with me after that."

Lou dabbed her nose with a tissue and sniffed. "Our condolences on your loss, dear."

Buddy frowned sympathetically. "Savannah told us that's why you had to miss the wedding."

Walt viewed Gloria with compassion. "That must have been a hard time for you."

"Yeah…" Gloria pursed her lips and hugged Mr. Noodles more tightly.

"We're sorry," Walt said soothingly. "We certainly don't need to talk about it."

Gloria gratefully met Walt's eyes, and she immediately felt better. He was such a reassuring guy, and genuinely caring, as well. Both these features clearly went into making him a great dad to Noelle and Joy. "I know. Thanks, everyone, for your sympathy."

"How old is your dog?" Buddy asked her.

"Five!" Gloria's heart felt lighter just thinking of her big, furry friend. "My brother David got Gitana for my aunt after my uncle passed and she complained of being lonely."

"Gitana?" Lou asked with surprised. "That's a fun name. What does it mean?"

"Gypsy!" Gloria laughed lightly, recalling how cute the little pup had looked when David had first brought her home to Titi Mon. "When David picked her up from the breeder's, the puppy was all dressed up with a bright red bandana around her neck. My aunt joked it made her look like a little gypsy, and so the name stuck.

"David's house-sitting for me now, and watching Gitana while I'm away. I would have left Gitana at his house, but pets aren't allowed in the parsonage."

"David's a pastor, then?" Buddy asked.

Gloria nodded. "Nondenominational."

"Well, what do you know!" Lou's entire countenance brightened. "We have a nondenominational church right her in Christmas Town! It's just down the street on the corner."

"Yes," Gloria said. "I saw it, when I was coming in." Gloria stifled a yawn, suddenly realizing how tired she was. She'd begun driving before dawn. "I'm sorry, I—"

"No need to apologize," Walt said. "You must be pretty exhausted."

"After the drive," Buddy added.

"And, from seeing Savannah!" Lou chirped. She paused and then asked, "You have seen her today?"

"Oh, yes," Gloria answered. "I went by to visit her as soon as I got in."

"How is Savannah?" Buddy queried in his rich baritone.

"Doing well." Gloria smiled softly. "And really ready to have that baby!"

"I'm so glad you mentioned that!" Lou's eyes lit up. "That's another one of the reasons why we're here." She glanced around the room then addressed Gloria. "I wanted to invite you to a surprise baby shower that I and some of the other women in town are hosting."

"Oh, what fun!" Gloria said, deciding not to mention how well prepared for the baby Savannah already appeared to be.

"It's not precisely for the baby, though," Lou went on in thoughtful tones. "More like in the honor of little him or her. The gifts will principally be for Savannah. Kurt's told me they're pretty well set with baby things."

Gloria was touched by Lou's generous gesture and especially pleased to be included. "That sounds wonderful, Lou. I'd love to attend, and will be happy to help out in any way I can."

"Mainly, you can help by getting Savannah to the Snow Globe Gallery on Friday evening at seven."

"This Friday?"

"Yes."

Gloria nodded, realizing that was only a few days from now. "Is there something I can do to help with the planning?"

Lou shot her a pleased grin. "How very kind of you to offer! Hmm. Let me think on it and also talk to Sandy. She and Liz are the main ones organizing the shower; they might have some ideas."

"I'll be seeing Liz tomorrow," Gloria said. "Savannah and I are meeting her for coffee."

"Fab!" Lou's expression grew serious. "Just don't let the cat out of the bag to Savannah," she said in a hushed whisper. "Mum's the word."

"No problem." Gloria winked at the older woman. "I'm very good at keeping secrets."

"Are you?" Lou seemed extraordinarily delighted by this. Her gaze swept quickly over Walt and then Gloria. "How grand!"

Walt set down his drink on the table beside him. "Yes, well," he said, hinting at his parents. "Mom, Dad…" He nodded at each. "Thanks so much for stopping by."

"I think that's our cue, dear," Lou told her husband. She grabbed her purse and got to her feet, and Buddy stood as well. He strode toward Gloria and held out his hand.

"Gloria, it's such a pleasure."

Gloria left Mr. Noodles on the loveseat and shook hands with Buddy, saying goodnight. When it was Lou's turn, however, Lou wanted another hug. Fortunately, this time, she wasn't wearing her wet coat.

"Lovely having you in town, Gloria!" Lou said, releasing her. "I'll be in touch soon."

"Oh!" Gloria glanced around for her purse, recalling she'd set it back in her guestroom. "Would you like my number?"

"That's all right," Lou said. "It's late and you're tired." She cast an impish gaze at her son, which caused his neck to flush. "Why don't you give it to Walt in the morning, and I can get it from him later?"

"Well…all right."

Walt escorted his parents down the hall to the coat closet and helped them on with their coats while Gloria waited in the foyer by the entry table. It wasn't until the group returned that she spotted the bag that she'd left there from the Christmas Cookie Shop.

"Why, what's this?" Lou asked merrily, noticing the bag at nearly the same time.

"Just a little treat that Savannah got me," Gloria explained. She shrugged timidly. "I didn't mean to leave it lying around. Sorry."

"No harm done," Walt said, though the color of his neck was even redder than before.

Buddy observed the paper bag and its pretty seal. "That looks like one of those cookies from Hannah's shop."

"It is!" Gloria confirmed. Next, she immediately felt embarrassed about it. She clearly wasn't going to confess that it was a Commitment Cookie, and that

Savannah had expressly given it to her to share with Walt. She sure hoped Walt wasn't putting those thoughts together in his head, but Gloria worried that he might be.

"How delightful!" Lou said with spunky cheer. "Would you mind telling us which kind it is, dear?"

Buddy hooked his arm through one of hers. "Come along now, Louise. We won't want to overstay our welcome!"

Noelle scurried into the foyer. "You're leaving already?"

Lou glanced momentarily at Buddy, who gave her a firm look. "I'm sorry, Noelle, yes," Lou said a bit sadly. "But we'll be back again soon. In the meantime, you're always welcome at our house. You know that."

Walt eyed his daughter with concern. "You weren't cleaning up in the kitchen all that time?"

"No, I had a phone call from Joy."

"Joy?" Buddy and Lou asked, their faces animated.

"How is she, dear?" Lou wanted to know.

"Doing really, really well!" Noelle glanced around at the group, clearly weighing whether or not to tell them, before further volunteering, "She's got a boyfriend. An Italian boyfriend."

The blood drained from Walt's face. "What?"

"So soon?" Buddy queried.

"It hasn't been that soon." Lou swatted him with one of her gloves, after tugging the other one on. "She's been over there…" Lou rolled her eyes toward the ceiling, mentally counting. "Four months!"

"I'm…not so sure I like the sound of this," Walt stammered.

"Da-ad…" Noelle shook her head. "He's a very nice guy. Legit. An architecture student and everything."

"Buddy has ancestors in Italy," Lou told Gloria.

"Yes," Buddy said, "but they go way, way, way back." He rubbed his snowy white beard. "Maybe even further than that."

Walt set a hand on his hip, looking shell-shocked. He appeared prepared to say something, but all that came out was, "Huh."

"Well," Lou said brightly. "We'd better get going!" She gave Noelle a quick hug and headed for the door. "Ta-ta!"

"See you, Grandma!"

Noelle hugged her grandpa, too.

"Good seeing you, sweetheart," he said.

After the senior Christmases left, Gloria and Noelle surveyed Walt, who hadn't moved a muscle since uttering, *Huh.*

Noelle raised her eyebrows at Gloria, then she saw the Christmas Cookie Shop bag on the table. "If that's yours, you'd better take it back to your bedroom for safekeeping," she said with a mischievous grin. "Once Dad comes to, he might not be able to stop himself."

Walt pointedly cleared his throat. "I heard that, Noelle." But Gloria noticed Walt viewed his daughter with patient indulgence rather than with true agitation.

"It's okay," Gloria told Walt kindly. "We all have our weaknesses."

He stared down at her with his deep blue eyes, and Gloria's heart pounded.

Walt's Adam's apple rose and fell and his voice sounded ragged. "Gloria..." he began. Then somehow he was unable to continue.

"I'll just go and finish up in the kitchen!" Noelle announced from beside them, though neither one turned her way.

"Thanks, daughter," Walt said, finding his voice.

"Yeah, thanks, Noelle!" Gloria called after her, when she heard the girl walking away.

Walt studied Gloria a long moment, seemingly trying to decipher something in her eyes. "I'm sorry," he eventually said. "I didn't mean to."

Gloria felt tipsy from his heady perusal. "Didn't mean to what?"

"Give you the wrong impression."

But his look belied his words. Walt's gaze poured over her and Gloria feared she was getting swept away again. To that tropical paradise written in Walt's eyes. Gloria was no babe in the woods. She was over thirty, and she'd dated plenty. Yet, she'd never had a man affect her so strongly, simply by standing so near. It was like Walt could see something deep in her soul... something that even she couldn't grasp completely, because she'd never experienced this level of connection before. "Walt?" Gloria asked, tilting her chin up at him. "Is there something going on here I should know about?"

"Yeah," he said hoarsely. "I mean, no." Walt's gaze darted to the cookie bag on the foyer table. His voice was husky when he asked, "That's a Virginia Cookie, isn't it?"

"What if it is?"

"I…I just want to make clear… Just so there's no misunderstanding—"

"Yes?"

Walt swallowed hard. "I'm not interested in sharing your cookie, Gloria."

Well, of all the nerve! An arrow shot straight through her heart at Walt's sudden disregard. It wasn't like she'd been trying to attract Walt. *He'd* been the one acting all weird about things, *not her*. And, if he believed she had designs on him and had intended to act them out by employing some silly Christmas cookie rumored to inspire true love, then the man had another thing coming.

"I don't know what you're thinking," she said stonily. "But, whatever it is, you're most likely wrong. I didn't buy that cookie. I already told you Savannah gave it to me as a gift."

"Yeah. I pretty much guessed that she did."

"And, I brought it back here for *me*." Gloria snatched the bag off the foyer table in confirmation. "To enjoy *by myself*, perhaps with some milk!"

"Okay."

"I did not bring it back to share—with *you*, if that's what you imagined."

"Hold on, I never said—"

"Oh yes, you did." Gloria huffed, her agitation growing. What did Walt Christmas think he was, anyway? Irresistible? It was Gloria's turn to think, *Huh!*

"Look, Walt. Let's just get this out in the open, all right? Savannah's been trying to matchmake us for nearly a year. She's said things to me, and no doubt she's also said them to you. But hey, you know what? We're both adults here, and—as grown-ups—we both know the score. You've built your life in Christmas Town and I've got mine in Miami. There's no point in thinking about things that could never be."

"I agree." Then why were his blue eyes twinkling, like Gloria was the most fascinating woman he'd ever seen?

"You've been incredibly kind and welcoming. A really terrific host, but I don't want you to feel pressured to take care of me while I'm in Christmas Town. I can manage perfectly fine on my own."

"But, meals here are included."

"Breakfast and dinner," Gloria corrected.

When his brow rose questioningly, she informed him, "I read the brochure online."

Walt viewed her with interest, his blue eyes gleaming. "Gloria Chavez, just what are you telling me?"

Gloria held her cookie bag tightly. "That I don't want you to go to any extra trouble on account of me. I want you to treat me like any other guest."

"Like any other guest?"

"Yes."

For some odd reason, he appeared to be resisting the urge to smile. "Anything else?"

"Well, yes! Of course," Gloria said, feeling foolish that she was forgetting her manners. "I wanted to say *thank you*. Thank you for putting me up here. That's incredibly generous and kind. Certainly beyond the call of duty, as Savannah's brother-in-law, and I know she appreciates it." Gloria paused a moment and then added, "I do, too." She sauntered over to Mr. Noodles and plucked him off of the loveseat in the living room.

"Now, if you'll excuse us," she said, cuddling the ugly creation close, "we've had a long day."

Walt chuckled warmheartedly at the vision of Gloria holding the wacky snowman his mom had made. "I didn't mean to offend you, you know."

"You didn't."

"You're sure?"

"Yes."

"Well, I apologize anyway!"

She paused to study him a minute more than she should have, taking in that rugged frame and his way-too-handsome hairy face. *Gosh.* Why did someone so obnoxious have to look so appealing? *In another life, maybe*, Gloria told herself, fuming, *he might have looked sexy, and hot, and like he could totally rock my world. But, nope. Not in this one! I wouldn't give Walt Christmas part of my special cookie if he got down on his knees and* begged *for it.*

"Sleep well!" he said as Gloria strode down the hall.

Yeah, well. Whatever. But, instead of saying that, she gave a cheery wave. "You, too!"

Whew! At least that part's over with and now Walt knows where I stand. Not at all interested in him! Huh! Gloria had not come to the Christmas Inn for *romance*; she'd come to Christmas Town to help her friend. She passed by the library at a fast clip, then stopped outside her open bedroom door. When she looked up, she saw something she hadn't seen hanging from the doorframe before: a pretty green and white sprig of mistletoe.

Later that night Walt sat at his desk in the library. He'd just finished going through the mail, and an empty tumbler rested at his elbow. He'd poured himself a short glass of peppermint schnapps as a nightcap, and had just finished it up. Fortunately, the correspondence that had come today was no longer "restless." In part, Walt attributed this to the fact that he'd carried the peppermint candle in from the living room, after Gloria had said goodnight. The instant he thought of his pretty brunette houseguest, a smile crept up on his lips. Despite his best efforts not to be taken in by her, Walt couldn't help but be charmed by Gloria. Particularly since she obviously had the hots for him.

Walt leaned back in his chair and shook his head, small snippets of information coming back to him. While he hadn't known Gloria's thoughts completely, somehow he'd gotten wind of passing fragments. It was like hearing something across an old-fashioned telephone wire with a very poor connection. Though he'd sensed no complete sentences, Walt had distinctly intuited some very telling thoughts: *hot, sexy, rock my world.* Walt's neck steamed at his open collar and the tops of his ears burned hot. Though he couldn't help but be flattered by Gloria's generous assessment of him, he was also privately embarrassed by it.

Walt hadn't had anyone consider him "hot" or "sexy" in...well, in forever, as far as he knew. Walt had kept himself out of the dating game, and distanced himself enough from the opposite sex so that women rarely came on to him. And, even when he thought they were, it turned out that Walt was sometimes wrong. Just like that time last Christmas when he'd believed Savannah was hitting on him at the church bazaar. Of course, Walt hadn't been alone in his faulty assessment. The rest of the parishioners who'd witnessed their exchange had come to the same conclusion. It had taken a bit of work, on everyone's part, to finally straighten that misunderstanding out.

While he had many strong suits, one of Walt's shortcomings was that he sometimes misread social cues. He'd clearly misread some of them with Gloria, because when she went to bed tonight she'd seemed awfully perturbed with him. Maybe Gloria thought him rude in making that remark about the cookie. Upon reflection, Walt could see how that might have seemed presumptuous on his part. And, the truth was, Walt hadn't meant to presume things at all. He'd merely been trying to let Gloria off the hook. As she'd admitted out loud, Savannah had been putting pressure on her about Walt, just as she'd been dropping hints to Walt about Gloria.

Since Savannah's matchmaking antics had been hovering over them, perhaps it was good that Gloria had brought it up, so she and Walt could discuss that and clear the air. Although, Walt hadn't felt like much of a participant in the conversation. It was more like Gloria had *told* him that she and he didn't stand a chance. Just like she'd basically *told* him that he should take Noelle to Italy! Man, she was a bossy woman. Rose hadn't been like that at all. She'd had a sweet, compromising nature, and went out of her way to avoid conflict. Walt had an inkling that Gloria was quite the opposite. Not that she appeared confrontational. It was more like she was a woman who held her ground, and who stated her opinions firmly. Like when she insisted Walt treat her like any other guest.

Gloria clearly didn't want special treatment from Walt, so she wasn't going to get it. But, what Gloria didn't understand was that all guests were treated royally at the Christmas Inn, Walt thought with quiet chuckle. Walt reflected on Gloria's arrival in that flurry of mail, and that soul-deep connection they'd shared when looking in each other's eyes. No matter what she said to Walt, or what Walt told himself, it appeared that a huge snowball had already started rolling, and it was growing larger by the minute.

A lot had gone on here today, much more than Walt had been prepared for. And, though the peppermint remedy seemed to be keeping certain problems at bay, Walt worried that this fix wouldn't work indefinitely. He'd need a more permanent solution. That's why he intended to make an appointment to see Kurt at the clinic tomorrow. Though Kurt was his younger brother, he'd been a very eligible bachelor before reconnecting with Savannah, so he'd had plenty of experience with dating and women. Kurt also was familiar with Walt's unique family heritage, and the myriad things that could go right—and wrong—because of it.

Chapter Seven

Gloria slept more soundly than she could recall sleeping in a while. The moment her head hit the pillow, she'd sunk into the cozy queen-size bed with its big fluffy pillows and billowy comforter, and dozed off immediately. The extra weight of the beautiful patchwork quilt kept her snuggly and warm. There was also a gas fireplace in this room, but Gloria hadn't bothered to turn it on. After taking her leave from Walt, she'd washed up and had gone straight to bed. Gloria stretched under the covers, feeling rested and alive. Then, she opened her eyes, and—*yikes!*—sat bolt upright in bed. The most horrifying stuffed doll had been lying beside her on the pillow, gazing straight at her with big button eyes. Gloria covered her mouth and giggled when recognition dawned. Of course! Lou's loan! She snatched up the stuffed snowman and held it out in front of her. "Good morning, Mr. Noodles!" she said, making his stubby legs dance on the covers. "Sleep well?"

"Yes!" she had the little guy say in a high, squeaky voice. "Just fine! And, you?"

Gloria laughed at her own playacting. "Excellently! Thanks!"

She set Mr. Noodles down beside her and fell back in bed, going over her plans for the day. Gloria was meeting Savannah at the theater on the top floor of the Grand Hotel at a little after ten, so Savannah could show her the space and explain how things were set up for the Christmas puppet show. Gloria wanted to be fully on board with the particulars of the production, so she could take over for Savannah as director last-minute if need be.

After that, the two of them would have lunch at the Main Street Café on the hotel's first floor, before going shopping. Savannah had mentioned several shops she wanted to stop into, but she was especially dying to check out the new ladies' clothing store in town. It was called the Merry and Bright Boutique, and Gloria thought she'd passed it while driving down South Main Street. It was located in between the pharmacy and a cute eatery named Santa's Sandwich Shop. Jolly Bean Java was also close by, and they had plans to meet up with Savannah's good friend, Liz, later for coffee.

Gloria stretched her arms above her head, thinking she was in for a full and happy day. With the curtains drawn, she couldn't tell if it was still snowing outside, though she suspected it probably was. No matter! Gloria had come prepared for the snow, and just about anything else in Christmas Town—except for perhaps Walt Christmas. She covered her face with a groan as she recalled Walt's irritating suggestion that Gloria keep her Commitment Cookie to herself. Naturally, that was her intention, and the fact that Walt had dared to assume otherwise really got under Gloria's skin. Yeah, he was a good-looking guy. And yeah, he was single. So was Gloria for that matter! But it wasn't like they were two pandas in a zoo who could be forced into mating just because they shared accommodations. Gosh!

Luckily, the Christmas Inn was a huge house, and Gloria didn't even know where Walt's room was. As her guest suite appeared to be the only sleeping quarters downstairs, Gloria guessed the family area was somewhere upstairs. Not that Gloria really cared about where Walt slept, nor was it any of her business. She actually could get along just fine without having to see Walt much at all! He was clearly uncomfortable around her. Surely through no fault of her own. If Walt thought Gloria was interested in him romantically, he'd obviously misread her signals. Because she wasn't. *Nuh-uh. Not one tiny bit!*

"I mean that would silly! Stupid!" She turned to Mr. Noodles. "Right?"

Gloria lifted Mr. Noodles off the pillow and made him nod his goofy head, his black top hat bobbing to and fro.

Something buzzed on the nightstand and Gloria realized it was the cell she'd left there to charge overnight. This reminded her about giving Walt her number before she left that morning, so he could share it with his mom. Lou had been very kind and welcoming to Gloria, including with her "loan" of Mr. Noodles. While she and her husband, Buddy, seemed a tad on the quirky side, both struck Gloria as very lovable people. Gloria slapped her forehead, also remembering the host gift she had for Walt: that bottle of wine. She'd give him that, too, before leaving for the

Grand Hotel. First, she needed to shower and change and make herself presentable.

Gloria reached for her phone, thinking the text might be from Savannah. Instead, it was from her brother, David, in Miami.

Make it there okay?

Gloria felt bad for not contacting him sooner. She'd agreed to let him know once she'd arrived safely in Christmas Town, but yesterday had been such a whirlwind of activity, contacting David had completely slipped her mind.

Yeah! Sorry I didn't let you know sooner!

He replied seconds later.

How's Savannah?

Good! Really great. Gloria pursed her lips then giggled. *Still very pregnant.*

Glad you made it in time.

Next, David attached a photo. It was of her sweet yellow Lab, Gitana, lying under the Christmas tree and looking forlorn. Under the pic, he typed:

Somebody misses you.

Aww! Gloria replied. *I miss you guys, too.*

Then, Gloria had a funny idea. She took a quick snapshot of Mr. Noodles sitting on her pillow and sent it right back. When she read David's reply, Gloria roared with laughter.

If that's the best you can do in Christmas Town, then you'd better step up your game.

Walt showered and dressed, unable to recall when he'd experienced a more restless night. Every time he'd turned over in bed, he'd woken up. Walt felt like he'd done more flip-flopping than a flapjack on a hot griddle. This gave him the idea to make pancakes for breakfast. Maybe he'd toss in a few chocolate chips. Chocolate chip pancakes were Noelle's favorite, and Gloria didn't seemed opposed to chocolate, either. Walt ran a comb through his hair and stared in the bathroom mirror, thinking that he looked different this morning. Younger somehow, though that seemed an absurd thought. Having Gloria in the house certainly hadn't been invigorating. Contending with the issues she'd unwittingly caused had honestly been wearing. In fact, the process of dealing with her should have aged Walt years—and not had the exact opposite effect.

Another problematic result of Gloria's being around was the intensification of Walt's deep craving for cookies. When she'd first stood in his kitchen before going to Savannah's, he'd experienced a dire urge for cookies and milk. Then—*poof!*—they'd suddenly appeared! Walt probably shouldn't have been thinking about cookies before bed, and he had Gloria and her

Commitment Cookie to thank for that. If she hadn't left that bag from the Christmas Cookie Shop on the hall table, Walt wouldn't have seen it, and they wouldn't have had to entertain that uncomfortable Commitment Cookie discussion.

It was clearly too early to be talking about commitments with Gloria, even in a joking way! She'd only just arrived in Christmas Town, and certainly wasn't intending to stay. Which was fine with Walt, actually. Because he was having difficulty controlling that insatiable urge for rolled sugar cookies that had hit him at two a.m., or that hankering for snickerdoodles that had arisen at three. Then, there was that voracious hunger for gingerbread men that had nearly consumed him as it approached dawn and his stomach loudly rumbled.

Walt had forcefully tugged a pillow over his head and had tried humming a non-Christmas tune to shoo the unwanted visions away. He'd finally fallen asleep right around sunrise. But that was only after dreaming up every possible kind of Christmas cookie that he absolutely adored. Walt was frankly stunned that he appeared fresh-faced, rather than having bags under his eyes!

Walt exited his room, noticing that Noelle's door was closed, which meant his daughter was likely still sleeping. He and his girls had bedrooms at the back of the upstairs hall. His master suite was to the right at the top of the staircase and Joy and Noelle shared the room to the left. Both of the family bedrooms overlooked the backyard and had a small private sitting room at the back of the house connecting them.

The sitting room contained comfortable den-type furniture, a flat-screen TV, and an adjoining mini kitchen with a table that sat four and a small refrigerator, sink, and half-size oven with a two-burner smooth-top stove. During the inn's renovation, Walt and Rose had designed things this way, so the family could maintain a separate enclave away from paying guests.

Although it wasn't open to public view, Walt and his daughters made a habit of also decorating this area for Christmas, and it, like many of the other rooms at the Christmas Inn, had its own prettily bedecked Christmas tree. It helped that Walt had a good source of fresh Fraser firs in his brother, Ray, who owned a Christmas tree farm, and had a very green thumb in that regard.

Walt had built up an enormous supply of Christmas ornaments over the years. Before they retired as shopkeepers, Buddy and Louise had run the holiday curio store in town, All Things Christmas. Savannah's sister, Olivia, owned it now, and had continued the tradition of gifting Walt and his family with a selection of pretty new ornaments each year.

It was getting to the point that, even with five Christmas trees in the place, including the smaller one on the sideboard in the dining room, Walt had more ornaments than he could possibly employ in one season. So, he'd begun rotating them, by putting out different ones each year. Someday, when his girls were grown and had moved on to have families and homes of their own, Walt could gift them with some of his healthy holiday decoration supply.

The thought of Noelle and Joy permanently moving away made Walt's heart heavy. It was hard enough having them gone for college most of the year. And now, Joy had gone abroad for a full nine months. He couldn't believe Joy had another boyfriend already. An Italian boyfriend to boot! Walt worried over what that could mean for the future, fretting that Joy might fall in love—both with the country and the man—and decide to stay in Europe forever. He told himself not to get carried away. Joy was only in college. Then again, he'd been in college when he'd met Rose. Not only that; they'd married before they graduated.

Suddenly, the notion of him and Noelle going to visit Joy in Italy during Noelle's spring break began to hold appeal. They could lend Joy support during her grand adventure, while simultaneously reminding her of the love and support she had in family. And, Walt would get a chance to check this Italian boyfriend out. Assuming he was still in the picture by then. With young love, who knew?

Walt descended the back staircase that connected the family living quarters to the kitchen at a clip. He was eager to put on some coffee and get started with his day. First, he planned to make an appointment to see Kurt. Then, he might just spend some time online investigating airline tickets. But, before anything else, Walt needed to cook breakfast.

Walt walked into the kitchen and halted abruptly. Everywhere he looked, there were cookies! Cookies, cookies, and more cookies! There had to be nearly twenty bundles of them. Lovely, little packages of red or green cellophane tied up with festive checkered bows, and each was accompanied by a cute miniature old-fashioned-looking bottle of milk.

He heard footsteps behind him, then Noelle appeared at the bottom of the back staircase, joining Walt in the kitchen. She wore reindeer pajamas and her cranberry colored glasses, and her hair was in a ponytail.

"Whoa," she said, looking around.

"Yeah." Walt swallowed hard, wondering what on earth he was going to do with all these cookies. Not to mention twenty small bottles of milk! "I know."

Noelle's gaze roved over him. "Does this have something to do with, you and…" She lowered her voice. "*Gloria?*"

Walt unsurely viewed his daughter. There was only so much he could deny without looking transparent. Noelle could see things with her own eyes, after all. And she was obviously putting things together. None of these odd occurrences—like fluttering mail or magically appearing cookies—had ever happened around here. At least, not to Noelle's knowledge. And clearly not before the arrival of one very special visitor from Miami. "It might."

Noelle beheld him with awe then whispered, "Well, what does it mean?"

"I'm not exactly sure!" Walt fibbed in part. Because in a certain way he *did*, yet not completely. "But I intend to ask your Uncle Kurt about it."

"You're going to see him today?"

Walt nodded. "If he can work me in." He glanced around the kitchen and its confectionery array, which rivaled the display cases at the Christmas Cookie Shop.

"In the meantime, what are we going to do with all these cookies?"

"Hmm, yeah," said Noelle. "And, also all those bottles of milk."

"What about taking them to the soup kitchen?"

Noelle shook her head. "Olivia just took thirty tins of cookies over there on Sunday, remember?"

"Oh, yeah." Walt remembered hearing something about that, because Kurt and Savannah had helped her and Nick make the delivery.

After a moment, Noelle's eyes lit up. "I've got it! I'm working at the courthouse today. I could take those by!"

"To?"

"To the folks who work there," Noelle returned. "As a little holiday cheer! I'm sure everyone would appreciate the gesture, as a Christmas giftie from the Christmas Inn."

"Well, I—"

"Sheriff Carter, and Deputy Cho…their secretary Tilly. Then, there's Judge Ben Winchester … And, the ladies at Jingle Bells Booties!"

"Why, yes! I see what you mean. That's a very good idea, Noelle. Our civil servants deserve our heartfelt appreciation, as do the dedicated employees at the daycare."

"And of course, I can stop by Grandma's office over in the courthouse building, too."

"Oh!" Walt thought on this, wondering if Lou would grow suspicious if she knew about Walt's sudden propensity to create cookies and milk. She was already a bit of a busybody, and had seemed awfully interested in Gloria's arrival. Likely, Savannah had mentioned something about Gloria being great for Walt to Lou, too. Or, perhaps Lou had thought that idea up all by herself. She was, after all, Christmas Town's legendary matchmaker. Or, one of them anyway… Their numbers seemed to be multiplying lately. "Maybe you should skip stopping by the mayor's office."

"Skip it? But, why?" Noelle curiously eyed her dad. "Oh, I get it. You don't want Grandma to know that something freaky is going on."

"It's not *freaky*, Noelle."

"No?" She pinned him with her blue gaze. "Then, what is it?"

Walt uncomfortably cleared his throat. "It's...personal."

"Hmm."

"Well, will you look at all of this!" Gloria appeared in the doorway to the hall, all dressed in white again and looking lovely in white jeans, white boots, and another white sweater. She held a big bottle of wine in one hand, which Walt thought was a little unusual for this time of the morning. Until he realized it had a ribbon tied around its neck and a gift tag on it. Gloria also seemed in good spirits, and Walt hoped that meant she'd forgiven him for his presumptive statement about her cookie. Walt certainly didn't want to be at odds with Gloria since she was staying here. And, from all appearances, she seemed to want to be mature about things, too.

Gloria walked into the kitchen and stared around at the loaded-down countertops, and also at the bags and bags of cookies covering the breakfast table, along with those many mini bottles of milk. "Wow! Somebody's been a busy bee this morning!" She glanced at Noelle, who shrugged, then fixed her gaze on Walt. "Goodness! I had no idea you were such a baker."

Walt hesitated a beat, then said timidly, "Actually, neither did I."

"And, you managed to not eat them all! Well, good for you!" She winked at Noelle. "Of course, we don't know how many your dad started with."

Noelle chuckled merrily. "That's true!"

Gloria strode toward one of the little packages and picked it up to study it more closely. "What sweet little gingerbread men! And...oh!" She set that package down and went to examine another. "Snickerdoodles?"

Walt stared at her blankly. "Uh-huh."

"There must be every kind of cookie here you can imagine!"

"Pretty much! Yup."

Gloria grinned at Walt, who seemed a bit dazed. Then again, she could certainly understand that if he'd been up since the crack of dawn cooking. He must be a real whiz in the kitchen to have gotten so much accomplished in such little time. Gloria hoped they could start today off on better footing than they'd ended things last night. Now that she and Walt had established that they were not romantically interested in each other, they could simply proceed with their interactions in a cordial way. She was willing to give it her best try, and it appeared that Walt was, too.

"Oooh! Look at those cute little milk bottles!" she said, noticing them for the first time. Gloria glanced curiously at Walt. "But how did you make those?"

"I..."

"He didn't," Noelle said. "It's a kit that he orders from a supplier."

"A supplier? I see."

"Yeah," Noelle continued. "There are places we buy from, in stocking the Christmas Inn."

Gloria nodded, guessing that made sense. "Well, the homemade cookies are a wonderful touch. What do you plan to do with them?"

"Send them to the folks at the courthouse," Walt said.

"I'm taking them in with me," Noelle supplied. "When I go there for my internship. It starts today."

"How great!" Gloria told Noelle. "Just what will you be doing?"

"Writing stories for the local paper on Christmas Town happenings and such. I'll get news from the sheriff's office and also the court. The town mayor is generally a good supply of information, too!" she said with a wink, and Gloria laughed warmly.

"I loved meeting your grandparents. They're both so sweet."

Walt walked toward the full coffeepot on the counter. "Can I pour you a cup?" he asked Gloria.

"I'd love one, thanks." She remembered the bottle in her hands. "And, oh! Here! I totally forgot about this yesterday, sorry. This is for you. A small host gift."

Walt handed Gloria a coffee mug and accepted the wine that she gave him. "Wow, thanks!" he said, scanning its label. "This looks very nice. I love a good pinot noir."

"It's the least I could do." Gloria sipped from her coffee. "I understand you normally don't keep guests here this time of year, so thanks for making the exception."

"But you're not a guest!" Noelle kindly protested.

"Quite right," Walt agreed. "You're a family friend."

"Well, thank you." Gloria took a seat on a stool by the center island. "Is there anything I can do to help you this morning?"

"Not really," Walt said. "I was just about to start breakfast. Do pancakes sound all right?"

"I adore pancakes," Gloria said sunnily.

"How about I toss in some chocolate chips?"

"Even better!"

Walt grinned, and Gloria couldn't help but think he appeared even more handsome at first light, if that were possible. Not that his handsomeness really mattered one way or another. She wasn't interested in dating Walt— and last night, she'd made that crystal clear.

"That's my favorite, too," Noelle confided from behind the back of her hand.

Walt opened the pantry and stepped inside. After a moment, he reappeared with a box of pancake mix, some syrup, and two different bags of chocolate chips. "Look what I found!" he said leadingly. "A bag of semi-dark morsels and another one of mint—"

"Ew, Dad!" Noelle said, cutting him off. "No."

Walt's gaze snagged on an open package of candy canes that sat on the desk. "I could crush in some candy canes?"

"You know what?" Noelle viewed him, aghast. "I think regular ol' chocolate chips will be great!" She shot Gloria a telling look. "Don't you, Gloria?"

"Umm...er... Yeah! Good old-fashioned regular chocolate chip pancakes sound great to me."

"All right! Sounds good!" Then Walt set his baking supplies on the counter by the sink and went to retrieve a candy cane, which he unwrapped and plopped in his coffee. Noelle scrunched up her face at this, but opted to say nothing.

"So?" Walt asked Gloria, as he began preparing pancake batter. "How did you sleep last night?"

"Really super, actually! How about you?"

Walt viciously swirled the candy cane stick around in his mug and took another sip. "Fine! Just fine. Really super, too."

Chapter Eight

"So, how's it going?" Savannah asked Gloria, as their lunch salads arrived. "Staying at the Christmas Inn?" They'd just enjoyed a yummy crab and corn chowder as a warm up and were now moving on to the main course. It was snowing hard outside.

"Fine! Just fine!" Gloria said, lifting her fork.

Savannah leaned forward, a naughty gleam in her eye. "Notice any of that mistletoe hanging around?"

"Shut up," Gloria said, but she was laughing. Up until now, Savannah had behaved herself with no mention of Walt or the Christmas Inn. She'd promised Gloria she wouldn't pester her about either of those things this morning. Since it was after noon now, apparently all bets were off.

The two ladies sat at a front window table in the Main Street Café, which was located on the ground floor of the Grand Hotel. The posh bistro had high ceilings, dripping chandeliers, and pink and magenta wallpaper, teeming with climbing green vines and white roses. The ceilings had elaborate plaster moldings fashioned after blooming flowers. And, against an outside wall, the enormous fireplace blazed with warmth.

After Gloria met Savannah on the building's fourth floor, Savannah had shown her the darling children's theater space. It had a spot for a stage, which was presently set up as a puppet theater, several rows of folding chairs, and two separate rooms used for storage of props and supplies. The farthest one to the back was also where the actors could change into costumes, and two individual changing booths had been installed. The theater further housed a galley kitchen that opened onto an enclave off of the main seating section. Savannah explained that refreshments were served through the pass-through window from the kitchen.

Savannah had additionally filled Gloria in on the nuances of her office area, which was basically a desk with a few filing cabinets located in one corner of the prop room. She kept all her scripts in one cabinet, and rosters including the names of the children in her theater camps, along with business receipts in the other. The space was cramped but well laid out, and Savannah had glowed with well-earned pride while giving Gloria the tour. She'd shared which children were performing in the Christmas puppet show, and who their parents were, and had even let Gloria examine a mock-up of the program that was to be handed out during the show.

Lily Winchester would also be there to help. Lily was a junior assistant at the theater, who worked there a couple of hours a week, keeping the more boisterous children on task. Sixth grader Lily turned twelve next month and she was extremely mature for her age. Lily was old enough to babysit now, and in high demand with Christmas Town parents, as she'd gained ample experience in assisting her parents with their toddler girls, Holly and Rose, at home. Lily also held a part-time job at Sleigh Bell Stables, where she kept a horse. Ben and Sandy's daughter was evidently an industrious girl.

Savannah took a sip of her water and viewed Gloria with a smirk. "You certainly look like you slept well."

"What's that supposed to mean?"

"Nothing! Just that you showed up at the theater all chipper this morning, and normally…you're not much of a morning person."

"Speak for yourself."

"Ha!"

Gloria dug into her chicken salad, which tasted delicious. It was prepared with pecans, grapes, and dried cranberries, which added a festive holiday flare. "The truth is, I did have a good night's sleep if you must know. Me and a certain fellow snuggled in nice and tight."

"What?" Savannah gasped with delight. "You're kidding!" Then she said in low tones, "I want every single detail, Gloria. I mean it. Now."

"Yeah," Gloria said, sounding sultry. "The only thing is…that top hat of his kept getting in the way."

"Hat?" Savannah's forehead shot up and Gloria burst out in giggles. Sweet, trusting Savannah. In many ways, she hadn't changed.

"And, his scarf was kind of itchy, too, to tell you the truth. And, that big round belly—"

Savannah pointedly arched an eyebrow. "You're not talking about Walt, are you?"

"Walt? No!" Gloria laughed and covered her mouth. "Mr. Noodles!"

Savannah's jaw dropped open, then it was her turn to chuckle. "Oh...my...goodness. Don't tell me. My mother-in-law stopped by."

"Boy did she ever! And, Buddy, too. I've got to say, they're both terribly sweet people."

"So last night...?"

Gloria shook her head and Savannah swatted at her with her napkin.

"No fair, Gloria! Teasing me about Mr. Noodles." She placed her napkin back in her lap then sat up primly. "Besides, I saw him first."

"Who?" Gloria asked, intrigued. "Mr. Noodles?"

"Yes, indeed. Lou brought him to me, when I first came to town."

"My, my!" Gloria said, laughing again. "The little man certainly gets around."

"Not only that, before me—he was with Hannah!"

"Really?"

Savannah thought for a sec. "Hmm. Maybe even with Ben, too."

"Hoo boy!" Gloria starting laughing so hard, her sides were splitting. "Savannah, stop."

"But it's true!"

"Well, I *like* him."

Savannah lifted her water glass then said cagily, "Mr. Noodles or Walt?"

"Walt's okay..." Gloria answered. "He's been a very good host."

"I hear he's a great cook," Savannah said leadingly.

"He is! But—gosh—does he ever have a thing for sweets!"

Savannah's eyes lit with interest. "What do you mean?"

"Well, don't look so surprised. You're the one who told me about the men in the Christmas family and cookies."

"What type of candy?" Savannah appeared utterly intrigued. "Exactly."

Gloria lifted a shoulder then began buttering a roll. "I don't know. Whatever he has around, I guess. A lot of minty stuff."

"Minty?"

"Yeah, like…peppermint bark, and candy canes… This morning, he even suggested putting mint chocolate chips in the pancakes." Gloria grimaced with disgust. "Fortunately, Noelle put a stop to that one."

"Peppermint, hmm." In one way, Savannah seemed to be watching Gloria, yet in another, she appeared to be far, far away. "That's pretty interesting, isn't it?"

"I'm not so sure about interesting," Gloria said. "You would have thought the peppermint schnapps would have been enough!"

"Schnapps?"

"Yeah, last night during dessert. Walt poured some on his ice cream."

Savannah thoughtfully tilted her chin. "Did Walt, per chance, have any peppermint candles burning around the place?"

"Yes! Two of them."

Savannah stunned Gloria by dropping her fork and grasping Gloria's free hand. "Why, Gloria! That's such great news."

"Huh?"

"Stellar." Gloria wasn't sure if it was her imagination, or if Savannah was literally on the verge of tears. "I've hoped for this for so long."

Gloria was almost afraid to ask. "Hoped for what?"

"You and Walt!"

"There is no me and Walt, Savannah. You and I already discussed that, remember? And, last night, I talked it over with Walt, too."

"You what?" Savannah looked positively wounded. "Why?"

Gloria squeezed Savannah's hand. "Because of all of the reasons I told you about."

"Those weren't reasons," Savannah said in pouty tones. "Those were excuses." She withdrew her hand from Gloria's grasp and began disconsolately poking at her salad.

"Savannah, honey. Please."

When Savannah looked up, she appeared resigned. "Okay. All right. If you say so." She tucked a tendril of red hair behind one ear and Gloria noticed the pretty barrette she wore near her part, pulling back one section of her hair on top. It was a small, heart-shaped gingerbread cookie, and the lettering across it said: *Forever Yours.*

"That's a darling barrette," Gloria told her. "Where did you get it?"

Savannah brightened at the change of subject. "Oh, this?" she asked, lightly fingering the accessory. "Liz made it for me."

"Liz Martin? How sweet."

"Yeah," Savannah said. "Liz is very talented. She's been making Christmas-themed barrettes for a couple of years now and selling them at Olivia's shop. More recently, she began making ones that look like Hannah's Virginia Cookies. With Hannah's permission, of course."

"I love that idea," Gloria said enthusiastically. "How cute!"

"You should buy one for yourself," Savannah told her.

"I'll have to get at least two! Maybe three," Gloria said after a beat. "So, I'll have the whole set." She thoughtfully eyed her friend. "What other designs does Liz make?"

"Christmas trees, candy canes...reindeer... You name it! I believe she's even done penguins, too. I think Carter's secretary Tilly has one of those."

"But, she's not an artist full time?"

"Not yet." Savannah eyes sparkled merrily. "But, I've been trying to encourage her to consider it. All of us—her girlfriends—have. You know that empty artist's studio on the third floor?" Savannah asked, mentioning the one unoccupied space in the Grand Hotel. The former guestrooms on the second and third floors had all been converted to working artists' spaces, where craftspeople could create and sell their wares. There was a musician who made string instruments typical to this region, a jewelry maker, another person who sold handmade note cards, an oil painter, a toymaker, a puppeteer, and more. Devon Slade, who had just started woodworking full time, had just taken the second-to-last spot, leaving just one remaining studio.

"Yes," Gloria said, recalling seeing the empty room on her journey up the grand staircase. All of the studios looked fantastic, and she thought it was so cool that shoppers got the chance to observe the artisans at work, while making conversation with them. Though there wasn't time for it today, Gloria looked forward to coming back later to explore each studio in greater detail. "What about it?"

"I think that spot would be perfect for Liz," Savannah chirped, her cheeks aglow. "Though she enjoys her work at the nursery, her artwork is her passion. She's just not confident that she could make enough money doing only that."

"Oh, I bet she could," Gloria said.

"I agree!" Savannah smiled happily at Gloria. "I can't wait for you to meet Liz. She's the first real friend I had here in Christmas Town, besides Olivia and Carter."

"Don't forget about Kurt!"

Savannah laughed at this. "He was hardly a *friend*, Gloria."

"Right from the beginning, there was a spark, huh?"

"Yep. Right from the beginning." She sadly surveyed her friend. "I'm just sorry you don't feel that for Walt."

"What...what do you mean?" Gloria lifted the dessert menu to hide her blush. What she'd experienced while looking deeply into Walt's sexy blue eyes didn't matter one iota. It meant even less because the feeling apparently hadn't been mutual.

"Well, he obviously feels something for you."

"How would you know that?"

"Woman's intuition." Savannah shrugged. "And, believe it or not, Gloria, a lot of my intuition's gotten stronger since I married Kurt."

Yeah, right. That's precisely why Walt had suggested Gloria keep her cookie to herself. *Huh!* "I hate to burst your bubble, Savannah. But, I think you're wrong. Walt isn't the least bit interested in me. Not interested at all."

"No?" Savannah asked doubtfully and Gloria firmly shook her head.

"I'd lay money on it."

"I'll pay you anything you want, if you'll just tell me how to stop this madness." Walt gazed worriedly at his younger brother as he sat on the examining table at Kurt's clinic. "Seriously, money is no object at all."

"I don't want your money, and you know it."

"But—!"

Kurt shushed him and pressed his stethoscope to Walt's chest one more time. Next, he listened to Walt's back. "Breathe," he instructed stoically, before withdrawing the stethoscope and removing its earpieces from his ears.

"I'm telling you, it's crazy, man," Walt said to Kurt. "I can't seem to get thoughts of Gloria out of my mind."

Kurt folded his stethoscope and tucked it in his pocket. "When did this begin?" he asked, picking up his clipboard. "Monday, you say?"

"Monday evening, that's right." Walt nodded, his throat feeling raw. "Pretty much the minute that Gloria arrived."

"She's very pretty, isn't she?"

"What? No! I mean, yeah... I suppose," Walt stammered, feeling flustered. "And, anyway! What's that got to do with it?"

"Maybe nothing." Kurt shared an enigmatic smile. "Then again, perhaps a whole lot."

"Listen, man. This isn't funny. Are you going to help me or not?"

"I'm here for you, brother." Kurt laid a hand on his arm. "In your time of need."

Good. Finally Kurt was talking sense.

"I don't want you to panic," Kurt went on.

Just the word "panic" sent Walt into an emotional tailspin. This was worse than he thought! Maybe even incurable. The blood drained from Walt's face. "Tell me," he said weakly. "I want to know."

Kurt's expression was ultra serious, but one corner of his mouth twitched. "I'm afraid you've got a bug. The love—"

Walt hopped off the examining table, fuming.

"You think this is totally hilarious, don't you?"

"No."

"Then why do you look like you're watching a slapstick comedy on television?"

"I don't know."

Walt wheeled on him and shook his finger. "When you were in your time of need, I was there for you!"

"What?"

"I helped you with your problem with Savannah."

"As I recall, you *caused* it."

"Yeah, but that was in the distant past. In the more recent past, I solved it."

Kurt chuckled and shook his head. "Whatever."

Walt latched onto Kurt's shoulders, feeling desperate. "You've got to tell me. Not just as a doctor, but as my brother and my friend. What else can I do?"

"You've already tried pepper—?"

"Please, don't even say it. I don't think I can stomach any more."

"There's always chewing gum, you know."

That was a brilliant idea. Walt didn't know why he hadn't thought of it. *Because I'm beside myself with angst, that's why.* "I'm not convinced peppermint will be enough," Walt added unsurely.

"You could be right," Kurt agreed. "It might not be." He set his clipboard down and took a seat on the stool, then motioned for Walt to sit back on the examining table, which he reluctantly did. "Look, I'm sorry you're so stressed about this, but I think a lot of it has to do with your age."

"My age? I'm only forty-two."

"Bingo."

"Bingo, what?"

"I don't want you to go all crazy on me." Kurt appraised him decidedly. "But, I think you're going through something called *peri-man-o-pause*."

"Peri-*huh?*" Walt raked a hand through his hair. "You've got to be kidding me. Men don't go through that. That's a female condition."

"No," Kurt said seriously. "Menopause is a female condition. *Man*-o-pause, however, afflicts males..." He paused then continued cautiously. "With certain abilities, and of a certain age."

Walt gaped at him. "Is that even a real thing?"

"For some people, yeah. But the outcome's a bit different for us Christmases." Kurt thoughtfully stroked his chin. "Five will get you ten the Clauses are predisposed to it, too. Given that we're from the same line."

"This is unbelievable. What does it mean?"

Kurt leaned forward on his stool, resting his elbows on his knees. "Walt, you're still a young man in many ways. You keep yourself fit. Eat what you should…" He paused momentarily. "For the most part. But, time marches on, my friend, and certain abilities of yours have lain dormant for years."

"Well, of course they have! I'm a widower."

"I'm well aware of the hard times you've been through," Kurt said sympathetically. "But that doesn't change the facts."

"Oh? And, what are those?"

"You're entering a special window. A 'use or lose' time." Walt could tell Kurt was trying to put this as gently as he could. "Think of your special powers like a fire's flames. Once, your light burned brightly. Lighting up the night! But as you've grown older, you've neglected to tend that fire. So, it's likely to go out, eventually. Poof!"

Poof? "What? Permanently?"

"It's not inevitable, but—at this point—probable. In the meantime, you'll experience these little flickers along the way." Kurt paused then said dramatically, "*Last gasps of magic*, as it were. That's how these gifts of ours work. You don't use them, after at a time they atrophy."

"Well, they sure haven't shown evidence of that lately!"

"Yes, and maybe you should ask yourself why?"

"Gloria," Walt said hoarsely.

"For better or worse, she's bringing something out in you. From my perspective, I'd say it's for the better." Kurt cleared his throat. "Speaking professionally."

"But, I can't...won't. What I mean is..." Walt said, feeling at an utter loss. "I'm not ready to start dating again."

Kurt's eyebrows shot up. "Aren't you? It's been ten years."

"That's not exactly true! I've been out." Walt hedged then added awkwardly, "A time or two."

"Yeah, but you never really wanted to go. Your heart wasn't in it."

"What makes you think my heart would be *in it* now?"

Kurt addressed him with bold dark eyes. "I think your heart already *is* in it. That's what it's been trying to tell you. And, why your entire system has been out of wack. Every romantically inspired ability you've ever experienced happened to resurface right out of the blue, and on the very day that a certain woman arrived on your doorstep. If that's not some kind of message about your destiny then I don't know what is."

"Destiny, ha!" Walt viewed him with dismay. "I come to you for medical advice, and you prescribe poetic platitudes."

"That's right!" Kurt said with interest. "You used to write poetry, too. I'd nearly forgotten that part. Has the muse been bothering you, too?"

"No. And it won't. Thank you very much. Brother. Doctor. Friend."

"You don't need to get testy. I'm honestly trying to help."

"How? By telling me what I'm experiencing is completely beyond my control?"

"I never said that."

"No, but you didn't tell me what I could do about it, either."

Kurt shot him a daring look. "Own it."

"Whaaat?"

"Own. It." Kurt spoke more firmly. "You cannot control something effectively when it has its grasp around you. By running away, you're ceding control. You need to take those abilities by the reins, and let them know who's boss."

"But, I—"

"I know you never had to do that before, because you had Rose. And, she helped you. The two of you somehow managed together, but that's just the thing. It was never really Rose's problem. It was yours."

Walt's emotions kept churning inside him, rolling around and around like some big prickly tumbleweed. What Kurt said made sense in a way. But how could Walt learn to master things he'd never had mastery over to begin with?

"I know it's rough," Kurt said kindly. "It took me a long time to learn how to deal with my abilities...to understand them, and what they mean for me. But, in the end, I view them as assets. They're part of who I am and I can't change that. What I could change—and did—was understanding how to make my unique heritage work to my advantage."

Walt stared at him blankly. "And you honestly think that I can do that?"

"I'm not saying it's going to be easy," Kurt admitted. "Apart from Nick, you've always had some of the strongest gifts among all the cousins. Although most of them don't know it, because you've never flaunted your talents."

Walt hung his head. "I've never wanted these 'talents.'"

"Yeah well, you know what? That's just too bad, because you've got them."

When Walt stared in surprise, Kurt continued. "Your body's sending you some pretty strong signals, bro. You've got a chance now to address things you brushed under the rug before. Things you never completely dealt with when you were married to Rose."

"I loved Rose." Walt's voice cracked. "Desperately."

"I know you did, and she loved you. But it's been ten years now. A decade, man. You're forty-two years old. Your life isn't over yet."

Walt eyed Kurt fretfully. "Are you saying these disturbances will only get worse?"

"That depends wholly on how you handle them."

"I was kind of hoping you'd just give me a pill, or something."

Kurt chuckled warmly. "Oh, that it were that easy."

"Yeah."

Walt scooted off the examining table and Kurt stood and gave him a bear hug.

"Chin up, Walt. This is not a *bad* thing." He stepped back and cracked a grin. "In fact, it could be the start of something very, very good."

Before Kurt left the room, Walt stopped him. "You won't say a word about this."

"Of course not."

"To anyone. I mean it, Kurt. Not even Savannah."

"No worries, brother. My lips are sealed."

Chapter Nine

Gloria laughed merrily as she and Savannah strolled out of the pelting snow and into Olivia's shop, All Things Christmas. The place was darling, with all sorts of holiday knickknacks for sale. There were small furniture pieces, like hand-carved end tables with bases that looked like prancing reindeer…beautifully hand-stitched Christmas stockings…and ornaments hanging on a row of artificial Christmas trees located near the back of the store. Olivia appeared from a stock room behind the Christmas trees as they came in the front door.

"Well, look who the cat dragged in!" Olivia said brightly. She wore a long red braid slung forward over one shoulder, and had Savannah's dark green eyes. "My baby sister and her very best friend from Florida!" Savannah's pretty older sister was a bit taller than petite Savannah and more athletic-looking, due to her sporty nature. Gloria was aware that, apart from being a dedicated horsewoman, Olivia was also an avid cross-country skier. Savannah had hinted that Olivia had recently picked up another interesting pastime connected to sleigh riding, but had been kind of fuzzy on the details.

"Welcome to Christmas Town, Gloria." Olivia strode forward and took Gloria's hand. "It's so good to see you again." The two had met previously during one of Olivia's trips to see Savannah in Miami, when Savannah had been showing Olivia around the high school where she worked.

"Thanks, Olivia! It's great to be here. It's nice seeing you again, too."

"What have you two been up to today?" Olivia glanced at the bulging shopping bags Savannah held in both hands. "A bit of shopping, I see?"

"Yes!" Savannah said gratefully. "That new store in town? It's to die for!"

"The Merry and Bright Boutique?" Olivia asked, and Savannah nodded. "I've been meaning to stop in, but haven't yet had time."

"They've got some really great stuff," Gloria said. "All very chic!"

"A lot of it imported from New York!" Savannah glowed brightly when she said this, and Gloria was so happy to see her having such a good time. Shopping seemed to take Savannah's mind off her other worries, and—luckily—she hadn't experienced one Braxton Hicks contraction all day.

Gloria noticed the pretty snowman barrette in Olivia's hair. "Is that one of Liz Martin's creations?"

Olivia lifted her hand to her hair, and laughed with recollection. "Why yes, it is!" Olivia's eyes sparkled. "Liz does beautiful work."

"I know," Gloria said. "I was hoping to buy a few barrettes of my own."

"Awesome! I stock plenty." Olivia gazed toward the back of the store. "There are a couple of small pivot stands on the display case back there to the left of the Christmas trees."

Gloria nodded. "Great, thanks." Next, she addressed Savannah. "Do you mind if I go and take a look?"

"Of course not!" Savannah said sweetly. "Go on, look around. Seriously. Take all the time you need."

But, when Gloria slipped away, she detected whispering behind her.

"So," Olivia said in hushed tones. "How's everything going with Walt…?"

Savannah attempted to speak even more quietly, but Gloria could still hear her. "Nothing yet, but I haven't given up hope."

Walt stood in Christmas Town Drugs, picking out several packs of peppermint-flavored gum. He found some sugarless mints as well, and tossed them in his basket. He still wasn't sure how he felt about Kurt's advice. Essentially, Walt needed time to mull it over. In the meantime, he wanted a bit of insurance in his pockets. An ounce of prevention, and all that. Even if peppermint couldn't prevent things from happening entirely, it at least might tamp down any resulting activity.

"Wow. Stocking up?"

Walt looked up with a start to find his older brother, Ray, watching him with chestnut-brown eyes. Ray was shorter than Walt, but—like Kurt—just over six feet tall. Unlike the blond doctor, Ray's hair was dark brown, even darker than Walt's. Ray wore a heavy field coat and boots, and held a prescription bag in his hand, apparently having just picked it up.

"Oh! Hey, Ray!" Walt's gaze scanned the stapled-shut white bag. "I hope you're not sick?"

"Not me. Kyle," Ray said, mentioning his fourteen-year-old son. "He's come down with strep throat, apparently. It seems to be going around at school."

"Bummer!"

"This time of year, what can you do?" Ray shrugged. "In any case, he'll get better."

"Were you just at the clinic?" Walt asked, worried that Ray had seen Kurt, and that Kurt had spilled the beans. It wasn't that Walt didn't trust Kurt; it was more like Kurt sometimes had trouble keeping his trap shut. Particularly, when it came to matchmaking people. An unfortunate trait that Kurt had inherited from their mom...

"I stopped by late this morning after picking Kyle up at school. The nurse called and said he had a fever. I dropped Kyle off back at home before coming out to get his meds." Ray scanned Walt's features. "Why did you ask about the clinic?"

"It was a natural question. I mean, I just assumed—"

Ray perused the contents of his basket, more carefully this time. "Peppermint. Hmm."

"It's not what you think!"

Ray eyed him astutely. "Were *you* at the clinic?"

"Me? Well, I..." Walt's face warmed.

"For a check-up or something?"

"Yep! Check-up! That's what it was! Gotta be sure the old system's in order!"

"In order." Ray clucked his tongue. "Right."

"I went by after lunch," Walt told him. "That's probably why we missed each other."

Ray viewed him with concern. "I hope everything's okay?"

"Oh, yeah. Just fine and dandy!"

Ray shot him a disbelieving look. "If there's something going on, I might be able to help, you know."

"Thanks, but I've got it!" Walt swallowed hard. "Got it all under control."

"I hear Savannah's friend is in town." Ray paused a moment then added with emphasis, "Her *very beautiful* friend from Miami."

"Who told you that?"

"Meredith," Ray said, referring to his wife. "She was at the Grand Hotel this morning, and ran into Savannah and Gloria as they were leaving."

Walt knew that Meredith, who helped Ray manage their Christmas tree farm, also volunteered at the Christmas Town Consolidated School where Kyle was enrolled. In conjunction with the school art teacher, Ms. Thurston, and Sandy Winchester of the Snow Globe Gallery, Meredith had helped organize the student art show currently on display in the ballroom of the Grand Hotel. Walt guessed Meredith had dropped by to check on the show, which was undergoing installation.

"It's true," Walt said, responding to Ray's earlier statement. "Not only is she here, Gloria is actually staying at the Christmas Inn."

"Do tell!" Ray's entire face lit up. "Now, how did I miss that part?"

"Maybe because you don't pay attention to town gossip as much as other people do."

"Meredith claims that's a good thing."

"You should listen to your wife. She's a very smart woman."

Ray laughed heartily and patted Walt's shoulder. "Yeah, she is, and I'm lucky to have her." He carefully scanned Walt's eyes. "You're sure you're all right?"

"Yeah, yeah. As right as rain!"

"Okay, if you say so. But, if you change your mind." Ray shared a warm smile. "You know where to find me. After I run this home to Kyle," he said, indicating the prescription, "I'll be heading back to the nursery and will be there for the rest of the afternoon."

"Thanks, Ray!" While Walt wasn't ready to talk about his problem to yet another sibling, he was genuinely grateful for Ray's support. "Please tell Kyle I hope he feels better soon."

After purchasing his gum and candy, Walt decided to stop by the Jolly Bean Java for coffee, rather than going straight back to the Christmas Inn, where he might run into Gloria. Kurt had given Walt a lot to ponder during that appointment, and Walt intended to give his brother's advice some serious thought. Walt had no clue how to "control" his abilities, and Kurt had not precisely provided a road map for that. It seemed Kurt was telling him this was more of a mind over matter situation. Which meant Walt had to get his head in the right place to be able to conquer his runaway fears. Walt had to *believe* he was in charge in order to *be* in charge of his abilities. *But, how?* Just stewing on the problem made him anxious.

Walt unwrapped a piece of peppermint gum and popped it in his mouth as he stood in line at the café counter. He met eyes with the barista and smiled at the kindly older gentleman with cocoa-colored skin, warm dark eyes, and short-shorn gray hair. Caleb Smith was the former sheriff in Christmas Town. He'd retired from the position six years ago, which was when Mayor Louise Christmas had recruited her godson Carter Livingston to run for the job. Caleb was also Jade Smith Scott's dad, and Jade was good friends with Olivia, and—by extension—Savannah.

Caleb hadn't lasted in retirement more than a few years before growing antsy. At first, Jade had given him a temporary position at the Elf Shelf Bookshop, which she owned. When Devon Slade left managing this coffee shop to man his woodworking studio full-time at the Grand Hotel, the slot had come open, and Caleb had leapt at the chance for regular employment, where he didn't feel beholden to his daughter. Besides, Caleb had joked, being the former sheriff had prepared him for serving up joe. He'd certainly had enough experience sipping coffee while in uniform, since actual occurrences of crime in Christmas Town were so low.

"Walt Christmas!" Caleb proclaimed as Walt sidled up to the counter. "What's your pleasure today?"

"I'll take a mocha, please. The medium size."

Caleb nodded and started fixing his order. "And, how are things at the Christmas Inn?" he asked conversationally. "Word is you've got a pretty houseguest staying with you this season."

The doorbell tinkled and Caleb's grin warmed the room as he looked that way. "My goodness. Is that her?"

Walt's heart pounded as he peered over his shoulder.

It was Gloria, all right. Standing there dressed in white, including that crazy winter hat and those knee-high boots. She was with Savannah, and both were chatting, oblivious to the other customers standing in front of them in line.

Caleb leaned toward Walt and whispered, "Very pretty, indeed."

Something in Walt's hand rattled, and—to his horror—he realized the noise was coming from the shopping bag he'd gotten at the pharmacy. The one that contained his peppermint candy and gum... Walt double-folded the crease of the bag, gripping it harder.

"Um..." He turned quickly to Caleb. "Better add some peppermint syrup to that. And, make it a large. P-p-p...please."

"One large peppermint mocha, coming right up!" Caleb said a bit more loudly than Walt would have liked. The barista's announcement caught the attention of the ladies who'd just entered the shop.

"Why look, Gloria!" Savannah cried pertly. "It's Walt!"

Walt spun slowly on his heel and shyly waved. "Ladies!" Savannah's belly bloomed so large, it was poking out from between the front flaps of her coat, which she'd been unable to button completely. Only the top several buttons were secured, though Savannah didn't appear the least bit chilly. Her cheeks glowed brightly below her blue knit cap, which matched her scarf and gloves, and she wore a broad smile on her lips. Her eyes danced with mischief when she said, "We weren't expecting to see you here! Maybe we can all have coffee together?"

"Sure," Gloria added, attempting to be polite. "That would be great. Liz Martin is also joining us in a bit."

"Wonderful invitation," Walt said, as Caleb handed him his drink. "But I'm afraid I can't stay." His shopping bag rattled again and he tucked it under his arm, pinning it down while he extracted his wallet to pay. "I have some paperwork that needs tending to this afternoon." Walt stuffed a few bills in a tip jar by the register. "Back at the Christmas Inn."

"Well, that's too bad." Savannah's face hung in a frown. "Perhaps some other time?"

"Sure," Walt said, ready to get out of there. He didn't know if it was the gum or candy that was acting up, but something in that bag under his arm was getting restless. It was squirming a lot, too. In a way that was starting to…tickle. "Hahaha! Ho! Hoo!" Walt sputtered, unable to stop himself. Several patrons in line gave him odd looks, as he scurried toward the door with pursed lips, and his arm clamped down hard. *Stop it!* he thought firmly. *Stop that, right now!* But that only caused the bag to twitch more fiercely. "Hee-hee! Ho! Ho-ho-ho! Ha-ha!"

"Are you all right?"

Walt called himself up short in sheer mortification. Gloria stood right in front of him, examining him curiously with her big, dark eyes. Walt took a quick sip of peppermint mocha. But—*ouch!*—it was too hot. That also forced him to swallow the wad of gum in his mouth, which he'd forgotten all about until precisely this minute.

"Walt?" It was Savannah's turn to view him worriedly. This was not good. Not good at all. Walt stared straight ahead at the door, less than an arm's length away. As soon as he was out and through it, he'd be in good shape. At least, he wouldn't be making a fool of himself in front of a café full of people.

"Yeah, uh-huh. Sorry! I've just got a lot on my..." He glanced suddenly at Gloria then quickly looked away. "Mind."

"Here, let me," Gloria said, attempting to hold the door open for him.

"That's all right! I've got—" But what Walt didn't have was the candy bag tucked under his arm, as his sudden movement in reaching for the door caused it to slip, and tumble onto the floor. The force of the fall caused the flap to burst open, and packets of gum and rolls of mints spilled out in an array.

"Wow, Walt," Savannah said in stunned surprise. "That's a lot of peppermint."

"Yeah, right. I know." He handed Savannah his mocha and she held it, as he squatted down to scoop it up. To Walt's dismay, Gloria bent low to help him.

"Here you are," she said sweetly, passing him a clear plastic container of tiny white mints that seemed to be doing a merry dance inside their case. Walt hurriedly took the object from her.

"Uh, thanks!"

"Oh! And, there's another!" Gloria said, stopping a roll of hard candies that was spinning its way toward a chair. Sweat beaded Walt's brow as he hoped really, really hard that Gloria wouldn't notice anything amiss about the wandering candy. He shoved the rest of it in his bag, and stood with an embarrassed flush.

"Well, thanks for your help," he said, retrieving his mocha from Savannah.

"No problem," Gloria replied. She appeared very amused…or intrigued, or something…Walt couldn't quite put his finger on it, until he caught wind of this thought:

You really are pretty cute, you know that?

Walt nearly stumbled out the door, backing onto the snowy sidewalk where tiny white flakes continued to cascade from the sky. "B-bye!"

"See you later, Walt," Savannah said with a knowing smile, as he scurried off.

Walt took a chance with another sip of mocha, which luckily was drinkable by now. In fact, he nearly drained the whole thing before reaching the corner with Santa Claus Lane. He hesitated there, remembering Ray's earlier invitation to lend an ear. Ray's place of business, the North Pole Nursery, was in the old train depot at the end of Santa Claus Lane, and at the foot of a mountain pass. Walt could either go home and try to handle this on his own, or he could seek the advice of his older brother. Ray was a very sound and reasonable person. Perhaps he'd know what Walt should do. Kurt's suggestions were all well and good, but clearly they weren't working. Walt needed a lot more help than that. He required specific instruction. And, who better to give him that than his older and wiser brother, Ray?

Chapter Ten

"You are *not* going to tell me Walt's not interested in you." Savannah gave a self-congratulatory giggle. "Not after what I just witnessed with my own eyes." She and Gloria sat at a small table by the front window. The table was really meant for two, but Jolly Bean Java was so packed, they'd grabbed the first empty table they could find and had pulled up an extra chair for Liz to have when she arrived.

"He was acting awfully strange," Gloria admitted self-consciously. "Almost embarrassed, or something."

"Probably because he wasn't expecting to run into you."

"Why would that make a difference?"

"It would if he'd been thinking about you all day." Savannah giggled again. "I've never seen Walt looking quite like that, to tell you the truth."

"Never?"

"There was only one time…" Savannah stopped herself. "Never mind. That doesn't matter."

"What doesn't?" Gloria leaned toward her, her interest piqued. "Come on, tell me." Not that *she* was interested in Walt. Although, it did feel pretty good to turn an attractive man's head. Especially, an attractive and *mature* man, who was a successful entrepreneur.

Sure, Gloria dated in Miami, but honestly not that much. She'd grown weary of going out with guys just because they seemed nice and had asked her. While it was fun to get out, after a couple of dates, she generally cut things off, because she didn't want to lead anyone on. Though she was in her mid-thirties, the men who asked Gloria out tended to be on the younger side. Some were in their early thirties, and others in their late twenties. All were super sweet, yet none of them seemed settled enough to Gloria somehow.

"Well…" Savannah began in coquettish tones. "If you must know, the only other time I've seen Walt looking flustered was on account of me. But not *me* me, really. It was more like on account of you."

Gloria blinked, not understanding.

Savannah dropped her voice into a whisper. "It was at the Christmas bazaar last winter," she confided quietly. "I was talking to Walt and thinking about you…"

"What?"

"I was remembering all the stuff you'd told me, Gloria…about how much you'd love to see snow…taste those teeny, tiny snowflakes on your tongue…"

"Yeah? So?"

"So, I was speaking with Walt at the time, and thinking about what a great match the two of you would make. I closed my eyes, imagining it, just as I thought of the snowflake thing…"

"Oh, no." Gloria chuckled softly.

"I kind of did this…" Savannah shut her eyes and opened her mouth, rolling her tongue around in the air.

"Savannah!" Gloria chirped quietly, but she was laughing oh-so-hard. "You didn't!"

Savannah opened her eyes then said seriously, "Oh, but I did. And, Walt?" She giggled at this. "He actually thought I was hitting on him."

"*No.*"

"Yes. And, right in the middle of the Fellowship Hall at the Corner Church."

"Gee."

"I know, right? It was so, so embarrassing. And, of course! Nobody would believe me. I mean, nobody but Liz."

"Did I hear my name?"

Gloria suddenly saw that another person had appeared, a pleasant-looking woman who appeared around their age, or perhaps a few years older. Liz Martin had curly brown hair, which tumbled to her shoulders in ringlets, and honey-amber eyes. Laugh lines crinkled around them and the edges of her mouth when she smiled. "You must be Gloria!" she said, pulling back the extra chair. "Welcome to Christmas Town." She set her paper coffee cup on the table then removed her hat, scarf, and gloves, before unzipping her coat and sitting down.

"Thanks, Liz," Gloria replied. "It's so great to finally meet you."

Savannah stared at Liz with wonder. "I didn't even see you come in."

"Of course you didn't," Liz said with a twinkle. Gloria noted there was a hint of southern sass in her tone. "That's because y'all were too busy gossiping about me."

"We were *not*." Savannah laughed and rolled her eyes. "I was just telling Gloria about that time at the Corner Church." She hesitated then added impishly, "With Walt."

Liz burst into chuckles. "Oh, *yeah*. I remember that episode, all right." She laughed again and took a sip of her coffee. "I'm actually surprised anyone in town could forget it."

"Liz came to my rescue," Savannah said, her green eyes sparkling.

"Well, I don't know about that." Liz grinned. "Although, I did get us out of there pretty quick."

Savannah and Liz laughed at their mutual memory, and Gloria joined in just trying to imagine it.

"Poor Walt," Gloria said.

"Yeah," Savannah concurred. "He was pretty flustered." She squared her small shoulders and shot Gloria a playful look. "Sort of like he was in here a few minutes ago."

"Oh really?" Liz asked with a smile. She glanced at Gloria. "So you and Walt are—?"

"No, no!" Gloria said quickly. "Not in the real world, anyway. Only in Savannah's very vivid imagination."

"Ha-ha." Savannah scrutinized her then turned to Liz. "I do think Walt has a thing for Gloria. You should have seen him, Liz! He was all thumbs in her presence."

"He was just in here getting coffee."

"Nope," Savannah said. "Peppermint mocha."

"Peppermint...oooh," Liz replied, like she was in on some kind of secret. Gloria only wished she knew what it was.

"Walt loves it apparently," Gloria said with a shrug. "Peppermint gum. Candy." She thoughtfully viewed the ceiling. "Peppermint bark, too."

"Isn't that the craziest thing?" Liz said like a cat that had swallowed a canary.

"Ye-es," Savannah agreed in low tones.

Gloria set her coffee cup on the table. "Okay, you two. What's going on?"

"Nothing!" Savannah said brightly.

"That's right," Liz agreed. "Nothing at all!" But Liz definitely looked like she was hiding something. She obviously wasn't as practiced at concealing things as Savannah. Savannah didn't used to be so sneaky. Yet, ever since coming to Christmas Town, she'd developed a habit of skirting around certain issues. She'd hinted at Kurt's *talents*, but failed to enumerate what they were. Apart from his good looks and doctoring skills, she'd intimated there was something more.

Gloria knew she didn't live in Christmas Town, and that Liz did. And, she was glad that Savannah had formed another close friendship. Though, Gloria couldn't help but admit to herself that she'd be a little hurt if Savannah had shared intimate secrets with Liz that she hadn't told her.

"Gloria, hey." Savannah reached out her hand and took Gloria's. "Why so glum?"

While Gloria had tried to hide her dejection, she apparently hadn't been very good at it.

"Why do I get the feeling that something's going on? Something that you two know about, and I don't?"

Savannah and Liz exchanged glances, then Liz said kindly, "I don't actually *know* know a lot of things. But, when you've lived here as long as I have, you start guessing." She shot a sidelong glance at Savannah and then continued. "You're not the only one Savannah's been tight-lipped with about certain things. Trust me on this, there's tons she hasn't told me, either. It's not because she doesn't want to; it's because she can't."

There was a really fine line between *can't* and *won't* in Gloria's mind. She and Savannah had been friends forever. And not just regular friends: best friends.

"It's true." Savannah reassuringly squeezed Gloria's hand before settling her grasp back on her coffee. "And, Liz is right, Gloria. There's nothing I'd keep from you if it weren't necessary."

"Necessary?"

"Family secrets." Liz lowered her voice in a whisper. "Christmas family secrets. I've got a hunch there are plenty in the Claus family, too."

Gloria shook her head, perplexed. "And, peppermint?"

"It has something to do with those," Liz said knowingly, as if Savannah wasn't even there. "Those family secrets."

When Savannah looked surprised, Liz shot back. "Sugar plum fairy! I can put things together!" Next, she told Gloria, "When I see someone in this town ingesting huge amounts of minty stuff, my *love*-ometer goes off! Beep-beep-beeping wildly!"

"*Love*-ometer?" Gloria giggled in spite of herself.

Savannah cracked a grin. "Oh, Liz!"

"It's true." Liz angled closer to Gloria. "Somehow lots of peppermint is connected to a new relationship forming, and—ultimately…" She sighed dreamily. "*Love*."

Gloria's face warmed. "Well, I hardly think in this case—"

"Oh yes, it does," Savannah said. She appeared to be hinting at something with her eyes. Maybe at some of those family secrets. But, what did any of this mean? Fear seized Gloria around the middle and latched on tight. *Maybe Savannah's gone nuts, and Liz Martin has, too. Maybe this entire town is some kind of giant loony bin dressed up for Christmas and drenched in never-ending snow.*

Liz fixed Gloria with earnest brown eyes. "Savannah's probably right about Walt." The thing was, Liz didn't actually seem mentally unbalanced. Neither did Savannah. She was pretty much her same old self.

"Oh! Oh, no…" Savannah grimaced and let out a moan, setting her coffee cup on the table and gripping her bulging belly. "Oh, dear!" She heaved a breath and started panting heavily.

"The baby?" Liz asked with surprise.

"Or, maybe Braxton Hicks," Gloria quickly confided. She lightly touched Savannah's arm. "Honey—?"

"Owwwww!" Savannah let out a shriek that filled the room and heads turned their way.

Liz darted a worried look at Gloria. "Maybe we should call Kurt?"

Gloria nodded, pulling her cell from her purse. Before leaving the Christmas Inn this morning, she'd given Walt her number to share with Lou, and he'd provided his and Lou's numbers in return. Walt had suggested Gloria enter Kurt's number in her phone, so she had it handy in the event she needed to reach Kurt in an emergency.

"No Kurt!" Savannah said, huffing badly. "I don't want to bother him again at work."

"Maybe just to be safe?" Gloria asked, but Savannah stubbornly shook her head and pushed back from the table. She attempted to stand, then groaned and hurriedly took her seat again.

Liz's gaze swept over Savannah then she addressed Gloria. "Yeah, you'd better call."

Despite Savannah's protests, Gloria did, and Kurt appeared within minutes, wearing a camel-colored car coat and an extremely stylish fedora.

"My, you got here fast!" Gloria said, amazed by his speediness.

Kurt nodded cordially at her and Liz, then knelt down by his wife, taking her hand. "Savannah, sweetheart? Is it very bad?"

Savannah nodded, her cheeks puffed out with air.

"Why don't we go down to the clinic and have a look?"

"Ooooohhhh!" Savannah squeezed Kurt's hand so hard her knuckles went white.

Kurt helped her to her feet while Gloria and Liz watched helplessly.

"Can we do something?" Liz asked.

"Yeah," Gloria said. "Maybe help you both to your SUV?"

"Thanks," Kurt said. "Won't be necessary."

Gloria frowned worriedly. "You will keep us posted?"

"Absolutely," Kurt said, ushering Savannah toward the door as coffee shop patrons granted them a wide berth.

"Savannah's got both our numbers in her cell!" Liz called, as they stepped outside.

Once Kurt and Savannah had gone, Gloria and Liz agreed that they should head out, as well. Liz needed to get back to work at the nursery, and Gloria was ready to put her feet up at the inn. Her feet were absolutely killing her from walking around all day in these high-heeled boots!

After she'd put on her coat, hat, and gloves, Gloria held out her hand. "Liz," she said sincerely. "It was so nice to finally meet you."

Liz's sweet face lit up in a grin. "Gracious, Gloria! Nobody's that formal in Christmas Town." Then, she pulled Gloria into a hug. "So great meeting you too, hon. You're Savannah's nearest and dearest friend. I'm so glad you could be here for her."

In that moment, Gloria's heart melted and any momentary resentment or jealousy she'd felt toward Liz completely evaporated. Savannah had needed a good friend nearby, and sweet Liz had volunteered for the job. Liz was funny, generous, and kind, and Gloria now saw there was never any competition between them. Nor would there be any in the future.

When Liz pulled back she confirmed this with a bright twinkle in her eye. "We're all going to be very good friends. I just know it!"

Liz bit her bottom lip as she suddenly recalled something. "Jumping jelly beans! I nearly forgot!" She stunned Gloria by fishing in her purse for a pretty oblong box tied up with a shiny gold ribbon. Gloria read the seal on the package: Nutcracker Sweets.

"These are for you," Liz said warmly. "A little 'Welcome to Christmas Town.'"

"How nice!"

"Their chocolate truffles are *divine*. I hope you'll enjoy them."

Liz's unexpected gesture warmed Gloria's soul. "I know I will. Thank you."

"I used to eat them a little too often myself," Liz confessed. "Back when I lived at Sisters' Row, the candy shop was right around the corner. I'm sure it's better for my figure that I'm holed up with my brother's family temporarily. They live out in the country," she further explained. "A ways down River Road and past the Christmas tree farm."

Gloria remembered that Sisters' Row was undergoing a renovation. That's why she hadn't been able to stay at the rental unit located there. "How long will it go on?" she asked Liz. "The construction work?"

"Nick's hoping they'll be done by summer. He's the architect in charge of the project, and also married to Olivia. They actually live right next to Savannah, and very near the Christmas Inn."

"Yeah, I've seen their house!"

"In any case," Liz said, slipping on her gloves. "Although I dearly love my brother, I'll be happy for the peace and quiet when I get to move back into town."

"Peace and quiet?" Gloria asked, puzzled. "I would have thought you'd have a lot more of that living in the country?"

"Not at Stan and Della's house, I don't," Liz said, naming her brother and his wife. "They've got four kids: all elementary age. It's as loud as the dickens around there!"

Gloria laughed sunnily, understanding why Savannah enjoyed Liz's company so much. She was such an earthy and congenial person. "I get why having your own place might seem appealing, then."

"Yeah, it's nice. Although sometimes it's a little lonely." Liz sighed heavily. "It was mighty fun when Savannah was in the rental next door. Jade Scott and her husband Wendell live on the other side with their two boys, Josiah and Alexander. They're staying with Jade's father for the time being." She shot a look at the barista behind the counter. "That's him, Caleb Smith, over there."

Liz tugged on her hat and shared another grin. This time, Gloria noticed the dimples etched on either side of her smile. "I hope to have a chance to see you again real soon, Gloria."

"Thanks, Liz. You, too! Maybe at the baby shower? Lou mentioned that you were involved in the planning, and I'd certainly like to help."

"Oh, that would be great! Lou's going to be sending out a group text tomorrow. Does she have your number?"

"Walt's giving it to her, yeah."

"Super!"

As they headed toward the door, Gloria noted it was snowing heavily outside and adjusted her bulky hat. "Thanks again for the yummy chocolates. I can't wait to try one."

"No problem! Enjoy."

"I'm also excited to wear one of your barrettes."

Liz appeared extraordinarily pleased. "You bought one?"

"I bought three!"

"Ha-ha. That's awesome. I appreciate it."

"You're very talented, you know. Savannah showed me your whole collection at All Things Christmas, and it's really, really gorgeous."

"Aww…now you're buttering me up."

"Speaking of Savannah, I hope she's okay." Gloria dropped the truffle box in her purse and yanked out her phone to make sure there were no missed calls.

"They've only been gone a few minutes," Liz assured her. "Plus, I wouldn't worry too much. Kurt's an excellent doctor. Savannah's in really good hands."

Gloria nodded in agreement. "I'm sure Kurt will let us know if there's news."

"I'm sure he will, too."

Chapter Eleven

Walt hurried home, eager to put his new plan in place. Ray had provided plenty of useful tips in this regard. It really *was* a question of mind over matter. All Walt had to do was put his mind to it. By failing to focus on his gifts, Walt had begun to let his heart rule his head, causing all these unnecessary disruptions. He hadn't experienced these problems before, because no other woman besides Rose had ever awakened his heart. Until now.

Perhaps Gloria was slightly alluring, but that didn't mean Walt had to get all discombobulated every time he saw her, like some silly schoolboy with an adolescent crush. Not that Walt was *crushing* on Gloria. No. No. Not even close! She was merely attractive and engaging…and more than a little bossy, Walt reminded himself. Good. That was a good. He should hang onto the negatives. But then, sometimes negatives could become positives, depending. And, Walt was going to *positively* stop thinking this way. This was nuts!

He hustled up the sidewalk to where his mailbox stood, still clutching the bag of candies and gum from the pharmacy. Walt glanced up the street to the right and then down the street to his left, then stepped off the curb and opened his mailbox flap. A neat pile of mail sat inside the box, but—the moment Walt peered in at it, it began to flutter. "Nope! Not today you won't." Walt slammed his hand down on stack of correspondence and slid it out of the mailbox. Next, he pinned it tightly against his chest along with the pharmacy bag and scurried into the house.

When Gloria returned to the Christmas Inn, the pretty candle-style lights in its windows were already shining brightly. Beyond them downstairs, she spied the two Christmas trees in the front rooms, one each in the parlor and living room, with their colorful lights aglow. With the snow dancing down from the sky, this old house really did look like a magical place out of a fairy tale. It was so different from Gloria's single-level Mediterranean-style villa in Miami.

Her place had pale yellow exterior walls and a red clay tile roof, and was located on a cul-de-sac in a quiet neighborhood. The enclosed patio area in back had room for a small garden teeming with lush local vegetation like low-growing ferns, waving palms, and plenty of flowers, including black-eyed Susans, amaranth, and colorful hibiscus blooms. She even had a small orange tree in the corner, which provided partial shade and delivered delectable fruit, perfect for making fresh-squeezed orange juice, which was delicious served chilled on sweltering days. In Miami, there were plenty of those. You certainly didn't get snow like here in Christmas Town!

Gloria was grateful that David had been able to house-sit for her and look after Gitana while she was away. Gitana was a very spoiled pup, who'd never been kenneled, and Gloria hadn't wanted to start with that now. Particularly, since she'd planned to be gone for such a long period and that would have been hard on the animal, who was about as much of a "people person" as a doggie could be.

Gitana was the smaller and stockier version of a Labrador that stood lower to the ground than a field Lab and had a hefty neck and powerful shoulders. The breed originally had been used as swimmers trained to drag heavy fishing nets in from the cold Canadian sea. Gitana did enjoy a good swim whenever possible, and also had those retrieving instincts intact. She'd taught herself to bring in the morning paper, when she'd lived with Titi Mon, and had carried on with that tradition since coming to live with Gloria.

Though she'd only been gone a day, Gloria realized she already missed her pet. She also missed David. While they didn't see each other every day back in Miami, she and her brother made it a point to meet for lunch or coffee at least once a week. It was how they kept up with each other, since David didn't much enjoy talking on the phone. He wasn't big on e-mail or social media, either, and only texted when he felt it necessary. Basically, David was a face-to-face kind of guy. He enjoyed personal connections, saying they were more warm and genuine. This was one reason he made such a good pastor.

Gloria reached the front door of the Christmas Inn, then hesitated. Walt had told her that she could come on in without knocking, but this still felt odd to her somehow. Then again, this wasn't simply a private house; the inn was accustomed to hosting guests, who were encouraged to make themselves at home. Walt had said he never locked the front door until late in the evening, so visitors could feel free to come and go. Christmas Town was evidently a safe place, so there was no real worry about intruders. That thought was a little hard for Gloria to get used to as well. She always locked her doors in Miami, whether or not she was at home.

Gloria turned the front doorknob and it opened easily. The moment she stepped indoors, she was greeted by the sweet aroma of peppermint mixed with the fresh scent of pine. The house smelled all holiday-like and homey, but she didn't see either Noelle or Walt. Gloria placed her purse on the entry table, preparing to call out and announce her arrival, but something caught her ear first.

"No! Stop! *Stay.*" That was Walt's voice, commanding authoritatively from the library. "*Good. Now, stand…heel…place.*" What was he doing? Training a dog? Walt had no pets as far as Gloria knew, and she certainly hadn't seen any around the inn. Perhaps Walt was pet-sitting for a friend, or fostering a shelter animal? But when on earth had he brought the creature home? Could it have been after leaving the coffee shop? Gloria knew it was rude to eavesdrop, but curiosity got the better of her. She removed her hat and gloves, setting them down on the hall table, then tiptoed through the living room.

"Excellent! Nice job!" Walt sounded so pleased. He must have accomplished something terribly grand. And, whatever he was training appeared to be very compliant. There were no complaining whines or whimpers. Nor excited yelps or barks, either... Hmm. Though she was hesitant to interrupt what was clearly some sort of instructional session, Gloria decided she needed to let Walt know she was here.

"I'm sorry to inter—" Gloria froze on the threshold to the library and her mouth dropped open. Walt stood beside his desk waving a pencil like a conductor's wand, and fanned out in front of him—just floating in midair—were a whole bunch of letters standing at attention and on end!

"Gloria!" Walt called out in shock and the entire assortment of correspondence tumbled to the floor, making a surprisingly loud crash-landing near his feet.

"Wha...what?" Gloria could barely utter the word, and no more were forthcoming. What in the world had just happened here? She reached up and rubbed her eyes, wondering if she'd been sleeping. Perhaps this wasn't real. She'd been so worn out from shopping, she'd dozed off somewhere and this was all some nutty dream.

Walt bent to pick up the letters, red-faced. "I...didn't hear you come in!"

Yeah, she'd pretty much gathered that part. "What was that?" she asked, still agape. "Some kind of parlor trick?"

"Nope. Nuh-uh." Walt pinned the letters to his chest, and motioned with his chin to some point over Gloria's shoulder. "The parlor's over there!"

She goggled at him, speechless for the second time in less than two minutes. And, that almost never happened to her.

"Let me just… Hang on!" He set the letters down on his desk and settled a heavy paperweight on top of them. The bulky item was designed to look like a Christmas stocking, but appeared to be made of bronze. "There. *Good*." He patted the letters and cut them a quick glance. "*Stay*." Walt gulped. "Did I just say that out loud?"

Gloria nodded numbly. "Are you…? What I mean is, what *are* you?"

"Just…just a regular guy." His voice squeaked a bit on that last part.

"Okay."

"And, whatever it was you think you just saw?"

"Yes?"

"Didn't really happen!"

"What?"

Walt's brow furrowed and he massaged it with his left hand. He met Gloria's eyes with a new thought. "Holograms!"

"Holograms?"

"Those were illusions, yeah!"

"Projected from where?"

Walt soundly patted the top of his roll-top desk. "Right in here."

The projector's right beside that tape recorder, sure, Gloria thought, but didn't say. *If I believed that, Walt could probably sell me swampland in Florida.* Fortunately for her, Gloria knew all about swampland, and Florida. She also knew when she was being hustled.

Walt blinked at her as Gloria strode over to examine the mail he'd secured beneath the paperweight on his desk. "They sure look real enough to me." She reached out and fingered the edge of an envelope. "Feel authentic, too."

"No, please!" Walt's face was a rash of panic. "Don't touch those."

"Why not?" Gloria challenged. "Because they might disappear?"

Walt looked caught out. "Er...maybe."

Gloria set her hands on her hips. She still wore her heavy winter coat and boots, which hopefully made her look a tad taller and more formidable. "If this is your idea of a practical joke, Walt, I don't think it's funny."

His face drew an absolute blank, and then Gloria worried over another conclusion. Walt could be losing his mind, and somehow dragging her down with him. *But, no! Wait!* That didn't make sense. She had no reason to get caught up in Walt's zany fantasy. At least, that's what Gloria thought until she gazed into his eyes. They were a tidal pool of blue and Gloria felt herself spinning around and around inside them.

"Oh!" She pressed her palms to her temples and quickly looked away. Then, immediately, she turned back again, facing Walt straight-on. It was like his eyes had this special power to suck her in and make her...*oof*...lightheaded.

Gloria stumbled in her boots and Walt reached out and caught her by her elbows. "Gloria," he said, gazing down at her. "Maybe you should sit down."

"Not until you tell me..." Balmy, warm breezes rifled her hair and Gloria felt caressed by warm sunlight. She felt dizzy and odd, yet at the same time sort of happy and free. "Wha...what's happening?"

"I think that you and I..." Walt paused and licked his lips. "Might share some kind of connection."

"Walt, no."

He nodded, and she heard ocean waves, and the gulls calling above them.

"I'm sorry," he said hoarsely. "I can't help this."

Gloria stared down at her feet to see they were standing in sand. Ocean winds ripped off the tumbling waters, swirling around them, as white-tipped waves beat a steady rhythm pounding against the shore.

Gloria's voice quaked and her whole body trembled. "Help what?"

"Wanting to be with you so badly it's upended my world."

"I think mine's pretty mixed up right now, too." She searched Walt's eyes, waiting for him to tell her this was another illusion, or a form of hypnosis he'd learned somewhere. Instead, he viewed her with remorse.

"I apologize for that," he said with a sigh. "Really, I do. I'm trying to get a handle on it, as quickly as I can."

"A handle…?"

"I promise you," he said more urgently. "I'm working on it."

"Working on what, Walt?"

His gaze was soulful and deep. "My attraction to you."

In that moment, Gloria felt something, as well. A deep primal calling… Something that rushed through her brain like a song she couldn't get out of her head. But the only lyrics were his name: *Walt…Walt…Walt…* It played over and over again, causing her pulse to race and her heart to skip a beat. Gloria stumbled and Walt shored her up in his embrace, holding her against him.

"Have you hypnotized me somehow?"

"Nope, sorry. Can't do that." Walt's expression was sincere; still, she doubted his words.

"Then, how are we—?"

"Dad! Gloria! I'm home!" It was Noelle calling from the hall, then—*whoosh!*—they were back in the library with dizzying speed and Gloria's knees buckled completely. Walt scooped her up in his arms and carried her to a chair by the hearth.

"Hi guys!" Noelle said in chipper tones. "What's going...on?" She entered the library and stopped cold.

Gloria stared at Walt's daughter, her heart pounding as she wondered if Noelle could do these crazy tricks, too. Or, whether the whole entire existential episode had been in Gloria's mind. Noelle eyed her worriedly.

"All you all right, Gloria? You look a little pale."

"She's just worn out from her big day of shopping," Walt said obliquely.

"You poor thing!" Noelle said, striding toward her. "You *must* be wiped out. You're still wearing your coat!"

Gloria glanced down, realizing that she was. Then, she saw the scattered taupe beads of sand sticking to the tips of her damp white boots, and she fainted dead away.

"Dad!" Noelle cried with alarm, rushing toward Gloria.

Walt stepped forward. "I'll see to her. You go and fetch some water from the kitchen. A tall glass with ice in it."

Noelle nodded and began to step past him, then halted. "Weird! What's that on the floor?"

"Where?"

"There! By Gloria's boots! It looks almost like…" She adjusted the frames of her glasses. "Sand!"

"I'll clean that up." He shot Noelle a pointed stare. "Water?"

"Water, right!" She crossed quickly through the room to the door to the hall. "I'm on it."

When Noelle vanished from sight, Walt pulled a hanky from the hip pocket of his jeans and bent down at Gloria's feet to gently wipe the sand off her boots. Next, he swept the grains that had landed on the carpet into his hand and quickly deposited them in the wastebasket, before shoving the hanky back in his pocket.

Walt drew close to Gloria and laid his palm on her forehead. "I'm sorry to have to do this," he said, "but you really can't remember." It had been a long time since he'd performed a memory wipe, but his dad had taught him how to do it. It was a rare skill only to be used under the most pressing circumstances. Walt's dad, Buddy, had learned it from his cousin, Cole, who was Nick's father. Christmas magic was something to behold, but it wasn't something ordinary folks were allowed to remember. For them, the season needed to be about belief in the unseen, and trusting in miracles of the heart.

Walt's heart pounded like a steel drum as he gently pressed his fingers to Gloria's cool brow. Her beautiful face caught the fire's glow and the flickering flames in the hearth caused a hint of auburn to shimmer in the coils of her rich dark hair. Walt shut his eyes and counted backward from ten, steadily reeling the beach memories in. Next, he recalled the letter sequence, putting Gloria back in the hall. He opened his eyes just as Noelle entered the library with a tall glass of water. She handed it to him and he took it with a grateful nod.

"Gloria," he said. His voice was low and rough. "Gloria, wake up now."

Her eyelids fluttered open and Gloria latched onto the glass Walt held in front of her. "What? Where am I?"

Walt didn't release the glass just yet. He held onto it, helping her take a sip. "Drink," he instructed. "Just a sip."

She tentatively took a gulp, her eyes warily watching Walt and Noelle all the while. "Did...did something happen?"

"You passed out," Noelle told her.

"What?"

"You were probably dehydrated," Walt said. "Here, have another drink."

She did, then wiped her mouth with the back of her hand. "How long was I out?"

"Only a few minutes."

"Gosh."

"Maybe we should call Uncle Kurt?" Noelle suggested.

"No, no." Gloria started to lean forward with her protest then slunk back against the chair. "Don't bother."

"You sure?" Walt queried with concern. He hoped he hadn't overdone it. His intention hadn't been to weaken Gloria. He'd been trying to protect her in a way. Protect her from knowing things her mind likely couldn't handle just yet. Possibly even *ever*.

"I'll be okay." Gloria took another long sip of water, draining half the glass. "I'm feeling better already. The water helps."

Walt nodded and sat down on the sofa, while Noelle sat in the other wing chair. Noelle was also still wearing her puffy down coat. She'd unzipped it but hadn't taken time to remove it during her haste to get Gloria's water. Both watched Gloria worriedly as she finished her water. Then, she set down her glass and stared at them.

"Guys! I'm really all right." She unbuttoned her coat and shrugged out of it, and Walt stood to help her.

"Let me hang that up for you." He glanced at Noelle. "I'll take yours, too."

Noelle nodded, clearly understanding Walt didn't want to leave Gloria unattended. She removed her coat and passed it to her father, and Walt momentarily left the room. As he did, he heard Noelle trying to lighten the mood.

"So! Was shopping with Savannah really that bad?"

Gloria's musical laughter spilled out into the hallway. "I must have been more tired than I realized. The last thing I remember, I was walking in the door. Then, I was waking up in this chair."

When Walt returned, he told her, "You came in to say hello and sat down to remove your boots. Don't you remember that part?"

"No." Gloria's eyes went wide. "I must have been on autopilot or something." She gave an embarrassed laugh. "I guess I dozed off. I'm sorry to have worried you."

"Where did the sand come from?"

"Sand?" Gloria asked, perplexed.

"There was some right…" Noelle adjusted her glasses and stared at the floor. "There."

Walt cleared his throat. "I cleaned that up, and it wasn't sand; it was sawdust, like the kind on the floor at Sugar Plum Feed Supply."

"Oh!" Noelle appeared surprised. "Did you and Savannah go to the hardware store?" she asked Gloria.

"No. No, I don't think so?" Gloria's eyebrows knitted together. "Some parts of the afternoon are kind of fuzzy. Although I do recall seeing *you* at Jolly Bean Java!" She stared at Walt and his face warmed behind his beard.

"Right! I was getting a coffee."

"No, you were getting a mocha. A peppermint mocha, as I recall. I do remember that part."

"You remember everything that happened in the café?" Walt locked on her gaze and Gloria gave a coy smile that bordered on flirty.

"Pretty much, yeah."

Noelle observed the exchange with interest, before scolding her dad. "I hope you at least ordered it with nonfat milk."

Walt shot Noelle a bashful look, but failed to answer.

"Gosh, Dad!" She stood then hauled the candy jar loaded with peppermint bark out of the room. Even without its lid, the container was still useful. Walt had fully restocked it just this morning.

"Hey, where are you going with that?" Even though he didn't think he could stomach more candy just yet, it didn't hurt to have it handy, just in case.

"To put this in one of my hidey-holes, so you can't find it." She paused in the doorway to the living room and sternly arched an eyebrow. "I think you've already had enough peppermint for today."

Noelle didn't know the half of it. He'd eaten two candy canes right off the tree soon after bringing in the mail. Ray said that might help him better focus his abilities and Ray had been right! Walt had been making great strides with those letters before Gloria appeared unexpectedly. He hadn't anticipated her return until much later in the afternoon.

"I think it's sweet how she looks after you," Gloria said to Walt once Noelle had gone. "Is Joy that way, too?"

Walt laughed and shook his head. "Noelle is the mother hen around here. Joy is a bit more chill. She's happy with whatever I do, and never interferes." He smiled fondly, thinking of his extroverted daughter. "But then, she'll go and tell the whole town about it."

Gloria giggled in reply. "Really?"

"Yeah," Walt said warmly. "Daughter number two is a little bit of a blabbermouth, but she's awfully sweet, and talented too." He sighed happily. "Noelle and I will keep her."

"It sounds like both your girls are talented."

"Oh, absolutely! They just have different…um, gifts."

"Joy's is art, and Noelle's is writing?"

"Yes, that's right."

"It must be fun being a twin. Your girls are so lucky to have each other. I always wanted a sister growing up."

"You have just the one brother, then? David in Miami?"

"Yes, he's a pastor there."

"Our pastor here is retiring next year," Walt said, before catching himself. He hadn't meant that to sound like a suggestion that David fill the opening, but he feared it had.

"Oh?"

Walt uncomfortably cleared his throat. "Pastor Wilson's been in charge of the Corner Church for as long as I can remember. He baptized all three of us boys. Officiated at our weddings, too."

"How sweet! Were you all married at the Corner Church?"

"Yes, it's a great place, with a very welcoming congregation. It's too bad you missed the annual Christmas bazaar. It was this past Sunday, the day before you arrived. It's a good time with a covered-dish supper, craft tables, and a pageant put on by the kids."

"Sounds great! I'm sorry I missed it."

"You're welcome to attend church with me and Noelle sometime if you'd like."

She studied him a long while, and Walt wished to goodness he knew what she was thinking. Only, this time, he didn't. "Thanks, Walt. That would be great. I'd like that. Like that very much."

Chapter Twelve

Gloria went to freshen up before dinner, still feeling a little dazed. What on earth had come over her? She couldn't believe she'd just zonked out like that in the library. How embarrassing! Gloria turned on the cold water in her bathroom sink and splashed a hearty amount of it on her face. As she dabbed her face with a towel, Gloria viewed her reflection in the mirror. Her cheeks were glowing bright pink! And, not just her cheeks. Gloria held out her hand, then pushed up her sweater sleeve to stare at her arm. Next, she set the towel down on the sink basin and peered under her sweater at her belly. Oh, no! That was pink, too! And not just any pink, but some kind of weird shimmery pink that almost appeared sparkly. Gloria walked into her bedroom and sat in a chair, unzipping and removing her boots. When she pulled off her socks and examined her feet, they were kind of glowing, too! She was shimmering from head to toe!

Gloria raced back into the bathroom and darted to the shower, opening its glass door. A bottle of scented body wash sat on the shelf. Naturally, it was peppermint. She picked up the bottle and flipped up its cap, squeezing a tiny dab of the gel into her palm. It did seem to sparkle a bit. It shimmered even more brightly when she held her hand under the bright lights framing the sink. Gloria heaved a sigh of relief. *Ah, mystery solved!*

From here on out, she was using regular old bar soap. Luckily, there was an unopened package sitting on the shelf by the shower that held the clean towels, all folded nicely and stacked in neat piles.

Later that night, Gloria accepted a large cooking pot from Noelle and dried it with a dishtowel. Walt had prepared another delicious dinner, and Gloria had insisted that she help clean up. She'd volunteered to tackle the kitchen solo, but Noelle had suggested that they work at things together, and Gloria had agreed. The two women had shooed Walt out of the kitchen, and he'd gone into the library to read.

"I'm glad you're feeling better," Noelle said gently.

"Yeah, me too. I'm sorry if I gave you and your dad a scare."

"Well, Christmas Town can be pretty exhausting." Noelle's lips twisted wryly. "There are lots of high-energy folks in town."

Gloria laughed at the tactful way she'd put that, guessing Noelle included Savannah in that "high-energy" group. Gloria had received a phone call from her friend right before dinner. Savannah apologized for causing a scene at Jolly Bean Java, saying Kurt had verified that it had been Braxton Hicks again after all.

Her cell buzzed on the kitchen desk where she'd left it to charge during dinner. "I'd better check that," she said, thinking that it might be Savannah again. Gloria quickly scanned the text. "Oh! It's from your grandmother."

"Speaking of high-energy folks," Noelle said, laughing.

"Yeah, she's another one." Gloria smiled warmly at the young woman, thinking about how mature and welcoming she was. Noelle didn't make Gloria feel like a guest at the Christmas Inn, she made her feel like family, and—despite what she'd told Walt earlier about being just another visitor—Gloria appreciated that very much.

"What did my grandma want?"

"It's about Savannah's baby shower."

"Oh, right! It's Friday."

"Are you—?"

Noelle shook her head. "It's really for the older crowd." She thought quickly then apologized. "No offense!"

Gloria laughed sunnily. "None taken. I'm sure hearing a bunch of women talking about marriage and babies would be boring to you."

"Yeah. Besides, I'm needed elsewhere! I'm babysitting for Hannah and Carter's daughter, Amanda." She pulled another pot from the soapy water and rinsed it. "Hannah will be at the party, and Sheriff Carter's on duty that night, so I'll be watching their baby."

"How old is she?"

"Two now."

"That's a cute age."

"Yeah, it is. I love kids!" Noelle handed Gloria the pot to dry then added dryly, "In small doses."

Gloria gave a low chuckle. "I'll bet you're very good with them."

"How about you?"

Gloria was caught off guard. "Me?"

"You think you want to have them someday?"

"I...er, sure! Someday," Gloria replied, somewhat nervously. It was hard to imagine having kids when she couldn't even envision getting *married, married, married*...no matter how badly Savannah wanted her to. "How about you?"

Noelle shrugged and handed her the strainer Walt had used to drain the pasta. "I'd like to have one each: a boy and a girl."

Gloria was surprised Noelle had already thought that out.

A faint blush swept the girl's cheeks and she giggled. "Assuming the dad agrees, of course."

"Yes," Gloria said authoritatively. "It would probably be good to have his input."

"*And*, his DNA."

"Noelle!" Gloria playfully air-swatted her with the dishtowel.

"Well, it does take 'two to tango' as my grandma says." Noelle suggestively waggled her eyebrows and Glorious burst into uproarious laughter. She wouldn't have expected this sense of humor from Noelle, and it was delightful.

"What's going on in there?" Walt called loudly from the library.

Noelle cupped a hand to the side of her mouth and yelled back, "Nothing, Dad!"

Gloria's phone buzzed again and she checked it, seeing it was a second text from Lou. The first message had been long and addressed to a larger group, detailing when everyone should arrive at the Snow Globe Gallery on Friday and what each person could bring. But, this latest text was addressed only to Gloria. "Oh, how sweet!" she told Noelle. "You're grandma's invited me to lunch tomorrow. She wants to bring me up to speed on the shower planning."

"Yeah? Where you going?"

"A place called the Peppermint Bark," Gloria answered, thinking she shouldn't be surprised by the name. "Is that close by?"

"Very close." Noelle pulled the stopper from the sink and dried off her hands. "It's right around the corner on North Main, across the street from the Corner Church."

Walt sat by the hearth with his book, wondering what all the commotion in the kitchen was about. Noelle and Gloria seemed to be having a very good time doing the dishes. Who knew cleaning up could be so much fun? Walt wondered what they'd been talking about that had caused such an outburst of hilarity from Gloria. Had Noelle made a funny joke? Perhaps about her dad's penchant for peppermint candy?

"I just wanted to say goodnight."

Walt stared at the doorway to the hall and saw Gloria standing there, holding her cell and its charger, and wearing a smile. Her smile was really lovely, and it took Walt's breath away. Made him a little bit hungry, too. For milk and chocolate chip cookies. "Headed to bed already?"

"I've got an e-reader back in my room. I thought I'd just snuggle down under the covers, and…"

Gloria. Covers. Bed. *Blip. Blip. Blip.* More cookies. More cookies. More cookies.

Walt's stomach rumbled and Gloria stared down at the table beside him. "Looks like you changed your mind about dessert!"

Walt followed her gaze and blanched in horror. Not one, but *three* small plates of chocolate chip cookies sat at his side. A cold glass of milk stood beside them, along with a tall milk pitcher. "Oh, *yeah.*" He lifted the nearest plate and held it out in her direction. "Want one?"

"No, thanks. I've still got that Virginia Cookie from Savannah."

Yeah, and Walt knew which kind. The Commitment one with the big red heart. Walt had heard Hannah's cookies were awfully good; just thinking of that made him want one. "Well, you'd better hurry up and eat it! You heard what Noelle said."

"Yes." Her eyes roved over the plates piled with cookies, including the one that he held. "The evidence is pretty clear. You're a Cookie Man, all right."

Walt guffawed, delighted by the sound of this. He'd never heard the term *Cookie Man* before. Coming from Gloria, especially, he kind of liked it. "Cookie Man? That's a new one!"

She leaned into the doorframe, appearing very relaxed there. "Well, sure. There are some guys who like cakes…others who prefer pie. Then, there's—"

Walt thumbed his chest. "Yes, yes. I see."

"And, don't worry," she told him. "You won't be getting my Commitment Cookie."

Walt wasn't sure whether he should feel challenged or disappointed. "No?"

"No, sir," she said in a tone that was definitely flirty. "I've stashed it in a hidey-hole."

"Oh really?"

"Uh-huh."

"Back in your—?"

"Nope. Not telling you where it is." *Because you might just come after it, you sneak.*

Walt heard that thought loud and clear and it caused his face to steam. "Uh...sleep well, Gloria!" he said as she turned to go. "Pleasant dreams."

"You, too!"

At that precise moment, Walt realized she'd been standing under a big sprig of mistletoe. He took a bite of chocolate chip cookie, suspecting he was in for a long night. He'd either be thinking up cookies, or dreaming about Gloria. Gloria...with her gorgeous dark hair and eyes, and that big beautiful smile... And, those totally luscious lips he'd been hankering to kiss when he'd swept her away. At that last thought, the flames in the gas fireplace flared brightly then went out.

Gloria was halfway to her room when she heard Noelle's cry down the hall, after she'd apparently stepped into the library. "Dad! Seriously?"

Gloria chuckled and let herself into her room, thinking about how incorrigible Walt was. What Savannah had told her was true. The man had absolutely no self-control around cookies. Gloria placed her cell and charger on the dresser, then paused in thought. *Hold on. Where did those cookies come from?* Walt clearly hadn't gotten them from the kitchen, because she and Noelle had been in there the whole time cleaning up. Perhaps Walt had his own private hidey-hole for his sweet treats? But, that still didn't explain where that very cold-looking milk had come from.

Gloria sat on the bed, thinking things at the Christmas Inn weren't always what they appeared to be. There was something different about this place, but Gloria couldn't completely guess what it was. Despite its large size, this grand old house was homey. Savannah had told her that her brother Carter and Hannah had held their wedding reception here, and Gloria could only imagine how the inn must have looked all dolled up for a wedding. It was gorgeous enough decorated for Christmas.

Gloria had seen the three stockings hanging from the mantel in the library, finding it sweet that Noelle and Walt had hung one up remembering Joy. She also found it a bit humorous that Walt had a stocking for himself. He was a grown man, after all. But a grown Cookie Man, Gloria reminded herself with a laugh. Walt clearly had a big sweet tooth, and would appreciate a Christmas stocking stuffed with treats.

With the way he went through candy, Gloria hoped Walt brushed and flossed often. Though, from his very handsome smile, it certainly appeared he took really good care of his teeth. This made her think of her own megawatt grin, which she'd very nearly forgotten about until now. Maybe it was better for her not to dwell on it.

There wasn't a lot she could do except hope her teeth would lessen in super brightness over time.

Gloria kicked off the white flats she'd swapped out for her boots before dinner. She massaged her sore arches, deciding the high-heeled boots were fashionable, but a bit impractical in Christmas Town. When she ate lunch with Lou tomorrow, she could ask Lou about where she might buy another, more practical pair. With this much snow around, surely there was a place in town that sold them. A light ticking sound pinged against the windows and Gloria saw little white flakes hitting against the windowpanes, then instantly melting against them due to the interior warmth of the inn. It was really cozy in here, and Gloria could make it even cozier by turning on the fire. She was happy this room had a fireplace. It was another gas-log fixture with a handy remote. After changing into her PJs, and before climbing into bed, she'd turn it on.

Later that night, Walt lay in his bed staring at the ceiling. He was restless and couldn't sleep, but at least he'd gotten his cookie problem under control. Noelle had asked him why that kept happening: him creating cookies and milk, and Walt had said he didn't know. Which wasn't precisely true. He'd also told Noelle that he'd figured out how to fix the issue. Thankfully, that part was accurate.

After Gloria had turned in, he'd come upstairs to their private family quarters and had begun working on it. Since he wasn't about to eat another candy cane, Walt had opted for chewing some of that peppermint gum. He'd gone through nearly an entire pack of it, while trying to concentrate on controlling his urge to create milk and cookies. At first, he let himself imagine them, the most delicious kinds he could think of… Then, he sternly willed them to disappear. And—*poof*— they actually did. It took some practice, but soon Walt was learning how to keep the cookies and milk from materializing in the first place. It had been an exhausting effort, which had worn him out completely. Still, Walt was pleased with his accomplishment.

He was glad that he'd talked to both his brothers, because Walt was finally making headway, and not just with the milk and cookies. The mail was behaving much more appropriately, now that he'd made it clear that things addressed to a "Christmas" and those meant for a certain "Claus" were bound for two different destinations entirely. Walt never would have guessed that correspondence could be reasonable. Then again, he'd never attempted reasoning with it before.

Walt sighed and folded his arms behind his head on the pillow. The problem was, his troubles weren't over yet. Attempting to reign in his abilities was like playing a game of whack-a-mole. The moment one seemed under control, another flared up! Like the fireplace! Naturally, certain ancestors of Walt's had the ability to make fires go out. Generally only for a short time and under extremely specific circumstances. What Walt didn't get was why this was happening to him now. Walt clearly didn't intend to go dropping down any chimneys, so no one was in danger. Walt gasped at a new thought. Maybe this wasn't only about him? Could it be about Gloria?

Walt reflected on the fire going out in the library, considering exactly when that had happened. It had been when Walt was thinking about Gloria and mooning over how pretty she was. He wasn't only mooning, either. He was fantasizing about what it would be like to kiss her. Walt locked on the thought that perhaps *he* was the dangerous one in a way. A danger to Gloria, because what Walt had to offer her wasn't very much. He was a single dad over forty with some pretty unusual family heritage that he'd have to share with Gloria if they became involved. And, sharing that information might frighten Gloria out of her wits. Could she handle it? Walt wasn't sure. Gloria appeared to be a strong and confident person, but what Walt would be asking of her would surely prove too much. How could he expect her to throw away her sense of reality and believe in the impossible? To take what Walt said on faith?

He'd barely been able to share the truth with Rose. He'd fretted so badly over the outcome, Walt had made himself sick with worry. Gentle Rose was the understanding sort, and fortunately, not at all judgmental. But, even with Rose, it had taken a while for her to come around. She'd later confided she'd only pretended to believe in the beginning, because she sensed it was so important to him. Eventually, over time…Rose had begun to experience more of the magic herself. Yet, Walt had taken care to expose her gradually so she wouldn't totally freak out and think she was losing her mind.

Walt felt a pang of guilt at wiping Gloria's memory of what she'd seen, but too much magic too soon might have caused her irreparable harm. *"Too much, too*

*soon"! Just listen to me! Thinking this out like a
relationship between me and Gloria is bound to
happen.*

That's when Walt realized with an electric jolt that
he wanted it to happen. Very badly. He didn't know
how. He didn't know why. But Savannah had been
right about things on so many levels. Walt hadn't spent
this much time analyzing his interactions with a woman
since he was in college dating Rose. And, just look
what had happened there. Walt swallowed hard. The
relationship had ended in marriage.

Walt didn't know how Kurt had been able to swing
the playboy bachelor lifestyle while dating so many
women before reconnecting with Savannah. Then
again, maybe Kurt's abilities had never been an issue
with any of those ladies, since none of them was *the
one*. Suddenly, Walt felt hot all over, like his entire
body was on fire, and he recognized the sensation at
once. It was the heat of acknowledgment and it was
telling him one thing loud and clear.

He wasn't meant to simply *date* Gloria. He was
destined to *marry* her. After all this time of believing
he'd never get over Rose, in a truly unexpected way he
was. Whether he believed Kurt's bit about "peri-man-o-
pause" or not, something was going on here Walt
couldn't ignore. The best he could do was what Kurt
suggested. Man up and own it. These wild flare-ups of
Walt's abilities only had occurred one other time in his
life, and if he didn't treat what was going on now
seriously, Walt might never have the chance to
experience them again.

Is that what Walt wanted? To relinquish his skills
and surrender his heritage…? Was he ready to dismiss

the idea of him and Gloria being together, without truly assessing her interest in him—and learning whether a relationship between them stood a chance?

The answer to all those burning questions was easy.

And it was only one word.

No.

Chapter Thirteen

When Gloria walked into the kitchen the next morning, she was surprised to learn that Walt had already left the Christmas Inn. Noelle said he'd volunteered to help Olivia do something with the horses at Sleigh Bell Stables. When Gloria commented that was awfully nice of Walt to help his sister-in-law's sister, Noelle had responded, *Oh, it's not just that. Olivia and Dad are old friends.* Gloria had experienced an unexpected stab of jealously at that, which was totally ridiculous. Olivia was married to Nick!

Still, she couldn't help but query, "How long have they known each other? Olivia and your dad?" Gloria toyed with her coffee mug, hoping her query sounded politely interested and not overly nosy.

"Since forever! Dad's family and Olivia's, the Livingstons, used to do a lot of summer beach vacations together, or something."

Now Gloria remembered. Savannah had mentioned those times. One of those summers was when she and Kurt—as teenagers—had fallen in love.

Noelle pulled a tin of freshly baked blueberry muffins from the oven, which looked and smelled heavenly. She'd mentioned that Wednesday was a casual breakfast day at the inn: yogurt, fruit, and muffins. This suited Gloria fine, since she was going out to lunch with Lou.

"Dad and Olivia hadn't seen each other in years, when she decided to move to Christmas Town. But, Olivia still was in touch with my grandma, who suggested she come here to take over All Things Christmas," Noelle said thoughtfully. "Olivia wanted to try something different. Plus, she knew the Christmas family, so she said, yes!"

"That must have been fun for her to reconnect with your dad and his brothers," Gloria said carefully. "How long ago was this?"

"Hmm, let's see." Noelle removed her oven mitts and set them on the counter. "I was about fourteen then, so I'd say it's been roughly seven years."

Which meant Ray had been married and Walt was already widowed at the time, Gloria found herself thinking.

"Some people thought my dad and Olivia might get together," Noelle said with a giggle. "But Joy and I were kind of glad they didn't."

"Oh?" To her dismay, Gloria's voice sounded a little shrill. Plus, her palms were sweaty.

"It's not about Olivia, don't get me wrong! We *adore* her. She's *so* funny!"

"She seems very sweet."

"Definitely! She and Nick are perfect for each other. Everybody knows it, too."

Relief flooded Gloria's veins. Of course, Olivia was happy, and naturally she wasn't interested in Walt. He also must not have been interested in her, or else something would have developed between them before Nick came into the picture, which was just a few years ago, according to Savannah. And, why was Gloria even pondering this, anyway? It wasn't like she had designs on Walt herself. Despite her very lurid dreams...

"I meant to mention the fireplace," Gloria said, thinking of the one in her suite. "I tried turning it on last night, but I couldn't get it started. I thought maybe it's the batteries in the remote?"

"No, Dad says it's something else. None of the other ones were working this morning, either."

"Wow."

"Yeah, sorry about that! Dad's stopping by the hardware store after the stables to pick some things up. He says he thinks he'll be able to figure it out."

"Well, that's good! It's nice having the fireplaces going in here. Really cozy."

Noelle nodded and poured more coffee for herself. She offered some to Gloria but Gloria declined. "I'm afraid you'll probably miss him since you're going out to lunch at twelve. But, he'll be around later this afternoon."

"How about you?"

"I've got the evening shift at the Elf Shelf Bookshop."

Gloria wondered how long the evening shift ran, and whether that meant she and Walt would be alone for dinner.

"You should stop by after lunch and look around," Noelle encouraged. "It's a really cool place, and you could meet Jade," she said, referring to the store's owner.

192 A Glorious Christmas

"Thanks, Noelle. Sounds like a fun plan. Do they carry children's books?" Gloria asked, thinking she might pick out something for Savannah's baby.

Noelle grinned brightly. "Loads of them! And I know exactly where each one is kept."

"Isn't this place *da bomb*, Gloria?"

Gloria repressed a giggle at Lou's attempt at modern slang and glanced around the quaint bistro. The restaurant was fashioned from an old house with a covered front porch and a huge deck out back, which was visible through the window beside their table. At the moment, the deck was covered in snow. "It's very cute here, yes. Do they put tables outside in warmer weather?"

"Oh, yes!" Lou said merrily. "With big red umbrellas! And not only that…" She leaned forward with a grin. "People can bring their dogs, dear."

"Oh wow, this place is pet-friendly?"

"Pet-friendly. Precisely."

They'd recently put in their orders for lunch. Both had ordered the soup and sandwich special. Lou was having a club sandwich with lentil soup, and Gloria had asked for the Mediterranean turkey wrap with the pumpkin bisque, which sounded delicious.

Lou shot Gloria a thoughtful gaze, and then said sunnily, "You could bring Gitana!"

Gloria took a sip of water. "I don't think I'll be bringing her here. It's a long drive for a dog for just a visit."

"I wasn't talking about for a visit, Gloria." There was a sly twinkle in her eyes. "I was thinking of something a little more long-term."

"Huh?"

"Can I be frank?"

"Why, sure." Gloria wondered what Lou was up to, but she didn't have to wonder long.

"I think you would love living in Christmas Town."

"Me?"

"Despite what you might think, dear, it doesn't snow here year-round. Only from early November through late March." She thoughtfully tapped her chin. "Occasionally also in early April."

"But, I—"

"The rest of the year, it's quite lovely. Olivia runs a huge community garden down by the Lena Winchester Memorial Park."

Of course she did. Olivia seemed to be everywhere lately, and on everyone's mind.

"It's right on the river," Lou continued. "And, totally gorgeous in springtime. It's also fine in summer. Olivia and Nick had their wedding there, and…"

Olivia, Olivia, Olivia… Gloria's brain seized on the name as Lou prattled on. Why was the mention of Olivia's name getting on Gloria's nerves this way? She barely even knew the woman and she seemed very nice. Olivia was also extra pretty, and perhaps, at one point, she may have been interested in Walt. But, so what? Why would Gloria care? Even if something had gone on there, by now it was ancient history. Still, the thought of Walt taking Olivia in his arms made Gloria's blood boil and her face steam.

"Did I say something wrong, dear?"

Gloria blinked when she realized her brow had knitted. "No, I…was just thinking about something. I apologize, Lou. That was rude of me. I didn't mean to be distracted."

"That's okay. We're not here to talk about Olivia, anyway."

Well, good. That's progress.

Gloria picked up her water and took several long swallows. She felt as parched as she had after waking up yesterday, when Walt had helped her hold her glass. And, when he'd gazed at her with his dreamy blue eyes she'd nearly fainted dead away again.

"We're here to discuss Walt."

The glass slipped from Gloria's hand and crashed down on the table before smashing into a million pieces on the floor. "Oh! Oh, no!"

"Poor dear! You didn't hurt yourself, did you?"

"No, no. Not at all." Gloria slid her boots away from the spreading puddle that was approaching the legs of her chair, as two bussers rushed over to help clean up the mess. "I'm so sorry!" Gloria said, as other diners gawked in their direction.

"Well, go on!" Lou told the room full of people with a wave of her hand. "Go back to your food! Show's over!" Gloria was amazed by the way the other restaurant patrons obediently hung their heads and returned their attentions to their lunches.

"Some people have no manners at all," Lou said testily as their meals arrived. Their waitress set down their plates, and another server brought Gloria a fresh glass of water. "Well!" She shot Gloria a warm smile. "Doesn't this look nice?"

The food really did appear tasty and the presentation was superb, but Gloria had somehow lost her appetite. Lou wanting to discuss Walt made Gloria nervous, though she wasn't totally sure why. Gloria nodded and forced herself to take a spoonful of the pumpkin bisque, which was fabulous. She simply didn't feel hungry anymore. Gloria had been pleased when Lou had asked her to lunch, but she hadn't anticipated an ambush.

"I thought you wanted to talk about the baby—?" she asked Lou, thrown.

"Ohhhh! Will there be babies involved?" Lou merrily clapped her hands together, and her eyes danced with the question. "Hope so! That would be so nice!"

"We *are* talking about Savannah?"

"Savannah?" For a split second, Lou appeared lost. "Why no, dear. I'm talking about you! You and my son getting *married, married, married*."

Gloria wanted to fold her face in her hands. She couldn't believe Savannah had told Lou about their private conversation. "My," Gloria said, setting down her spoon in total shock. "You really are very direct."

Lou studied her a long while, then her face hung in a frown. "What's wrong with my Walt?"

"Nothing! Nothing at all."

"He's a very nice man, I assure you. Gentlemanly. Kind. And, a really great father, besides."

"Yes, I'm sure."

"Some would even go so far as to say *handsome…*" Lou said, cranking up again. If she'd been dispirited by Gloria's earlier lack of enthusiasm, it certainly hadn't kept Lou down for long.

Gloria stared at her food, unsure of how to answer. She didn't want to be impolite to the older woman, but Lou was clearly overstepping her bounds.

"Oh, dear," Lou said on a sigh. "I might have known."

When Gloria looked up, she continued, "You have a boyfriend, is that it? Back in Miami?"

"Well, I…"

"Naturally, you do." Lou sadly shook her head. "I only wish Savannah had given me the lowdown before I made an utter fool of myself."

"Lou—"

"I mean, look at you!" she went on. "You're smart! Pretty! Plus, a little bit exotic with that Latina thing going on."

"Well…er, thanks."

Lou *tsk*ed. "You and Walt would have made such beautiful children together."

"Walt has two children," Gloria said. "Very accomplished daughters."

"I know," Lou said with a titter. "But there's always room at the inn for one more!"

Gloria was absolutely tongue-tied. The last thing she wanted to do was think about making babies with Walt. But now, Lou had put the suggestion in her head. When Gloria was being honest with herself, she admitted it had been there since yesterday evening when Noelle asked her about wanting to have children. The notion had always been a vague idea, something that seemed nice to think about down the road. Then Noelle had asked that innocent question, and Gloria had gone to bed thinking about it. No wonder she'd had those sexy dreams about Walt. Gloria flushed with embarrassment remembering them, while sitting right here with his *mother*.

Lou took a few bites of her sandwich then set it down. "Please don't be angry with me, sweetheart," she said, obviously misreading Gloria's bright blush. "I only mean well, truly."

Gloria had to concede that Lou's apology sounded heartfelt.

"It's just that I've been so worried about Walt for so long that I don't know how to stop." Lou pushed her plate aside, apparently losing her appetite as well. "When he lost Rose, something happened to him," she confided softly. "I don't know how to put it other than to say the light went out of his eyes."

"I'm sure that must have been extremely hard." If there was anything Gloria knew about it was the heartbreak of losing a close family member. "Losing someone you love is always difficult," she continued, feeling a strange sort of bond with the woman, because she understood it had been Lou's loss, too. "How old were Joy and Noelle when Rose passed?"

"Eleven."

"So the girls got to know their mother."

"Oh yes, and love her dearly. She was a very fine person, Walt's Rose. When she went, it hit all of us hard."

"Was it an illness, or—"

"Cancer," Lou said. "Ovarian, and very quick. By the time it was discovered, there was nothing the doctors could do."

Gloria felt an ache deep in her soul for the entire Christmas family. "How tragic."

"Yes, it was a hard time, but my granddaughters came through it. They've blossomed beautifully despite not having a mother around, and I give Walt one hundred percent credit for that."

"I haven't had the pleasure of meeting Joy, but—judging by Noelle—Walt's done a fabulous job."

"Yes, he has. Hasn't he?" Lou's smile was melancholy. "But, that's just it. Walt's poured everything he's had into those girls, but they're growing up. Both are adult women now."

Gloria understood where Lou was going with this, and her heart went out to Walt. After being a dedicated dad for so many years, the role Walt played with his girls was changing, and would change even more in the future as Noelle and Joy began their individual lives and established their own homes.

"They're incredible women. Noelle is so strong and self-assured. No doubt having you and her granddad in town has played a role in that."

"I like to think we've been of help. Walt's brothers and friends have helped, too." Lou's eyes grew moist. "But there's a certain void friends and family can't fill." Lou extracted a tissue from her purse and blew her nose really, really hard. "I don't know why I'm telling you all this."

Gloria reached out and touched Lou's arm, rife with empathy for the woman, who'd clearly tried so hard to be a good mom to Walt and a caring grandmother to his girls. Lou may have come off as brassy at first, but underneath she had a heart of gold. Gloria could see that now. What's more, she could *feel it* in some very deep and intuitive way.

"It's all right," Gloria told Lou kindly. "I'm happy to listen."

"The world has too many talkers and not enough listeners." Lou's brown eyes sparkled. "That's what Buddy always says."

"I'm afraid Buddy's right."

Lou dabbed the corner of her eye with a fresh tissue then tucked it away. "Do you mind if I ask you a question?"

Gloria hesitated. "Is it about me and Walt?"

Lou resignedly shook her head. "No, dear. It's about the Christmas Inn."

This surprised Gloria, but in a pleasant way. Perhaps this bleak conversation was taking a brighter turn. "Why, sure! I'm glad to help, if I know the answer."

Lou seriously met her gaze, then surprised Gloria with her next statement. "When Buddy and I were over at the inn the other day, I didn't have the heart to look… But, you must have been in the library by now. Are three stockings hanging from the mantel?"

"Why, yes!" Gloria was suddenly silenced by Lou's dour expression.

"Two of them are for Joy and Noelle," Lou offered quietly.

Gloria's heart banged in her chest, as she anticipated Lou's next words.

"And, the third stocking?" she asked, although she already knew the answer.

Lou dejectedly dropped her chin, and the pain in her voice was palpable. All the hurt and anguish that Walt and his family must have experienced over the years rained down on Gloria like a billion prickly darts of sleet cascading from the sky.

"It belonged to Rose."

Chapter Fourteen

Walt breezed out of the Candy Cane Barbershop feeling chipper and spry. He'd gotten his haircut and his whiskers trimmed, and now he was off to see Ray! Which was extra convenient since the North Pole Nursery was at the end of the road right on the other side of the barbershop. As he approached the front of the building, he spotted Ray saying goodbye to Pastor Wilson, who had a tall Fraser fir tied with ropes to the top of his old-fashioned, wood-paneled station wagon.

The old man with silvery white hair gave Walt a friendly wave as he drove past him, and Walt approached Ray through the solidly packed snow. It had let up momentarily, but from the dark clouds looming overhead, Walt knew it was bound to start up again at any minute. But, Walt didn't mind. He loved snow, actually. And winter, too. And, wintry things… Activities. Sleigh bells. Carols—one in particular. He gave a jolly *"ho-ho-ho"* as he strode up to his brother and Ray did a double take.

"Did I just hear you say *ho-ho-ho*?" Ray asked, wide-eyed.

"I don't *know-ho-ho!*" Walt shot Ray a spirited grin. "Did I?"

"Oh, oh, *oh,*" Ray said, deadpan. Then he reached out and pumped Walt's hand. "Something tells me congratulations are in order."

Walt pursed his lips, feeling smug. "Maybe."

"So, tell me?" Ray asked eagerly. "What's going on?"

Walt's gaze trailed after the minister's taillights and he asked distractedly, "Was that Pastor Wilson? Buying a tree?"

"Yup."

"But the Corner Church is all done up for Christmas. So is the parsonage from what I hear."

Ray watched the departing vehicle then spoke admiringly. "Said he was buying it for a friend. Someone who couldn't afford one of his own... I suspect Pastor Wilson was talking about Ben and Hannah's dad, Tanner, but he wouldn't say."

After being estranged for many years, Hannah and her dad had only recently reconciled. Fortunately, it was in time for Tanner to get to know his new granddaughter, Amanda, and become involved in her life. It had taken longer for Tanner to reconnect with his son, Ben. But, they'd eventually worked things out, as well.

Tanner had experienced some down times, but he'd finally turned things around. Thanks, in part, everyone knew, to the support of Pastor Wilson and his friends at the local soup kitchen. While Tanner had initially partaken in the meals there, he currently worked as one of its managers, giving back to the community that had embraced him.

"I know he's got a job now," Ray said. "But the pay at the soup kitchen probably isn't that high. Maybe Tanner couldn't afford a Christmas with all the trimmings."

"I'm sure that Hannah and Carter would have stepped in. Ben and Sandy would have been happy to, too."

"True. But, it's possible that Tanner was embarrassed by his meager state, and he didn't want his kids to know."

Ray was so sage and intuitive. Really great at reading people, and Walt had always appreciated that about him. He also gave dynamite big-brotherly advice. Ray turned to Walt and rubbed his hands together to warm them. He wore a heavy field coat and a cap, but the fingertips of his gloves had been cut off to allow for more nimble handling of his merchandise, as well as the old-school cash register that stood on a counter just inside the door. While freshly cut Christmas trees lined the outside of the building, the inside was filled with pretty potted poinsettias in a selection of colors, fresh-greenery wreaths, and mounds of mistletoe tied up in individual bunches with silky white ribbon.

"So," Ray asked. "What's the good news?"

"Oh, ha-ha, yeah." Walt gave a dopy grin, thinking of Gloria. Next, he snapped to attention and stared straight at Ray. "I decided to man up, Ray. *Own it.*"

"What are you talking about?" Ray dropped his voice into a husky whisper. "Christmas magic?"

"Yeah," Walt whispered back. "I've been working on that, too. Thanks for the tips, by the way! They're working great."

"Ah, so." Ray grinned heartily. "This is about Gloria."

"Yes!" Walt announced like he'd just scored a goal in soccer. He hadn't actually *played* soccer, but he had helped coach Joy's recreational league team when she was in grade school.

Ray tugged him nearer and grinned. "Going that great, huh?"

"Actually, no!" Walt swallowed hard, his throat suddenly scratchy. "I mean, it's not going at all…"

Ray viewed him quizzically and let him go. "What do you mean?"

"I haven't asked her! Not…" Walt anxiously stroked his bead. "Yet."

"What?"

"But I will! I've been gearing up for it all day."

"Which part?" Ray asked, trying to follow.

"The *part* where I ask Gloria to go out on a date with me."

"That's a good start," Ray said matter-of-factly. Then he added with a snicker, "For two folks who are getting *married, married, married*." Ray said these last three words in a high falsetto Walt equivocated with nails on a chalkboard.

"Wait. Savannah told you that, too?"

"Nope." Ray chuckled irritatingly. "Savannah told Olivia, who told Sandy, who told Hannah…"

"I think I've got this one!" Walt said, holding up his hand. "Who told Meredith," he said, referring to Ray's wife, "who told you."

"Exactly."

"I can't believe this is all over town."

Ray shrugged nonchalantly. "Honestly, Walt. What did you expect?"

Gloria and Lou stood on the front porch of the Peppermint Bark saying goodbye. Each one held a doggie bag with most of her uneaten lunch in it. Remarkably, the snow had stopped for a bit, but it was still piled high on the neighboring lawns. Across the street, someone had built a snowman in front of the Corner Church.

"I'm so sorry to have been such a downer," Lou said. "It's honestly not how I hoped our lunch would go."

Gloria definitely believed that, and her heart ached for the Christmas Town mayor. Lou thought she'd be encouraging a nice, single person to marry her son, thereby alleviating his loneliness. But no one could make that choice for Walt but Walt himself. And, Gloria had no clue what Walt wanted. He seemed to say one thing, like, he wouldn't be eating her cookie, then do another, like stare deep into Gloria's eyes with that soulful look. It occurred to Gloria that Walt might not even understand his own motives. If what everyone in town said was true and Walt hadn't dated in all these years, the sheer prospect of going out with a woman might prove enough to unnerve him. "I know, Lou. Please don't worry about it."

"I hope you and your boyfriend will forgive me. I'm sure he's a top-notch fellow."

"Hmm…" Gloria said, before rapidly amending that to, "Um-hmm!" If Lou believed that Gloria had a boyfriend, perhaps she'd leave the matchmaking alone for a while. Which would be helpful, since Savannah was still secretly working on it. She'd practically said as much to Olivia in her shop, when Gloria's back was turned.

Gloria groaned, realizing she had thought of Olivia again, causing her temper to unexpectedly flare. Poor Olivia hadn't done a thing to Gloria! Why, then, did this notion keep popping into her head that Walt and Olivia had been planning something romantic together? Not in the distant past, either… Right here in the actual present!

"Are you all right, dear?" Lou asked, alarmed. "You're stomach's not bothering you?"

"No, Lou. It's not that."

"Then?" Lou's forehead crinkled concernedly and Gloria got the insatiable urge to hug her. She did and Lou blinked in surprise.

"Thanks for the lunch invite, that's all." Gloria said, patting Lou's back. "It was very, very sweet, and I appreciate the thought about me and Walt," *although it was misguided*, Gloria attempted to hint with the tone of her voice.

"And, I appreciated the ear," Lou said, returning Gloria's hug. When they separated, Lou's eyebrows arched. "All in confidence, I hope?"

"You don't even have to ask."

"Thank you, Gloria."

Gloria glanced at the street then down at her feet, remembering about her boots. "I meant to ask you about a good place to buy boots. The warm kind that I can wear around here without killing my feet."

Lou examined Gloria's three-inch heels. "Yes, I see what you mean." She looked up decidedly. "The Snowman Saddle Shop is right down the street."

Gloria couldn't help but chuckle at the name. "And, they sell boots?"

"Oh, yes. Apart from horse tackle, they have lots of outdoor wear, including things for cross-country skiing. Olivia shops there all the time!"

"Of course she does!" Gloria said, like she'd just pinched a nerve.

Lou eyed her perplexedly before continuing. "The store is right at the edge of town. That way," she said, pointing north. "Take a left at the corner when you reach the Gas and Go, and the Snowman Saddle Shop will be on your right."

Walt knocked at the open door of Kurt's office. The receptionist had said Kurt was finished with patients for the day, and was doing paperwork. "Well hey, bro!" Kurt said with a pleased smile. "Back for another check-up so soon?"

"Greetings, brother, doctor, friend." Walt strode confidently into the room, then answered Kurt's query. "And, nope. Don't need one."

Kurt leaned back in his chair and stroked his chin. "No. I don't suppose you do." Another grin graced his face. "You seem mighty happy. Mind telling me what's going on?"

"I've decided I'm going to do it."

"Do what?"

"Do *eeeet*, Kurt! Ask Gloria to go out with me!"

Kurt goggled at him. "You mean, go steady?"

"No! Goodness, no. Why would you even think…?" Walt pulled back one of the metal-framed chairs facing Kurt's desk and took a seat. "What I meant was, I'm going to ask her to go on a date with me."

Kurt opened his mouth to speak and Walt flagged a palm in his direction. "Don't even start with that *married, married, married* baloney. If I hear that one more time I think I'll lose my lunch."

"Yeah, let's not do that. I just cleaned my desk."

Walt stared at the piles and piles of manila folders Kurt had fanned out in front of him. "Right."

"So, what's it going to be?" Kurt asked enthusiastically. "Dinner at the Peppermint Bark?"

"No, she's already been there."

"What? When?"

"Today for lunch with Mom."

"Uh-oh."

"Uh-oh, what?"

Kurt seemed to shake something off. "Nothing. It's probably nothing."

"They're planning a shower, Kurt. For Savannah."

"If you say so, sure."

"In any case, that's not why I'm here."

"Why are you here? To gloat?"

"Huh?"

"Over your obviously conquering peri-man-o-pause. And, in just one day. Whoa! That must be some kind of record."

"I'm not totally over it." Walt cleared his throat. "I mean, not…not completely."

"But, you're obviously working on it."

"No truer words."

Kurt leaned forward and set his elbows on his desk. "So?"

"Oh yeah, right!" Walt unzipped his jacket, feeling suddenly overheated. "I wanted to asked your advice about something."

Kurt's forehead rose. "Medical advice?"

"No. More like romantic advice."

Kurt started to howl but stopped abruptly at Walt's glare.

"I know you think this is funny."

"No, I don't." Kurt did his best to play the consummate professional. The consummate professional *bachelor* who Walt wanted advice from, not the *brother. Doctor. Friend.* "Just tell me what you need?"

"I need to know how to start it? I've thought of wine and flowers, but is that too much?"

"For...?"

"The invite, Kurt!" Walt grew animated considering the elaborate plan he'd concocted. Luckily, Olivia had been a huge help. "I know what to do when I get Gloria on a date." He swallowed hard. "At least, I think I remember that part."

"Like riding a bicycle," Kurt assured him. "It will all come back to you."

Walt nodded and pressed ahead. "I'm talking about how to ask Gloria out to begin with?"

"Uh...just ask her?"

"What? No! That's so lame."

"A couple of practical points here," Kurt said reasonably. "Neither of you is seventeen and this isn't the prom."

Walt sighed heavily and ran his hands through his hair. "Yeah, at least there are videos on YouTube about how to ask someone out for that."

Kurt studied him agape. "Look at you. You're a wreck."

"Thanks, Doc. Is that your professional opinion?"

"Just a brotherly observation."

"Okay, fine. So, what? Are you refusing to help?"

"Walt," Kurt said more calmly. "Just ask her."

Walt pinned Kurt with his gaze. "What did you do the first time you asked Savannah out? I mean, how did you approach it?"

"We'd already dated in high school."

"Still, it had been a long time. You had to start over somehow."

Kurt threw up his hands. "Fine!"

"Fine, what?"

"I took her champagne and roses."

"Seriously?"

"It was under completely different circumstances."

"Maybe so. But it apparently worked for you."

"I wouldn't go there, Walt."

"Why not?"

"Because you're not me." Kurt tried to put this gently, but it still stung.

"Gee, thanks."

"I didn't mean it like that, come on. I'd had plenty of experience with women by then. I could pull off a move like that."

"And, you don't believe that I can?" Walt asked indignantly.

Kurt laughed in surprise. "Walt, do you hear what you're saying?"

"Yeah," Walt said. His tone was prickly with emotion. "I hear what *you're* saying, too. And, let me tell you something, Kurt Christmas," Walt said, his voice rising. "If you think there's only room for one *suave dude* in this family then you're dead wrong!"

"Wow!" Kurt appeared stunned but utterly pleased. "I like what Gloria's done for you."

"You're an enormous pain in the neck," Walt grumbled. But he couldn't help but love his little brother just the same. Walt stood grumpily and zipped up his coat, thinking Kurt was no help. No help at all. "Thanks a whole lot for nothing," he said, turning to go.

"Oh no, you don't." Kurt strode toward him and held out his arms. "Come here."

"No."

"Stop acting like a child, Walt. Give your baby brother a hug."

What Walt felt like doing was giving his baby brother a karate chop, or maybe a harsh flip—right onto his back. Walt might not have ever played soccer, but he'd studied martial arts as a teen and had become a black belt.

Kurt took a step closer and opened his arms wider. "You know that you love me."

But instead of embracing him, Walt socked Kurt in the gut. Hard.

"Ow!" Kurt doubled over in surprise. "You really pack a punch."

"Oh, man!" Walt was awash with shame as he rushed toward his brother. "I'm so sorry, Kurt! I don't know what came over me!"

Kurt straightened with a hearty laugh and rubbed his belly. "Passion, my friend," he said with a wink. "Hang onto it."

A wave of clarity hit Walt when he understood that Kurt had manipulated him. "Wait a minute! You made me feel all that on purpose?"

"Just *ask* her," Kurt said. "But when you do, really mean it. Trust me. When Gloria sees that there's fire in your veins, she'll say yes."

"I'm not sure that kind of fire's good for me," Walt said, rubbing his knuckles.

"Like everything else, you'll need to learn to control it."

"Huh." Walt scratched his beard. "Interesting."

"Just don't go karate chopping anyone or flipping them onto their backs."

"I was absolutely not thinking about doing either of those things."

Kurt met his gaze dead-on. "Liar."

Chapter Fifteen

Gloria decided to run a few errands in town before going back to the Christmas Inn to get her SUV and driving to the Snowman Saddle Shop. She'd suffered through wearing these boots up until two, so she could last a little longer in the day. First, Gloria wanted to drop by the Elf Shelf Bookshop as she'd promised Noelle. She had a few classic children's books in mind she wanted to purchase as a starter set for Savannah and Kurt's baby. When Savannah had shown Gloria the nursery, she'd noted a few picture books on the shelf, but little Julia or Jacob could certainly do with more reading material. No one could ever have enough books!

As Gloria hurried down the street, it started snowing again. This time, huge white flakes were falling in sticky clumps. She passed boarded-up Sisters' Row with tons of scaffolding shielding the pale pink structure with dark green gingerbread trim. The building consisted of three town houses snuggled together, and Gloria could imagine the fun times Savannah had enjoyed when she'd stayed there in the townhome next to Liz, with Jade and Wendell's unit on the far side.

Santa Claus Lane was just up ahead and the impressive Snow Globe Gallery perched on the corner. It had one showcase window facing North Main Street, which displayed an enormous yet intricately designed snow globe. Gloria guessed the piece was the mascot of the shop and it was unbelievably pretty. A small barn sat inside the glass bubble with a cute farmhouse beside it. Reindeer waited patiently in the yard, while real smoke appeared to rise from the farmhouse's little chimney. It was the most amazing curio item Gloria had ever seen. She couldn't wait to ask Sandy more about it on Friday. If she remembered, that was, in the midst of the happy celebration for Savannah.

Gloria rounded the corner, passing the gallery's front door and another display window on the Santa Claus Lane side. Several gorgeous winter landscapes were featured there, as were—hey! Gloria's eyes lit on a sweet still life portraying three heart-shaped cookies. One of them looked identical to the Commitment Cookie Savannah had given to her. The other two on the canvas had different designs. One had a pretty blond angel wearing a halo on its front, while the third one was decorated with a green Christmas tree adorned with colorful candy balls. Gloria thoughtfully viewed the portrait of what she guessed were Hannah's Virginia Cookies, then hurried on by, noting the gallery appeared packed inside.

The next shop on her right was just as loaded with customers standing in line behind a beautifully arranged candy counter. Of course! Gloria checked the marquee. That was Nutcracker Sweets, where Liz had purchased that wonderful gift for her. Gloria had tried one of the truffles last night while she was reading. It was called Christmas Orange and tasted so citrusy, yet chocolaty delicious and silky smooth. The candy had virtually melted on her tongue, and she'd had to exhibit great self-control not to devour the entire carton at once. Gloria had resisted because she wanted to take her time in savoring each new flavor as a delicacy. She was definitely trying another—maybe peppermint stick— tonight.

Gloria laughed, thinking that variety sounded right up Walt's alley. He seemed to love everything peppermint so, so much. He was such a nice man, and she was sad that life had been hard for him. If he was hurting inside, he took care not to let it show. For this, Gloria admired him all the more. Walt had been so nice to put her up and he'd been playing the perfect host besides. Gloria had brought him that bottle of wine, but wished she could think of something more she could do to thank him. Then, she stopped walking, realizing where she was. Right in front of the Christmas Cookie Shop!

Gloria congratulated herself on her bright idea. What better way to thank a Cookie Man than by bringing him what he loved? If he didn't want them now, Walt could always freeze them for later. Though Gloria seriously doubted that Walt would have the restraint for that. She still wondered about those chocolate chip cookies last night and where they had come from, and she intended to ask him.

The door chime tinkled as Gloria entered the crowded Christmas Cookie Shop. She glanced around the packed room and at two display cases that were teeming with every kind of Christmas cookie Gloria could imagine, and all were exquisitely made.

"Wow," she remarked to another customer in front of her who was standing in line. "Popular place."

"You don't know the half of it!" the perky woman said. She had long wavy blond hair, a smallish frame, fair skin, and big blue eyes. She seemed pleasant enough but was a little oddly dressed in a puffy white coat, mittens, and big sparkly white earmuffs. "You should see this place on the first Saturday after Thanksgiving!"

"Oh? What happens then?"

"Hannah unveils her newest version of her Virginia Cookies. They're very famous."

"Yeah." Gloria nodded knowingly as the line inched forward. "That's what I've heard."

The blonde studied her a long moment then broke into a happy grin. "Hold the phone! Are you Gloria Chavez?"

"Why, yes," Gloria said with surprise. "But, how did you—?"

The woman jutted out her mitten. "Sandy Winchester! Great to meet you!"

"You're Savannah's friend? Sandy, from the Snow Globe Gallery?"

"That's right!" They scooted up a bit further in line. "Welcome to Christmas Town."

"Thank you! I passed your gallery just seconds ago. It was brimming with people."

"Ms. Thurston, the art teacher from the high school, is running a Christmas Craft Workshop this afternoon. She and the puppet maker from the Grand

Hotel, Mr. Hadley, are helping the kids make their very own holiday puppets."

"How cool!"

"Yeah, a lot of kids around here are big into puppets. Especially with Savannah's theater camp, and the upcoming Christmas puppet show."

"I'm looking forward to that, too. Savannah's told me all about it, and I'll be helping out with the production." Gloria drew closer and whispered, "I'd also like to contribute to the baby shower. I'm baking a casserole to bring as Lou suggested, but I'd love to do something more."

"Oh, you're doing plenty by getting Savannah there! We all appreciate your taking on the job." She giggled like it was a chore, but it really wasn't to Gloria.

"Oh hey, Sandy!" An attractive brunette called from behind the register. She had a modern-cut, chin-length bob, a creamy complexion, and big dark eyes. They curiously darted to Gloria, and then the woman grinned. "Oh my goodness! Are you Gloria Chavez?"

"Yes!" Gloria extended her arm and shook hands with Hannah Winchester over the countertop. "And you must be Hannah! I've heard so many great things about you." She shot a quick glance at Sandy. "About both of you. Savannah is singing your praises all the time."

Hannah laughed sunnily at this and Sandy chuckled, too.

"We love having Savannah in town. Carter and Olivia are happy about it, too."

Gloria nodded. "It's nice when family can be together."

"Christmas Town is a very nice family place," Hannah said. "My brother, Ben, moved here a few years ago to become our new Justice of the Peace and marry Sandy."

"I hear your brother's here too," Gloria remarked to Sandy.

"He is! Which is really, really great."

Hannah smiled pleasantly at the customers who were waiting behind them and starting to grow impatient. "It will just be a second!" Next, she turned her attention on Sandy and Gloria. "I look forward to chatting more at the shower. But, for now, what can I get you ladies?"

Gloria visited the Elf Shelf Bookshop next, and Noelle showed her around, assisting Gloria with her selections. She also met Jade Scott, an elegant-looking woman with caramel-colored skin and warm brown eyes. Jade wore her medium-brown hair in a stylish cut that was cropped short and accented with copper highlights. She welcomed Gloria to Christmas Town just as warmly as the other women had, but Gloria didn't linger for long. The bookstore was busy and Jade and Noelle had to get back to work. Gloria also needed to return to the inn to deposit her shopping bags in her room and pop her doggie bag from lunch in the refrigerator. Then, she needed to scoot out to the Snowman Saddle Shop to buy those boots!

And, she had to accomplish all that by four o'clock, because she'd promised Savannah she'd come by to help her address notecards. Since the moment she and Kurt announced they were pregnant, the baby gifts had started pouring in. Savannah had been trying to stay on top of her thank-you notes, but she'd been falling behind, so Gloria was going to help by addressing envelopes.

Gloria was due back at the inn at seven for dinner, but she was unclear about what that would entail. In speaking with Noelle, it sounded like the young woman was working at the bookshop until closing and then helping Jade with inventory afterward, which could take some time. Gloria felt a little uneasy about having dinner alone with Walt, given the hints that Lou had dropped, and also with Savannah trying so hard to get the two of them together.

Gloria told herself not to be silly. Things would go just fine. She and Walt were two adults, weren't they? There was no reason they couldn't share a meal without an aura of romance looming over the table. She'd also purchased a nice gift for Walt and was excited about giving it to him. Hannah had arranged the loveliest box of Christmas cookies for her, all packed up in a little brown box and tied up with thin gold twine. Gloria hoped Walt would be pleased, and not think that she hitting on him, which Gloria wouldn't be doing of course!

Gloria was so deep in her thoughts, she lost track of where she was going. The next thing she knew, she'd collided with someone, her shopping bags crunching between them.

"Oh! Oops! Excuse me!"

"Gloria?"

Gloria blanched, the blood draining completely from her face. "Well hey, Olivia!"

"Are you all right?" Olivia's brow furrowed worriedly. "You kind of ran right into me."

"Oh no! I mean, oh gee…" Gloria's shoulders sagged. "I'm sorry. I didn't even see you coming."

"Yeah, I guess not!"

When Gloria glanced at Olivia, she started to get this little tingly feeling all over, and it wasn't a good tingle, either. It was negative to the point where it almost hurt. *Ouch.* Gloria rubbed her upper arm with her free hand. It felt like someone had just given her an injection of something. But Olivia just stared at her blankly with big green eyes. "Are you sure you're okay?"

"Yep. Uh-huh. Great! How about you?"

"I'm doing great today, thanks."

"I hear you saw Walt this morning," Gloria said impulsively. Then she kind of wished she hadn't.

"Oh yeah, *Walt*. Hmm."

Gloria didn't appreciate the dreamy way she'd said that.

"He went to help you at the stables?"

"He sure did!"

There was a lilt in her voice that Gloria found annoying. "Well, that was nice."

"It sure *was*." Olivia cagily bobbed her chin like she was trying to tell Gloria something. Whatever it was, Gloria didn't want to know. Particularly if there was something illicit going on between Olivia and Walt. Yuck.

"How cozy for the two of you."

"What?"

"I'm sorry, Olivia," Gloria said curtly. "But I'm kind of in a hurry. I've got to go."

Gloria scurried down the sidewalk shaking her head. She didn't know what it was about Olivia that got under her skin, but something did. Gloria sure hoped she was wrong about Olivia and Walt! What a disaster that would be—for everyone. Olivia's marriage would be wrecked, and Savannah would be so upset with her sister. And what about Walt? He appeared so conservative and upstanding. Was he really capable of having an underhanded tryst?

That didn't sound like Walt, or Olivia either for that matter. Not from everything Gloria had witnessed and heard. Yet, she couldn't shake that niggling sensation that Olivia and Walt were keeping secrets. Gloria also had a very big hunch that those secrets had something to do with her.

Chapter Sixteen

Walt crept into his darkened kitchen, furtively glancing around. He wore his heavy winter boots and field jacket and held the bagged bottle of champagne he'd picked up at the Merry Market. While he was there, he'd nabbed this nice bouquet of roses, too. What the heck. You only lived once, and Walt had only pursued a woman twice—this being his second time. His brother Kurt was not the only Christmas son with romantically persuasive skills. Walt had been quite good at that at one time. Didn't matter how many years ago. Like Kurt said, it would come back to him. It already was coming back to him. And, not in little bits and pieces, either. In one big rush!

He peered around the darkened kitchen, figuring Gloria was still out and about in town. Noelle was obviously still at work at the Elf Shelf Bookshop. Walt flipped a few switches and the shadowy kitchen bloomed with light. He'd need to get to work soon on preparing Gloria's special dinner. Walt had planned an elegant surf-and-turf repast, complete with pan-seared scallops and rib-eye steaks with a garlic-mushroom sauce. Twice-baked potatoes would serve as a side, along with grilled asparagus, and a salad. Walt hoped that Gloria would be impressed.

Walt had cooked plenty for his guests at the Christmas Inn and he knew what constituted a romantic meal. The roses would serve as a centerpiece on the candlelit table, and he'd seat Gloria beside him, facing the fireplace, rather than at the opposite end. Their being closer together provided greater intimacy. If the occasion arose, it would also give Walt the opportunity to reach out and take Gloria's hand.

Walt's heart stuttered at the thought of holding Gloria close and gazing into her eyes the way he'd done that time in the library. They'd been swept away to some magical place created by their joint imaginations. The stunning thing was, he and Gloria had both envisioned the same exact landscape perfectly. Walt didn't know why this was happening now. And, he didn't know why it was happening with Gloria. He only knew that being with her felt very, very right.

It was a feeling he had to explore, if Gloria would let him.

He'd know so much more after tonight.

"So, tell me," Savannah said as she and Gloria sat at her dining room table. "How are things going at the Christmas Inn?"

Gloria didn't look up. She just kept addressing envelopes. "Really well. Same as the last time you asked me."

"And, Walt?"

Gloria met Savannah's eyes this time. "He's been the perfect host, as well as a perfect gentleman."

"Shoot."

"Savannah."

"I'm just saying, Gloria, it looked like he had the hots for you. Walt was falling all over himself at Jolly Bean Java."

"Well, maybe looks can be deceiving."

"I don't think so. Not this time."

Savannah set down her pen, suddenly remembering. "How was your lunch with Lou?"

"Oh, er…" Gloria fumbled with how much to tell Savannah. Lou was her mother-in-law and also on the same mission as Savannah. At least she had been, until she came to believe Gloria had a boyfriend. "Okay."

"Only okay?"

"Neither of us was very hungry," Gloria admitted honestly.

"Gosh. Why not?"

Gloria shrugged. "We got to talking about things."

"Such as?"

Gloria heaved a breath. "Walt, if you must know, but it's not what you think. I mean, maybe it was in the beginning, but it definitely wasn't by the end."

"Gloria, you're not making any sense."

"Did you know about Rose's stocking?"

Savannah's lips took a downward turn. "Yeah. Sad, isn't it?"

"I'll say."

"Why do you suppose he still hangs it up? I mean, it's been years."

"Kurt says it has something to do with a tradition. The girls and Walt put notes to Rose in her stocking each year."

"Oh!"

"Yeah, it sounds depressing, I know." Savannah lifted a shoulder. "But maybe, for them, it's therapeutic."

"I see," Gloria said, thinking she did. It was hard to understand how other people dealt with grief. Different people had different ways of going through the process.

They both got back to work, then Gloria said after a bit, "I ran into Olivia today."

"Yeah?"

"I'm afraid literally."

"What do you mean?"

"We bumped into each other on the street."

Savannah eyed her quizzically. "O-kay."

"Savannah," Gloria said, braving it. "Do you think they're happy?"

"Who?"

"Olivia and Nick?"

"You bet! Ecstatic!" She worriedly scanned Gloria's eyes. "Why do you ask?"

"It's nothing. Just wondering, that's all." Gloria finished addressing a stack of envelopes and pushed it aside. "What are your plans for tomorrow?"

"I've got to catch up on some computer work at the theater in the morning, then Kurt's taking me to my OB-GYN appointment in the afternoon."

"Routine?"

"Yes."

Gloria laughed with relief. "So, no more Braxton Hicks?"

"Not at the moment!" Savannah knocked her knuckles against the dining room table. "Thank goodness." Savannah studied her friend. "How about you? Do you want to meet up?"

"I promised my school I'd do some work remotely. Since you'll be busy, maybe I should focus on that."

"All right. Then, how about Friday?"

"I'd love to take you to dinner!"

"Dinner? That's great! Let me ask Kurt—"

"I was hoping for just a girls' night." Gloria gave a play pout. "If you know what I mean."

"A girls' night? Sure! That would be fun. Where would you like to go?"

"What do you suggest?"

"There aren't too many options in Christmas Town." Savannah laughed heartily then considered this a moment. "The Peppermint Bark is open at night, but you probably won't want to go back there so soon. Would you be up for pizza?"

"I love pizza. Sure!"

"There's a really great place on the other end of town called the Reindeer Pub. Their pizza is out of this world. We can go there."

"That sounds perfect then. I'll pick you up around seven."

"I don't mind driving!"

Gloria gazed doubtfully at Savannah's stomach. "Are you sure you can still fit behind the wheel?"

"That is so not nice!" Savannah said, but she was grinning. Then, after a beat, she said, "All right, you can drive. If you insist, I'll let you."

"I insist."

"Then I'll see you on Friday at seven."

Walt was putting together the salad when Noelle walked in the kitchen.

"Well, well, what's this?"

Walt startled at her arrival, as her gaze snagged on the prettily arranged vase of roses. Thankfully, she couldn't see the champagne as he'd stuck that in the freezer. Walt wanted it extra cold when he presented it to Gloria with the dark chocolate mousse dessert. He'd just finished whipping it up and planned to serve it with ripe raspberries and fresh whipped cream.

"Noelle! What are you doing home? I though you were working until eight or nine?"

"I am." She surveyed him cagily. "I just came home to grab my sandwich. I made one earlier but I forgot to take it with me."

She opened the refrigerator and her gaze landed on the chocolate mousse. Next, she sneakily peeked in the freezer. "Champagne! Just as I suspected." Noelle turned slowly on her father. "You're preparing the Valentine's Day dinner tonight, aren't you?"

"Well, I..."

"Interesting, Dad. Very interesting." Something in Noelle's big blue eyes said she knew something was going on. Meaning, Walt was attempting to woo his pretty houseguest from Miami. "It's the surf-and-turf combo, right?"

Walt wiped his brow. "I just thought it would be nice! We haven't had shellfish in a while, and it should be a treat for Gloria. She's worn herself thin this week from...shopping."

"I know. She came by the bookshop today. She'd already been a few other places, too."

"Oh?"

"Like out to lunch with Grandma."

"Yes. Yes, I know." Walt nervously picked up the salad tongs and began mixing the greens around, while Noelle watched him oh-so-carefully. "Hope that went well!"

"You might want to add the rest of the ingredients to the salad before you toss it."

Walt stared at the countertop, seeing the rest of the washed and cut vegetables still remained on the cutting board. "Oh, right! Ha-ha! Right. Was about to do that. Actually."

Noelle's eyebrows rose. "You like her, don't you?"

"Who?"

Noelle folded her arms across her chest. "Gloria."

"Why, sure. Doesn't everybody?"

"Pretty much, yeah."

"Do you like her?"

"You know what? Yeah, I do. I think she's pretty cool." Noelle nabbed a brown paper bag out of the refrigerator. "I also think it's cool if you want to start dating again."

"You...what?"

"Joy does too, Dad. She and I talked about it last night."

"You did, did you?"

"Yeah, and here's what we both decided. You're not exactly a spring chicken anymore."

Walt's neck warmed at the gentle jab. "Thanks, Noelle."

"But that doesn't mean you're not the right age for someone like...Gloria."

Heat crept up Walt's neck and onto his face.

"Dad, listen. It's okay. Seriously. Joy and I aren't even around anymore most of the time. Maybe it's good for you to start thinking about a life of your own."

"I have a life!"

Noelle briskly approached him and kissed him on the cheek. "Bye, Dad! See you later!" When she was halfway out the door she turned to him. "And, I mean *much* later. I'm stopping by Grandma and Grandpa's after I get off work."

"Fi...fine!" Walt stammered, completely gobsmacked. "Have a good time!"

"You too-hoo!" she said in telling tones.

Chapter Seventeen

Gloria couldn't believe how gorgeous everything looked when she returned to the Christmas Inn. The décor was as festive as always, but there were extra special touches in the dining room, where the table was set for two with elegant china sporting a red poinsettia design. The lilies had been removed, and a beautiful bouquet of deep red roses served as the centerpiece. And, the smells coming from the kitchen couldn't be beat.

"Walt?" Gloria called, walking in that direction. "I'm back!"

She found him by the stove, wearing that dark green apron over jeans and a navy blue sweater. The collar of a white T-shirt was visible below the sweater's V. He turned to her as she entered the room. "Gloria! Hey!"

"What are you cooking that smells like something out of a gourmet restaurant?"

"Something out of a gourmet restaurant," he quipped. His blue eyes danced as he answered merrily, "I'm preparing surf and turf tonight: pan-seared scallops and steak."

Gloria's mouth watered at the prospect of such a delicious meal. Since she hadn't eaten much lunch, she was ravenous. "That sounds so good! I can't wait."

Walt smiled warmly. "Why don't you remove your coat and hat and join me in the kitchen? We can chat while I finish up with the meal."

"Only if I get to help."

His eyes twinkled. "You can help by drinking some wine."

"Okay," Gloria said with a laugh. "I think I can handle that part." She decided she wanted to freshen up as well. Gloria also had that gift for Walt she wanted to retrieve from her room. "I'll be back in a few!"

"Take your time." When Walt's eyes locked on hers, Gloria's heart pounded. "I'll be here when you return." Gloria's pulse beat double-time as she strode down the hall. There was something different about Walt tonight, barely perceptible but it was there. And, it made Gloria's skin all tingly in a good way. Not in that horrid manner that had happened when she'd run into Olivia.

Gloria didn't know what the real deal was between Olivia and Walt, but for now she decided to put any notions of an untoward affair between them out of her mind. She'd believed Savannah when she said Olivia and Nick were happy. And, Walt seemed like such a stand-up guy. He was certainly standing up pretty well in the kitchen. The man had looked absolutely gorgeous when she'd walked in.

Gloria left her coat and hat in the coat closet then went to her suite, where she touched up her makeup in the bathroom. *Now, that's weird!* Her cheeks looked all glittery again in the mirror. And, she'd stopped using the peppermint bath wash after switching to regular bar soap.

Gloria held out her blusher brush to examine it in the light above the sink. The shimmery sheen on her cheeks didn't appear to be coming from there. And, yet… Gloria stared at her reflection again. She was positively glowing, in an ultimately strange and happy way.

She heard her cell buzz in her purse and went to retrieve it from where she'd left it on the bed. It was David, checking in. He'd also attached another darling photo of Gitana.

Hi, sis! How's it going? Everything a-okay in Christmas Town?

Gloria rapidly typed back.

Everything's great here. Still no baby!

All right. Keep me posted!

Thanks, David. Will do!

Gloria set down her phone, hunting for the bag from the Christmas Cookie Shop. She had another, smaller package from the same store tucked in her nightstand drawer. Gloria decided she ought to eat the cookie Savannah had given her sometime soon, before it went stale. Clearly, there was no truth to the rumor about it inspiring true love. That cookie was simply another one of Hannah's gorgeous creations. Gloria thought that Hannah had been terribly smart to come up with that Virginia Cookie gimmick. Although Savannah said it was based on some legend about Hannah's great-great grandmother, it was Hannah who'd brought the idea forward into the twenty-first century. And the concept of those magical cookies had made Hannah a very successful businesswoman, for sure.

Gloria found the bag she sought in the side chair near the bed, sitting beside the bag from the Elf Shelf Bookshop. Though the "baby shower" was supposed to be more about presents for Savannah, Gloria intended to bring a little something for the expected child, too. She'd seen some stores in town she planned to explore over the next couple of days, while searching for gifts for Savannah. Jade had recommended a funky shop on Santa Claus Lane called Mystic Magi, and also South Pole Pottery, to the right of the Grand Hotel on South Main.

Gloria was awfully glad she'd come here. Primarily, she'd wanted to help Savannah. But Gloria also couldn't help but get caught up in Christmas Town's charms. Everyone she'd met had been so warm and friendly, and she'd really liked them all. Even meddlesome Lou! Then, there was the matter of Olivia...hmm. Gloria shook off that negative vibe, willing herself to focus on the positives.

A very handsome bachelor was in the kitchen cooking her a gourmet meal, and Gloria couldn't recall the last time that had happened to her. In fact, when she paused to think about it, it never had! Walt was such a nice guy. Wonderful, warm, and funny. Gloria hated that he'd been through such a rough time. She couldn't wait to give him his gift and see the expression on his face when he realized she'd bought him cookies. They seemed to be one of the things Walt loved best in the world. Apart from peppermint, Gloria thought curiously.

When Gloria reentered the kitchen, she looked stunning. She'd changed out of her other clothes and now wore a pretty red sweater and tightly fitted blue jeans that were tucked into calf-high leather boots. "I don't think I've ever seen you in anything but white!" Walt said jovially.

Gloria self-consciously studied her clothing. "Yeah, I decided it was time for a change. Ha-ha!"

The new outfit hugged her womanly curves perfectly, and Walt felt himself blush just from noticing that. "Can I pour you some wine?" he asked, clearing his throat. "We have red or white." Walt reached for the wine rack above the kitchen desk. "There's also that nice bottle of pinot noir you brought us."

"Oh, no! That's a gift. Why don't you save that?"

"For when?"

Gloria shrugged, holding a shopping bag with handles in her hand. "Maybe for Christmas?"

"It's a shame you won't be here," Walt said, knowing that she'd be back in Miami by then, assuming Savannah's baby came on schedule next week.

The thought of Gloria leaving so soon made Walt feel foolish for making this display of a lavish dinner. He also was slightly abashed by the elaborate date he'd planned. But, even if he only had one or two fabulous dates with Gloria before she left Christmas Town, Walt decided the risk of him asking her out would be worth it.

The two of them spending time together could be the start of something good. Walt didn't care to ponder the long term, or how things might eventually work out. He merely wanted to focus on the present and that fire burning through his veins. The fire that told him he needed to spend as much time as he could with Gloria. For however long that it lasted.

She could tell he was waiting on her response about the wine. "Whatever's open is fine."

Walt pulled a few wineglasses from the rack then ambled over to the sink. He'd recently uncorked a bottle of merlot and set it out to breathe on the counter. As he poured them both a glass, Gloria walked toward him with a sunny smile. "I got you a little something today," she said, lifting the bag in her hand.

Walt was both surprised and touched. He was even more excited when he spied the emblem on the bag, indicating it had come from the Christmas Cookie Shop.

"Gloria, you shouldn't have," he said in a warm way that indicated he was awfully glad that she had. He passed Gloria her wine and accepted his gift. "Should I open it now?"

"I think you'd better, but maybe hold off on indulging until after dinner." She chuckled sweetly. "We don't want to ruin your appetite!"

Walt eagerly dug into the bag and pulled out a dainty box. "Hannah Livingston makes the best cookies," he said in pleased tones.

"That's what I hear."

"Have you tried any?"

"Not yet!"

"Saving that Virginia Cookie for a special occasion, huh?"

There was amusement and intrigue in her eyes. "Maybe."

Man, she was a beautiful woman. So beautiful that her smile made Walt lose all sense of place and time.

"Go on," she said with a giggle. "Open it!"

"Oh, right. Right."

Walt pried back the gold twine and lifted the lid of the box. A gorgeous assortment of Christmas cookies nestled inside, and Walt's stomach immediately rumbled. "How did you know?"

"Wild guess." The way she said that was a little saucy, causing heat to flare at Walt's temples.

"I thought you might have run out of the chocolate chip ones by now," Gloria teased lightly. "Did you eat all of those that you had in the library?"

Walt gave an embarrassed flush. "Not all at once."

"Where did they come from, anyway? I was wondering about that, since Noelle and I had been in the kitchen."

"Oh, that!" Walt thought quickly. "We have another smaller kitchen upstairs. It's part of our private family quarters," he answered. His explanation obviously worked, because Gloria seemed satisfied with his reply.

She glanced around the kitchen and took a sip of wine. "Is there anything I can do to help?"

"Yes. Sit right over there," he said, motioning to a stool by the center island, "and keep me company while I cook."

Gloria complied, while holding her wine. "That hardly seems a fair division of labor."

"I'm not meaning to be fair." Walt shot her a telling look. "I'm intending to treat you to a very nice meal."

She laughed lightly then said, "You're really going overboard as the perfect host, you know."

Walt stared into her gorgeous dark eyes and his throat swelled up. "I'm not doing this as your host," he said huskily.

"No?" Fine color swept her cheeks. "Then, what?"

"As a man, Gloria," he said hoarsely. "A man who likes the opportunity to treat a really beautiful woman to an elegant meal."

Her blush deepened.

"I hope that's all right?"

Gloria shared a soft smile at this unexpected turn. "It's lovely."

Gloria giggled as the fizzy bubbles tickled her tongue. She'd never been treated so royally by any man—ever. "This is fun having champagne with dessert. Very high class."

Walt raised his champagne flute to hers. "Well, you're a high-class lady. You deserve it."

Gloria didn't know what had come over Walt in these past twenty-four hours, but he seemed more commanding somehow. He was also being more than a little flirtatious.

Gloria's cheeks warmed when she answered, "Thanks, Walt."

She took another bite of the fabulous chocolate mousse, thinking she'd never tasted anything better. And, it went perfectly with the champagne. "Did you make this yourself?"

"Yes. Do you like it?"

"Like it? I love it. I'd bathe in it if you'd let me."

Walt's neck reddened at his collar. "That could be arranged."

"Walt Christmas!" Gloria gasped, then she gazed at him with new eyes. "There's a whole different side to you that I wouldn't have guessed."

Walt lifted the champagne bottle and topped off her glass. "Maybe you underestimated me."

"Yeah," Gloria said softly. "Apparently, I did." It was hard not to be in awe of a man with so many skills.

Walt's grin broadened. "You don't know the half of it."

"Sorry?"

Walt coughed into his hand. "I had a hunch you were wondering what other skills I have."

Gloria playfully waggled a finger in his direction. "You're much more intuitive than you let on, you know."

"Were you?" Walt cocked one dark sexy eyebrow and butterflies took flight in Gloria's stomach. Next, little tingles raced down her spine. "Wondering about my skills?"

"I…er…" Gloria's face burned hot. "I know that you can cook!" Gloria heaved a breath, perusing the perfect table. *Boy, can you ever.* "And, Savannah says you're good with carpentry."

"That's true." Walt swirled his champagne around in its flute. "I even built a sleigh once."

"A sleigh?" Gloria asked, impressed. "The sort with runners?"

Walt nodded. "And, that's drawn by horses."

"Sounds amazing." Gloria sighed, trying to imagine it. "How long ago was this?"

"Oh, some years back."

"Do you still have it?"

"Believe it or not, I do."

Gloria bit into her bottom lip, wondering where it was. She'd never seen that kind of sleigh before in person. Only in the movies.

"I was wondering if you'd like to see it?"

"Oh, yes! Please! Where do you keep it? Out back in the garage?"

Walt shook his head. "It's been in storage at Sleigh Bell Stables."

"It has?" Gloria asked, thinking of Olivia, who had horses there.

Walt took a sip of champagne. "I went to check on it this morning."

This morning. Of course he did. And, Olivia was at Sleigh Bell Stables at the time. Gloria felt so stupid for making the wrong assumptions. She looked over at Walt to find him watching her closely with his intense blue eyes.

"Is something the matter?"

"No, I…was just thinking about how awesome that is! That you still have your sleigh at Sleigh Bell Stables."

"It had gotten out of condition and the runners had gotten rusty, but I went and worked on it today."

"Oh?" Gloria asked, desperately curious. "Why?"

He latched on her gaze then said with a sultry edge, "I was hoping to ask you on a date."

Gloria could have been knocked over with a feather. She felt giddy and excited and nervous, and that sounded like such a fun idea. But a date? That meant romantic, right? What about Walt's prior lack of interest in sharing her cookie? Gloria stared around the dining room again, thinking what a goofball she was. Tonight had been a totally one-eighty—and totally romantic, too. What's more, Walt had planned it that way. On purpose.

"That sounds so wonderful, Walt, but I'm—"

"Not staying in Christmas Town," he finished for her. "I know that."

"Then, why?"

"Because, I can't think of any other way I'd like to spend tomorrow afternoon." The way he looked at her made Gloria feel all womanly and beautiful, like some enchantress out of a fairy tale. Or, maybe a princess in some magical realm. And oh, how her heart wanted Walt to be her prince—if only for one day in a sleigh in Christmas Town.

"I'll pack a picnic lunch," he added temptingly, "and, a thermos full of cocoa."

"You're making it awfully hard to say no." Gloria swooned when Walt's blue eyes twinkled.

"That's the general idea."

After dinner, they decided to carry their drinks and the rest of the champagne into the library. Walt couldn't believe how well the evening was going. Kurt had been right. Certain things really were like riding a bicycle, and his old aptitudes were coming back to him. Walt had once had no trouble flattering beautiful women. He hadn't had any difficulty getting dates with them, either. Then, he'd met Rose in his junior year of college, and he'd lost interest in any other female but her.

As long as they were married, Walt never took Rose for granted. He always told her she was beautiful, because she remained so until the day she died. Walt wondered why he was thinking about her so much now, then his gaze fell on Rose's stocking. He noticed Gloria looking at it, too, and wondered if she'd guessed the truth, or had assumed, like so many did, that the third stocking was for him.

"I see you got the fireplaces going again," Gloria remarked, taking a seat in the wing chair. Walt felt a little disappointed she hadn't sat on the sofa beside him, but he decided to let it go. There was no need to rush things.

"I did," he answered. "There was a just a valve loose."

"On all of them in the house at the same time?" Gloria shook her head with surprise. "Gosh, that's weird."

"It's an old house."

"Yes, but those gas fixtures look nearly new."

Walt stroked his beard. "Maybe they just needed a good talking to."

Gloria laughed heartily at this. "Oh, Walt! Sure, right." She turned toward the hearth and addressed it in mock-scolding tones. "Now, you listen to me, Mr.

242 A Glorious Christmas

Fireplace. You best behave yourself right now, or go to your room!"

At that moment, the gas flames glowed brightly than instantly died out.

Gloria's mouth hung open and Walt's jaw nearly dropped, too. That was pretty impressive, and he wondered what had caused it.

Gloria viewed him wide-eyed. "Did I just do that?" She appeared forty percent proud and sixty percent petrified.

"*No-ho-ho.*" Walt coughed into his hand and stood. "I'm sure it's just the valve. Here," he said, sauntering that way. "Let me have a look at it."

Walt crouched low and reached under the gas log set, fumbling with some controls. As he did, he concentrated really hard. *Fire. Light. Now.*

The logs instantly flamed with bright light, and Walt stepped back. "There!" he said, dusting off his palms. "That should do it."

Gloria watched him with wonder as he strolled back toward the sofa. In truth, Walt had to resist the urge to strut. He was really getting good at this. Owning it, indeed.

"Wow," Gloria said, once he'd settled himself back on the sofa. "You're very handy. I'm glad you were able to fix the problem."

"I pretty much handle all the repairs around the Christmas Inn."

Gloria scanned the room as she sipped from her champagne. "You do a fine job keeping it up. I really love it here."

Walt caught and held his breath. "Do you?"

"Doesn't everybody?" Gloria's pretty dark eyes glimmered in the flickering firelight, and Walt experienced a powerful need to hold her. But, he wouldn't dare try. Not just yet.

"Perhaps in a passing way," Walt said. He let that thought linger, without adding anything more to it. When he caught Gloria's thoughtful gaze on the Christmas stockings again, he decided to say something about them. Sooner or later, he'd have to tell Gloria about Rose. Since they were going out tomorrow, maybe a light mention of his past would be good at this juncture.

"You're probably wondering about the stockings?"

"No, I…"

"And, why there are three?"

Gloria fell silent and waited for him to continue.

Walt raised his champagne flute and used it as a pointer. "The one on the left is Noelle's. The middle one is Joy's." He tipped up his flute and drained the rest of his champagne in one long swallow. "And, the third belonged to my late wife, Rose."

Compassion lined Gloria's face, but, oddly, she didn't seem surprised. "I've been meaning to tell you how sorry I am. I mean, I know it was a long time ago."

"Ten years," Walt said.

"But it still must be difficult sometimes."

He studied her a long while, taking in the contours of her face, her long and lovely hair, and her hypnotizing dark eyes. "It has been difficult, yes. But, things are getting better."

"I hope so." She stared straight at him and didn't look away, and all kinds of crazy emotions started rocketing around inside him. Gloria was more than pretty. She was sexy and desirable. And, how Walt got from thinking about his late wife to there, he'd never know.

Walt turned away, uncomfortable for having thought about desiring Gloria while they'd been discussing Rose. "In any case," he said, setting the conversation back on track. "About Rose's stocking… Each year, the girls and I write messages to their late mother on small slips of paper and stuff them in her stocking on Christmas Eve. The next morning, on Christmas Day, we cast those messages into the fire… At least, we used to."

"Used to?"

"You were right about the gas fireplaces being new. Nick suggested we replace the wood-burning ones due to fire hazard concerns. There are so many hearths in this house, and guests sometimes would leave the fires going in their rooms unattended."

"What do you do with the messages now?"

"We burn them in the fire pit."

"You have a fire pit?" she asked, pleasantly surprised.

"Yeah, out back. We have a large back patio area and a garden."

"No kidding! I do, too."

"I'll bet my backyard's got more snow in it than yours does," Walt said, and Gloria laughed.

"Oh yeah? Well, I'll bet I've got the better orange tree!"

"Touché!" Walt thought on this. "Wait. Do you really? That's so cool."

"There's nothing like fresh-squeezed orange juice in the morning."

"You should have told me that's what you like. I would have made you some."

"Seems like you're spoiling me rotten already."

"Somebody needs to spoil you, Gloria."

Her cheeks burned brightly. "Is that right?"

Walt shook his head and chuckled. "You mean to tell me the guys in Miami are so boneheaded that nobody's even tried?"

Gloria giggled in delight. "Oh, Walt. How do you do it?"

"What's that?"

"Make me feel like I'm the most special woman on earth."

Walt grinned, extraordinary pleased. This was going far better than he expected.

Gloria settled back in her chair, appearing relaxed and contented. They both watched the fire for a while, each lost in their own thoughts. Finally, Gloria looked around the room, examining the knotty pine paneling and packed bookshelves. "I love that there's so much history in this house. It's so special that it belonged to your great-grandparents."

"I know. I wish I could hold onto it forever."

"Why can't you?"

"Well, *I'm* not planning on leaving. They'll have to carry me out of this place feet first." He twinkled at Gloria. "But, I can't say about Noelle's or Joy's plans for someday, or what might become of this house in the future."

"It would be a shame to have it fall out of the family again."

"I agree."

"Walt," she said thoughtfully. "Thanks for telling me about Rose, and the stocking."

"I keep thinking I should take it down." Walt shocked even himself with his brutal honesty. "That, you know, it's time to move on."

"But you haven't yet." There was no hint of accusation in her voice, only understanding.

Walt shrugged. "One way or another it hasn't felt right."

Gloria viewed him with compassion and it warmed Walt's soul. "You'll know when it's time."

"Hi, folks! I'm home!" Noelle barged in the front door, then she shut it with a bang, loudly rattling her keys. "Dad! Gloria? Yoo-hoo!"

"Why's she being so loud?"

Walt winked and Gloria's pulse fluttered. "She's worried she's disturbing us."

Gloria cupped a hand to her mouth and giggled. "Oh."

"We're back here, sweetheart!" Walt called to Noelle. Seconds later, she appeared on the living room threshold.

"Hi, guys." She surveyed their champagne flutes and the empty bottle sitting in a bucket on the coffee table. "How's it going?"

"Very well," Walt said.

Then Gloria asked her, "How's your evening been?"

"Long!" Noelle reported with a yawn. "Grandma and Grandpa made me watch the old-people movie channel."

"Noelle," Walt said sternly. "That's not nice."

Gloria attempted to chime in on a chipper note. "Sometimes old movies can be fun!"

"Not these ones, though." Noelle playfully rolled her eyes. "In any case, I'm beat! I'll see you two in the morning."

"Good night, Noelle!" Gloria said.

Next Walt added, "I'll be up in a bit."

"This has been such a wonderful evening," Gloria said, meeting Walt's eyes. "But, to tell you the truth, I'm a little tuckered out, too."

"It's been a long day for everyone."

Gloria stood and Walt got to his feet, as well.

"I can't thank you enough," she said.

"I'm the one who needs to thank you."

"Me? For what?"

"The cookies."

Gloria's smile dazzled. "Don't eat them all at once."

"I won't."

"Good night, Walt."

"Good night, Gloria."

"I'm looking forward to tomorrow."

Her dark eyes sparkled and Walt's heart skipped a beat.

"So am I."

Chapter Eighteen

Gloria woke up the next morning in a giddy ball of happy nerves. She couldn't believe she was going on a sleigh ride with Walt! She strode to the window and threw back the curtains. Light wisps of snow were twirling and falling outside through the crisp morning air. If Gloria had wanted a big dose of winter by coming to Christmas Town, she was getting it, no question. The bonus today was that she'd have an ultra handsome man at her side.

Walt was so thoughtful and attentive, and when he'd made that comment about wanting to spoil her, the notion had thrilled Gloria through and through. So what if it was just for this week, and then it was over? No one in her life had made Gloria feel as pampered as Walt. She'd been loved, sure. Cared for, definitely. But, tended to—so as to cater to her every whim and need? No sirree!

Gloria danced happily around the room, thinking of Walt and their adventure. She also needed to put some thought into what she was going to wear. Walt had said there'd be blankets in the sleigh, but he'd still encouraged her to dress warmly. Although, just his heady perusal could warm her up in a jiffy! Gloria did have work to do, but she could tackle some of that this morning, and then maybe later today, assuming she could keep her mind on schoolwork.

In the meantime, Gloria wanted to put on something pretty to wear to the breakfast table. She was sorting through the clothes she'd unpacked and placed in the dresser drawers, when a strange knocking noise met her ears. Then it sounded again, louder. *Knock-knock, rumble. Bang!* Gloria jumped in fright and wheeled on her nightstand. The commotion seemed to be coming from in there. She stealthily approached the bedside table, concerned about getting too close. *Bang! Bang! Bang!* There it was again! Something was down inside the top drawer and fighting to get out!

Gloria gasped. *My Commitment Cookie!* She should have known better than to leave it in there. Clearly, a mouse had gone after it and was now trapped in the drawer. Yikes! Gloria hated rodents of all kinds, especially the kind that was apparently in her bedroom. She inched toward the nightstand, almost scared to take a look. If she slid the door open a tiny bit, she could take a peek. But when she did, the nightstand rocked sideways and tumbled onto the floor. *Eeek!*

The blunt force of the fall caused the top drawer to jettison open and Gloria ran screaming out of the room wearing her pajamas. "A mouse! Help! A mouse!"

Noelle met her in the hall and caught her by the shoulders. "Gloria? What is it? What's wrong?"

"It's big and furry and ugly!" Gloria's teeth chattered. "In there! Back in my room!"

"Hang on." Noelle strode confidently down the hall and walked into Gloria's suite, while Gloria stood there shaking in the hall, hugging herself tightly. She peered into the kitchen, but saw no signs of Walt.

"I think I found your 'mouse'!" Noelle called brightly.

Gloria tentatively inched back toward the room, where she saw Noelle had righted the nightstand and pushed its drawer back in place. She held up the bag from the Christmas Cookie Shop. "This was the only thing on the floor."

Gloria eyed Noelle unsurely. "Do you mind taking a peek? To make sure nobody's taken a nibble?"

Noelle smiled indulgently. "Sure. No problem." She pried open the bag and peered inside. "Nope. Looks good as new."

"Really?"

"You should probably eat it soon, though, while it's still relatively fresh. Savannah gave it to you on Monday."

Yeah, well. Maybe so. But, Gloria wasn't so sure she wanted that cookie now. She had not been imagining things. Something else had been down in that drawer with it. "I…er, never eat sweets before breakfast!" Gloria finally managed to say.

"Then, how about I toss it in the freezer for you? It will keep better that way?"

"That sounds like a good idea!"

"And don't worry about my dad, I'll put it in my secret compartment."

"Oh?"

"There's a carton of eggnog ice cream in there that's not really an ice cream carton." She winked in collusion. "It's really a hidey-hole."

"*Oh.*"

"Yeah. Dad's not much for ice cream. He's more of a Cookie Man."

"That's what I gathered, yes."

Noelle started to go. "We've got baked hot oatmeal in the kitchen, and Dad made some fresh-squeezed orange juice for you before he left."

"Did he? How sweet." Gloria felt overwhelmed by the gesture, and then she asked, "Where did he go?"

"Said something about making arrangements for an outing. Not sure. He was sketchy on the details." Noelle shrugged and Gloria's cheeks heated.

"Do you know where Dad's gone?" Noelle asked suspiciously, though she was grinning.

Gloria rubbed the back of her head. "Sleigh Bell Stables perhaps?"

"Huh." Noelle's gaze darted to the cookie bag in her hand. "That's weird. I thought he was out there yesterday."

Gloria showered and dressed and joined Noelle for a hearty breakfast, before deciding to catch up on some grading in the library. She'd received a text from Walt saying he was coming to pick her up at twelve, so Gloria had time to do some work. Focusing on concrete tasks would help keep Gloria's mind on something else so she would be less anxious about her date. Already, she was counting the minutes until twelve and repeatedly checking her watch.

Noelle was still doing something in the kitchen. She apparently had the evening shift at the bookshop again, and tomorrow she was working at the courthouse all day, before babysitting for Amanda. Gloria scooped up her laptop and her teaching folder, carrying them from her suite. She paused in the kitchen doorway to ask Noelle a question. "I've got some work to do. Do you think your dad would mind if I sat at his desk in the library?"

"Not at all. Make yourself at home."

Gloria settled into Walt's comfy swivel chair at his roll-top desk, thinking what a great room this was. Despite the house having a beautifully decorated living room and parlor, it seemed that Walt preferred to spend most of his time in here, and Gloria could see why. She scooted some items aside and set down her laptop, spotting the heavy paperweight shaped like a Christmas stocking that she'd noticed from a distance earlier. What she hadn't been able to see was that it had been engraved to Walt from Rose.

"Do you mind if I join you?" Noelle walked into the library carrying a laptop of her own.

"Not at all! Please do."

Noelle smiled and settled into the wing chair beside the fire. She then crossed her legs beneath her and settled her laptop on her knees.

"What are you working on?" Gloria asked. "More job applications?"

"No. It's just a little project of mine."

"Oh?"

"Yeah. I'm trying my hand at fiction."

"Fiction? That's cool."

"Thanks." Noelle adjusted her glasses and sat up straighter. "My degree's in journalism and I've mostly focused on reporting. But making up stories can be kind of fun."

"I'm sure it must be!" Gloria commented. "I'm an avid book reader, and also love to read scripts. But, I'm afraid I've got no talent for writing at all."

"I guess everybody has their strengths."

Gloria was curious about Noelle. She seemed so gifted in so many ways. "Have you had anything published?"

"Only articles for my college newspaper. I wrote in high school, too."

"Well, I think it's exciting you're trying something new. How many stories have you written?"

"Just a couple, so far."

"I bet they're fantastic."

Noelle's face lit up. "Would you like to read them?"

It touched Gloria deeply that Noelle would let her into her private world. "I'd be very honored, Noelle."

A short time later, Gloria turned over the final page of the hard-copy stack of papers Noelle had given her to read. Noelle's stories were whimsical and fun, and filled with fantasy and magic. "These are absolutely delightful. Some of the best work I've read!"

Noelle's smile was a burst of sunshine. "Really?"

"Oh yes. These are very, very good." Gloria shuffled the papers together and neatened the stack, handing it back to Noelle when she rose to retrieve them.

"Thanks, Gloria. That makes me feel really good."

"Have you thought of submitting them somewhere?"

"I've looked into it," Noelle said disconsolately. "There are tons of books on publishing at the Elf Shelf Bookshop, and from everything I've read short stories are pretty hard to place."

"Well, maybe you shouldn't worry about that at the moment. Maybe, for now, you should just have fun. Write from the heart. Build up your portfolio."

"Portfolio. Hmm. I like that idea." Noelle thoughtfully studied the ceiling before continuing. "Joy keeps a portfolio for her art, and I have a clip file for my articles, but building up a collection of my fiction is something different."

"Your oeuvre, yes."

Noelle laughed, delighted by this. "My oeuvre! I like it." Her gaze swept over Gloria, then she surprised Gloria with a compliment. "I'm really glad you came to Christmas Town. It's fun having you here."

Gloria felt for the girl, who'd been without a mother or regular adult female figure in this house for so long, and tears prickled the back of her eyes. "Thanks, Noelle. That's very sweet of you to say. And, you know what?" Gloria said, speaking from the heart. "I'm awfully glad I came to Christmas Town, too. And, not only because of Savannah."

Noelle stared at her a long while and then said, "I know you like my dad."

Gloria ducked her chin to hide her blush and pretended to focus on her computer screen.

"Hey, that's okay."

When Gloria looked up, Noelle's eyes twinkled.

"I think he likes you, too."

Chapter Nineteen

When Walt picked Gloria up in his SUV at noon she felt like a kid on Christmas morning. She'd dressed in warm layers as Walt had recommended, and wore her practical low-heeled boots.

Walt's blue eyes shone as Gloria got into the SUV and buckled her seat belt. "Looks like we picked a good day for a sleigh ride."

"Yeah."

"I'm not taking you away from Savannah, am I?"

"Savannah has her own plans today," Gloria said cheerily. "Theater work and a baby doctor check-up."

"Well! Maybe they'll have some news."

It was true that the doctor could confirm whether the baby was on schedule, or whether delivery might be delayed. Most first babies arrived late, but Savannah didn't like to hear this. Gloria thought of the gift she'd given Walt and wondered if he'd indulged yet. Perhaps late last night, while Gloria was enjoying another yummy truffle from Nutcracker Sweets?

"Have you tried the cookies?"

"Oh yes! They were delicious!"

Gloria giggled at his reply. *Were?* "Don't tell me you ate them all, already?"

Walt's Adam's apple rose and fell. "I left the inn pretty early—before Noelle made breakfast. So I just decided to grab some coffee and a cookie on my way out the door."

"*One* cookie?" Gloria's eyebrows arched and color swept Walt's temples.

"That's how it started, anyway…"

Gloria belly-laughed at the man's complete lack of self-control. "Oh, dear! You ate the whole box?"

"Maybe," Walt said with a grimace. "But they were amazing cookies, I assure you. Got my day off to a great start. Thanks!"

Gloria chuckled again. "Well, mine started out great, too. Thank *you* for the fresh-squeezed orange juice. That was a real treat."

"I'm glad you enjoyed it."

Gloria smiled happily then settled in, absorbing the view. Walt drove them down the main street and to the roundabout. He took the second turn past the library, and then they were on their way out into the countryside with snow-covered fields, scenic farmhouses, and faraway mountains coated in white. "It's beautiful out here."

Walt shot her a sideways glance. "I know."

"Thanks for setting things up for today," Gloria said. "I'm really excited about our adventure." This was so far from Gloria's everyday life in Miami she could scarcely believe it.

"My pleasure." He smiled her way then turned his attention back on the road. "So what have you been up to this morning?"

"I found a mouse!"

"A mouse?" Walt appeared startled. "Oh, no. Where?"

"In my suite."

"Whoa, Gloria. I'm so sorry about that. We have had issues in the past, but nothing lately. That sometimes happens with old houses."

"That's what I figured."

"I'll look into it when we get back to the inn."

"I think it's all right now! I mean, Noelle investigated, and she didn't find anything. But there was knocking in my nightstand!"

"Knocking?"

"Yeah, and rocking, too. The whole thing tumbled over."

"Gee. What did you have in there?"

"Only that Virginia Cookie."

"Ahhh."

"Ah?"

"Not to worry! I'll check things out when we return."

"All right." Gloria smiled sunnily glancing around at the lovely landscape, then she suddenly saw the sign. *Sleigh Bell Stables.* "We're already here?" she asked with a happy gasp.

"Yep." Walt grinned handsomely and Gloria's pulse raced. "It's just a hop, skip, and a jump from downtown."

Walt pulled up to the barn and who should come galloping out to meet them but Olivia! She wore a puffy green coat and a green hat and scarf to match. They all complemented Olivia's pretty green eyes and made her look terrific. Particularly with that natural blush on her cheeks and her thick red braid worn over her shoulder. Walt extended his hand and helped Gloria out of the SUV. He'd done the gentlemanly thing by rushing around the front of the vehicle to come and open Gloria's door, and she couldn't have been more impressed. Walt was giving her the first-class treatment. So, why was Olivia here?

"I'm so glad you made it!" Olivia extended her arms and pulled both Gloria and Walt into quick hugs. Her eyes danced excitedly and there was a playful smile on her lips. Olivia glanced back toward the barn and a phenomenal sleigh glided out of its open door. "Your carriage awaits!"

The sleigh was a cheery Christmas red with elegant gold trim and it appeared freshly painted. Two sturdy horses pulled it along, as a barn hand held onto their reins, guiding them in Walt and Gloria's direction. The horses' harnesses were bedecked with sleigh bells and a musical timbre accompanied every clip-clop, as the horses trotted through the snow.

Gloria covered her mouth with her hands. "It's remarkable!" Even in her wildest dreams, she hadn't imagined the sleigh being this grand. It had a low-slung bench with a high back, and the seat was cushioned with worn white leather. Neatly folded blankets sat in a stack on the bench, and there was a closed wicker picnic basket stashed on the floor. The small cargo area located behind the bench looked large enough to haul supplies of some sort, or even a passel full of gleeful children.

"Thanks for letting us borrow your horses, Olivia," Walt said.

Borrow? Horses? Is that what Walt and Olivia's recent interactions had been about?

"Aww, look at her," Olivia said in reference to Gloria. "She's so happy she's speechless."

Gloria pondered the mean-spirited thoughts she'd had about Olivia and her voice cracked hoarsely. "Oh gosh, Olivia. Thanks."

"Olivia even helped me with the new paint job," Walt said, twinkling her way.

"Hey!" Olivia said brightly. "Nobody can accuse me of not being a true romantic."

No, but they might falsely accuse you of other terrible things, Gloria thought, awash with shame.

Walt shot Gloria a curious glance, but she didn't know why.

"Gloria," Olivia said with a kindhearted gaze. "I hope you have the very best sleigh ride. *Ever.*"

Gloria couldn't take any more. Olivia's innocent generosity was too much. "Olivia!" she cried, lurching at her. "I'm so, so, sorry!" To the others' dismay, Gloria broke down in tears, blubbering against Olivia's shoulder.

Olivia weakly patted her back. "Er…Walt?"

But Gloria wouldn't let go. She gripped Olivia harder. "Sorry that you…" *Sob. Sob. Sob. Deep breath… There!* "Had to work so hard!"

"It really wasn't such a big deal." Olivia shot Walt a helpless look, and Gloria pulled back just in time to catch it.

Walt viewed Gloria warmly. "Why don't we run along now and enjoy our time outdoors, huh?" He held out his arm and Gloria took it, hoping she wouldn't fall down and face-plant on the way to the sleigh. She couldn't believe she'd just had that mini meltdown in front of Olivia and Walt. Okay. Maybe there was nothing "mini" about it. Gloria sniffed and Walt reached in his pocket, gallantly handing her a hanky. This only made Gloria whimper again. Was there nothing this man couldn't do?

"I apologize if this had been too much for you."

"No, no. It's fine!" Gloria wiped her cheeks. "It's just *so* different from Miami."

Walt helped her into the sleigh with a boost. "I'll bet."

As the horses trotted along, Gloria gradually regained her composure. Fortunately, Walt was too polite to say anything further about her breakdown with Olivia. He held the reins with a gentle repose that said he was used to doing this. Walt didn't have to work hard to steer the horses; they appeared to know where they were going all on their own. They followed a trail to the edge of a wood, then entered a deep forest, passing snow-covered brambles and thickets and pines. Songbirds perched on tree limbs, and somewhere far away a hoot owl called.

Gloria sighed at the majestic beauty of it all.

Walt called his team to a halt and they paused beneath the towering limbs of an oak tree. "Are you hungry?"

Gloria had been so swept away by the scenery she hadn't had time to think about food. "Not yet."

"How about some cocoa then?"

Gloria smiled softly, thinking she could use the warm-up. It was chillier than she'd anticipated outdoors with north winds blowing, even with the blankets that Walt had draped across their knees. "Cocoa sounds delicious."

Walt tugged the basket off the floor and onto his lap. Then he opened its lid and pulled out a travel mug, which he handed to Gloria after unscrewing its lid. Next, he extracted a thermos. As soon as he opened it, billowing steam filled the frigid air. It smelled warm, chocolaty, and heavenly! Walt filled Gloria's mug, then handed her another mug to hold, so he could pour cocoa into that one as well. Once he'd returned the thermos to the basket and the basket to the floor, Walt lifted his travel mug of cocoa toward hers. "Cheers!"

Gloria smiled happily, her heart light. "Cheers to you!"

He took a sip of his cocoa then wedged his travel mug into a spot in the open basket.

Walt surveyed her features. "Are you having a good time?"

"No."

When his face fell suddenly, Gloria couldn't keep up the ruse.

"I'm having a *great* time," she said, leaning into him with a teasing smile.

Walt took this as a cue to wrap his arm around her and Gloria didn't mind. She liked feeling him close, and was surprised by the power and strength of his grip.

Even through his thick coat, she could detect his solid and muscled chest. "I'm glad."

Walt cracked the reins and they got going again. As they moved along, he grinned at her. "You're wearing white again."

"This is the only coat and hat I have."

"I could take care of that if you'd let me."

"Absolutely not!" She gaped at him in surprise. "I am *not* hiring you as my fashion consultant."

"No? Why not?"

"Because, you silly! You'd muck it up." Laughter rumbled in his chest as she snuggled against him. It sounded deep, reassuring, and warm.

"If you think I'd buy you flannel and jeans, you're wrong."

"Oh?" she asked, her interest piqued. "What would you have me wear?"

"Anything your heart desires." He gazed into her eyes and then said huskily, "Because everything you touch—you make beautiful. Just like you."

Gloria's heart stilled, then it started beating overtime as her cheeks flamed. She'd never had a man look at her like this, or talk to her like this... In fact, she'd never really dated a *man*, Gloria realized with sudden clarity. All of the others had just been grown-up boys. Guys who lacked maturity...dudes who were still getting their acts together...

Walt Christmas had everything together in spades. And, it made her weak-kneed just looking at him. Thank goodness she was sitting down.

"You do know your eyelashes are turning white?"

"I'm not the only one," Gloria said with a saucy lilt. "Yours are, too."

"So's your hair."

"Well, I guess now you know how I'll look when I'm eighty!" Gloria said with a laugh.

But, Walt just smiled thoughtfully and said, "Yes."

"How far does this trail go?" Gloria asked, feeling like they were heading deeper and deeper into the forest.

"About twelve miles. It's a loop."

"That's good!" Gloria playfully rolled her eyes. "That means we won't get lost."

Walt viewed her a long while then a smile teased his lips. "Sometimes getting lost is not the bum rap it's made out to be."

"No?"

"Not when you're lost with the right person."

Gloria gazed up at his handsome face and that rugged beard, and those incredible blue eyes that took her breath away. "Walt," she said, feeling like she needed to tell him. "I have a horrible confession to make."

He glanced at her askew. "Go on."

"I...somehow got the wrong idea about you and Olivia."

"Olivia?"

Gloria wanted to sink into the seat cushion for having had such thoughts, but she didn't believe in keeping secrets from people you cared about. And, she was definitely starting to care about Walt. "I was totally mistaken, and I feel so stupid..."

"About?" His brow rose with the question and Gloria nearly swallowed her tongue.

"Oh gosh, Walt," Gloria said, wanting to bury her face in the snow. "I somehow got the idea..." She drew a deep breath and released it. "I thought something was going on there."

"Wait a minute." He gaped at her in incredulity, which only made Gloria feel worse. "Between me and Olivia?"

Gloria stared at him, on the verge of crying again. How could she have even thought such a thing of someone so kind as Olivia, and someone as wonderful as Walt?

Walt suddenly pulled his team to a halt and tied up the reins. He took Gloria's cocoa and set it down in the basket with his, then he turned to her in disbelief. "You were jealous?"

Gloria's chin trembled. "I can see now that it was ridiculous. But I kept getting all these weird feelings, tingles, vibes…"

"Gloria, listen to me. There has never been anything between me and Olivia. She's like a sister to me. We've always been friends." He paused and narrowed his eyes, thinking. "Tingles? Vibes?"

"Yes! They were so crazy, too! Like my skin was on fire! I just couldn't bear the—"

Walt stunned her by taking her in his arms. "Oh, my dear sweet woman…" His expression was needy, intense…sincere. "Don't you know I only have eyes for you?"

"What?" she asked, her head spinning. "Really?"

"Gloria Chavez, you're special. So special you've caused me to feel certain things I haven't thought about in years."

Yeah, he kind of made her crazy-headed, too. Gloria felt feather-light, like her heart was this great big balloon that was floating away, and tugging her off the ground. Like she was flying! And the sleigh was, too!

Walt reached up his glove and stroked her cheek. "Do you know where we are?"

Gloria shook her head. Then, she glanced around. Everywhere she looked, huge bushes formed a canopy above their heads, composed of dark green leaves and waxy white berries.

"That's mistletoe," she said on a breathy whisper.

Walt held her chin in his hand. "Yes."

His gaze roved over her and Gloria was swept away. Despite the sting of the cold and snow in the air, she felt sunshine warming her cheeks. "There are so many things I want to tell you," he said. "But I think I'm going to die if I don't kiss you first."

Gloria slid her arms around his neck as he pulled her close. "Walt," she said. The word was a warm invitation. "I want to kiss you, too."

His lips brushed over hers like silky smooth butterfly wings and Gloria moaned. "Oh my gosh."

Walt held her closer. "It's all right," he said, "I won't drop you."

"Drop me?"

Then he kissed her again, with more passion and force, and Gloria felt rocketed into outer space. Her world went spinning around and around with flashing moonbeams and shooting stars, supernovas and blazing comets...until she was left gasping for air. "What just...?"

Walt brought a finger to her lips and pressed his forehead to hers. "It's not over." Then he kissed her again, and she surrendered to him, lips opened wide and tongues tangling. Electricity shot through her veins and fire filled her belly, and every single erotic point burned hot. Her heart thumped harder and her body felt weightless. Soaring. Free. Gloria broke contact, panting hard, but her eyes were still closed.

Walt traced her lips with the thumb of his glove. "I'd kiss you again if you'd let me." His voice was hot, heavy, rough... Gloria tingled all over and her whole body warmed. She'd never experienced anything like this. She had no way to define it. She only knew that she needed more.

She *wanted* Walt.

Gloria opened her eyes to find Walt staring down at her with a longing look.

She reached up and stroked his face, running her glove down his hairy beard and then tracing his mustache. His smiled fondly as his forehead rose. "Too much?"

Gloria grinned, filled with heat, sexiness, and desire. All those things she'd absorbed from Walt, and was ready to give back to him full-throttle.

"Oh, no," she said on a sigh. "Just enough."

Walt's hand cupped her nape and he tugged her close. Then his mouth came down on hers and Gloria was lost to oblivion.

Chapter Twenty

The next day, Gloria picked Savannah up at seven o'clock under the guise of having a girls' night at the Reindeer Pub. All day long, Gloria's brain had been in a heady swirl. She'd tried grading term papers remotely, but all she could focus on was Walt's earth-shattering kiss. Where had the man learned to kiss like that? It was probably better for the world he'd remained off the romantic radar these past several years. Otherwise, Gloria could only imagine the number of women he might have devastated in his wake. Walt was one seriously sexy guy. The fact that you couldn't tell this at first glance made him all the more appealing.

After their romantic picnic outing, Gloria had hoped to spend the rest of the afternoon with Walt. Sadly, he'd apologized that his dad had asked for his help with something, so he'd gone to Buddy's aid. Buddy's car had broken down and he had a number of handmade toys to deliver to a charity in the next town. Lou was busy mayoring, and Kurt was at the clinic, while Ray manned the North Pole Nursery. Walt was the only one with enough flexibility to help out, and

Gloria of course encouraged him toward this worthy cause.

Once he'd returned yesterday evening, they'd shared a casual family-style dinner with Noelle in the kitchen at the breakfast table, with Walt and Gloria each casting furtive glances at the other while Walt's daughter stayed unawares. Ultimately, they all turned in early, but not before Walt gave Gloria one flaming hot kiss under the mistletoe by her guest suite.

Gloria sighed, wondering what she was going to do. Walt had asked her to have a scotch with him later this evening after the baby shower, and Gloria had agreed. Her heart thundered, imagining spending more time with him. After babysitting tonight, Noelle was going to a friend's house for a sleepover and wouldn't be home at all. This meant Gloria and Walt would be alone together and it set her nerves on edge just thinking about it.

"Thanks for picking me up!" Savannah said, maneuvering her bulky frame into the passenger seat of Gloria's SUV. "It's really nice of you to drive tonight."

"It's no problem. Really!"

Savannah lifted her nose and lightly sniffed the air. "What smells like macaroni and cheese in here?"

Gloria had the casserole concealed under a blanket on the back floor of her SUV. The baby books and the selection of gifts she'd purchased for Savannah, including a bath kit from Mystic Magi and a pretty scarf from South Pole Pottery, were with it. "I, er…gee! I don't know!"

Gloria smiled at her friend, attempting to get Savannah's mind on another topic. "How did the doctor's appointment go?"

Savannah frowned disappointedly. "Not great, actually."

"What do you mean?"

"He said the baby hasn't dropped yet. It could be at least another week. Maybe two."

"Oh! *Oh…*"

Savannah eyed her apologetically. "I'm sorry, Gloria. I know you didn't intend to stay here that long."

While that was definitely true, suddenly sticking around Christmas Town a bit longer didn't seem like such a hardship to Gloria. "But everything's all right? With the baby?"

"Oh yeah, perfectly fine. We're still on track!" Savannah set her chin. "I just wish we were on track sooner."

"I know you do, hon," Gloria said sympathetically.

"Listen." Savannah turned to her before she started the engine. "I don't want you to feel like you have to stay all that extra time. That could put you here through Christmas, and I know you have other plans."

Gloria thought of her brother David. While she hated leaving him alone, he did have many friends to rely on, and also several supportive connections through his parish. Gloria was Savannah's best friend, and the arrival of Savannah's first baby was a once-in-a-lifetime event.

"Savannah," Gloria said sweetly. "I don't want you to worry about it. Babies come in their own time. All of this is out of your hands."

"Yes, but you—"

"I can handle myself. Just fine. Here in Christmas Town." Gloria shoved her key into the ignition and cranked it. "For a little while longer if I need to."

"*Do* tell!"

"What?"

"Gloria Chavez, your face is as red as a ripe tomato!"

"Is not."

"Is so! Now, *spill.* What's going on?" Savannah's mental wheels seemed to be churning. "Oh my gosh, is this about Walt?"

"No!"

Gloria's instantaneous reaction was unfortunately a tip-off.

"Wow. Wow. Wow! Something happened…"

"Savannah, stop."

Gloria put on her blinker and turned left onto North Main Street.

"You have to tell me, Gloria. It's really not fair."

Okay, Savannah had a point. Since she'd been the one pushing to get Gloria and Walt together from the get-go, didn't she at least deserve the satisfaction of knowing she was right in foretelling their mutual attraction?

Gloria decided the answer was no. At least, not yet.

Gloria was still savoring the newness of her relationship with Walt, and trying to figure out what it meant. She wasn't ready to discuss her feelings about the handsome innkeeper, when she hadn't fully sorted through them herself. Especially not with Savannah, who was bound to go all crazy pressing her for details and reading happily-ever-after into the situation. "There's nothing going on," she said obliquely.

"Really!"

"You're sure?"

"Sure, I'm sure. Savannah—"

Savannah sat back in her seat and gave a little huff. "All right, if you say so."

It wasn't a long trip to the Snow Globe Gallery and, since it was on the corner, Gloria decided to stop a little before it at Sisters' Row. She pulled into a parallel parking spot and Savannah goggled at her.

"Why on earth are we stopping here?"

"I need to drop by the Snow Globe Gallery."

"What? Why?"

"I promised Walt I'd pick something up."

"Walt?" Savannah sounded positively gleeful.

"For Noelle."

"*Oh.*" Now Savannah looked like a deflated balloon. "What does Noelle need from Sandy's gallery and why couldn't she get it herself?"

"Some information for a story she's writing," Gloria fibbed. "And nobody asked me to get it. I volunteered! Since we were going right by."

Then Savannah thought clearly. "Wait a minute. The Snow Globe Gallery's not open this late."

"Not normally, no. But Sandy offered to stay a little late tonight."

Savannah's forehead shot up like this was the weirdest story she'd ever heard.

"Sandy's waiting on us, see?" Gloria said, pointing to the gallery window that housed the shimmering snow globe. "The lights are still on, but we don't want to keep her."

"O-kay. Well, why don't you just run in then, and I'll wait right here."

"No!"

Savannah wrinkled her brow. "Why are you being so grumpy?"

"I'm not being grumpy, Savannah. I just need you to come along."

Savanna jutted out her chin in a pigheaded fashion. "No, thank you."

What?

"Whatever your little errand is, just go ahead and run it, please." Savannah pushed her along with her fingers. "So, you and I can progress to the Reindeer Pub."

"Savannah!"

"What? Walking is hard these days, and it's frigid out there."

"But, you have to come with me!"

"Goodness gracious, Gloria. Why so bossy?"

"Because…" Gloria viewed the sidewalks illuminated by the streetlamps' glow, and the shadowy patches of brush separating Sisters' Row from the Snow Globe Gallery. Although it was just after seven o'clock, it was already pitch black in Christmas Town, where the sun set early during this time of year. "I'm afraid of the dark, that's why."

"Afraid of the dark? Since when? What are you? Five?"

Gloria found herself grasping for straws. Who knew it would be so hard to motivate Savannah out of her SUV and into the Snow Globe Gallery?

"Since I had that experience!"

"What experience?"

Gloria's mind was frantically searching for answers, so she made something up. "When that guy outside the club was trying to mug me. Remember?"

"What? No!"

"Savannah, *puh-leeze*. Don't be difficult."

Savannah stared at her haughtily. "You're the one being difficult from my point of view. I thought we were going out for pizza?"

"We are!"

"When?"

"After this!"

Savannah heaved a deep breath. "Gloria, what's going on?"

Gloria thought creatively. It was her last good card. And, bless Savannah's stubborn soul, Gloria had to play it. "Okay, you've got me." She gave a sheepish shrug. "I went out with Walt."

"What? Really? I *knew* it!" Savannah yelped happily. "When?"

Gloria giggled in spite of herself and her cheeks warmed. "He took me on a sleigh ride yesterday, out at Sleigh Bell Stables."

"Sounds romantic."

Gloria sighed. "It was."

"So, how did this come about?" Savannah asked, intrigued. "What happened? And, why didn't you tell me sooner? *Gosh.*"

"Why don't you walk with me into the gallery and I'll fill you in on the way?"

Savannah instantly unbuckled her seat belt. "All right."

Savannah clambered out of the SUV and Gloria went around to help her.

"So, what's all this about you and Walt?"

"He asked me out! I was...kind of caught off guard."

"But, you accepted?"

Gloria grinned shyly as they approached the corner with Santa Claus Lane and the door to the Snow Globe Gallery. "Yeah, Savannah. You were right. He's quite a guy."

"What's that mean?" Savannah's eyes lit with understanding. "Did he kiss you?"

"Savannah!"

Savannah's cheeks glowed rosy pink. "Oh my goodness, he did, didn't he?"

"Okay, all right, *yes*," Gloria said quietly. "Shhh!"

"I'll bet you've never kissed anyone like him!"

Gloria blinked at her, wondering how she knew. Could it be genetic? Were all the Christmas family brothers dynamite kissers? "It was pretty great, yeah," Gloria whispered. "But, could you please keep your voice down?"

Savannah waddled into the gallery looking as pleased as punch, as Gloria held back the door. "Well, it's good to know that I was right about the two of you after—ahhhhhhhh!!!" Savannah paused and gripped her belly. Her very best friends in the world were here: Olivia, Liz, Sandy, Hannah, Jade, and Lou! All were grinning brightly.

"Whaat? What's going on?"

Liz stepped forward and pulled her into a hug. "Surprise!"

Savannah squealed with delight as the women rushed her with piles of pretty packages and flowers, then she opened her big mouth and blabbed to everyone about Gloria's kiss.

Meanwhile, back at the Christmas Inn, Walt made preparations for a romantic evening with Gloria. He'd purchased some bourbon-pecan bonbons from Nutcracker Sweets, and had two cut crystal glasses and his best bottle of scotch at the ready. He'd also set a number of candles out around the room in the library. While the living room and parlor were elegant areas, something about the library felt more intimate, with books lining the walls, and its location toward the middle of the house and farther away from the street. Walt intended to light the candles a little later—closer to the time he expected Gloria home. Walt's heart warmed at the thought of Gloria coming home to him, and a happy anticipation filled his soul.

Gloria was such a special woman and Walt was pleased that their outing yesterday had gone so well. Okay, so she'd had that minor episode where she'd burst into tears and sobbed on Olivia's shoulder. Walt had been concerned about Gloria at the time, and also a bit surprised that she could be so emotional. But Walt would take Gloria's emotionality any day, because it came in such a beautiful package. Everything Gloria did and said was all a part of her, and Walt was growing to appreciate every aspect of Gloria's warm and winning personality more and more.

He'd even found it cute that Gloria had been so worried about a mouse being in her room. According to Noelle, she'd gone running down the hall screaming at the top of her lungs while wearing her pajamas. Walt kind of wished he'd been around to see that, and perhaps play the big strong fellow who could come to

Gloria's rescue. But, luckily, his competent daughter had taken command of the situation.

Walt wasn't sure what had happened, but it was unlikely that a mouse had been involved. Noelle said she hadn't spotted any evidence of a rodent. Walt had checked the guest suite carefully, too, and had found no telltales signs of a mouse having been there. Gloria said she'd left her Virginia Cookie in the nightstand drawer, but when Walt checked—purely for investigative purposes, of course—it had been removed and stashed somewhere else. He wasn't sure what that cookie being in the nightstand had to do with the disturbances Gloria had witnessed, but Walt couldn't help but wonder if there was a connection there somewhere.

He knew he'd have to talk to Gloria about Christmas magic sometime soon, and the weight of that responsibility was bearing down on him. Walt doubted that Gloria would be pleased that he'd wiped her memory. Even a small part of it, and for a very good reason.

Since the attraction between them was deepening, Walt felt like he owed it to Gloria to tell her the truth, but he worried over how she might take it. Would she be understanding like Rose was, or would Gloria run screaming out of the house like she'd seen a big, hairy rat? Whatever the outcome, Walt understood he had to risk it. He couldn't allow things to evolve romantically between him and Gloria while pretending he was a normal man. Because Walt wasn't. He could only hope in his heart that Gloria would view that as a plus, and not a solid reason for ending her budding relationship with him.

Walt glanced around the library, thinking he was forgetting something. Oh, yeah! Ice for their drinks, in case Gloria preferred her scotch on the rocks. Walt had a simple bar set up on an old chest against the wall near the smaller seating area. He kept several bottles of booze on it, as well as an ice bucket and a pair of tongs. He could go ahead and fill the ice bucket now to have that prepared. While he was at it, he'd set the pretty bonbons on a small silver tray and have them ready to carry into the library. Walt worried if he did that now, the delicate chocolates might melt under the heat of the fire. The library was not just the coziest room in the Christmas Inn, it was also one of the warmest, due to its snug position far from the front door and drafty foyer area.

Walt reached the kitchen with the ice bucket and took care of the bonbons first. He'd tucked them in the fridge temporarily, but they'd be just fine on a tray left in the kitchen. They'd also taste better at room temperature. Next, Walt opened the freezer compartment where the icemaker had two sections. The first was a closed container that fed into the ice dispenser on the outside of the freezer door, and the second was an open bucket in which Walt left a plastic scoop. Since entertaining guests at the inn often meant having to access large amounts of ice quickly, for pitchers of cold drinks and such, Walt had needed to purchase a specialized industrial-style refrigerator unit. The fancy stainless steel appliance coordinated seamlessly with the rest of the kitchen, but it was far larger than a standard refrigerator/freezer.

He pulled open the freezer door with the ice bucket tucked under one arm, after he'd left its lid on the counter. *Now, that's weird!* A carton of eggnog ice cream was sitting on a huge pile of ice and leaning up against the scoop. "How did you get down there?" he asked the inanimate object, reaching for it. That's not where the ice cream belonged! It was supposed to be stored on one of the freezer's shelves, or on one of the shelves inside the freezer door. Walt's gaze traveled to the spot inside the freezer door across from where the eggnog ice cream sat, and his arm froze in midair. *Holy cow!* Something had burst right through that industrial-strength shelf railing! Walt had only seen that happen once. It was when Joy had left a couple of cans of diet soda inside the freezer door to chill, and had forgotten all about them. The cans had exploded with a *bang* so loud it had sounded like a car backfiring in the kitchen.

"Walt! I'm back!"

Walt stood up ramrod straight and shut the freezer door. "Gloria?"

"Uh-huh?" She strolled into the kitchen in her coat and hat wearing a sunny smile. "Ohhh," she said, spotting the tray on the counter. "Chocolates!"

Walt stroked his beard, still puzzling over that ice cream container. There had been something very odd about it, something that sent all his senses tingling. "You're back early! I thought those hen parties went on for hours."

Gloria laughed at his choice of words and removed her hat. "Often they do, but not this time. Savannah had another episode of Braxton Hicks."

"Oh, no!" Walt surveyed her worriedly. "Are you sure it was that, and not the—"

"Yeah," Gloria said, stopping him. "Pretty sure! Savannah's doctor said she's running late. Her baby hasn't even dropped yet."

Walt ran some mental calculations. "So that could mean an extra—week?"

Gloria sighed happily. "Or, two!"

"Oh really?" A smile tugged at Walt's lips. He didn't know when he'd heard better news. "So then, you'll be here for Christmas?"

"I can't very well abandon Savannah. Not after already coming this far."

"I hope you know there's room for you at the inn."

"Thanks, Walt! I appreciate your hospitality, *but*—"

"But, what?"

"I don't want to overstay my welcome."

There was no way on earth Gloria could do that. Walt started to say this, but she barreled on ahead.

"So, I've decided that I'm going to help out."

"What?"

"Around here!"

Walt was transfixed by her penetrating dark eyes.

"You've been treating me like royalty and don't think I don't appreciate it. But, hey. I know how to cook, too."

"I can't let you do that. I'm the innkeeper, and this is my inn."

"No," she said forcefully. "You told me the other night that you didn't view me as a guest."

"I did?" Walt asked, perplexed. "When?"

Gloria rolled her eyes in annoyance. But she didn't appear seriously vexed. More like mildly perturbed. "When you made me the surf-and-turf dinner."

Oh yeah. Now it was coming back to him. That suave comment about him not seeing her as a guest, but rather a beautiful woman he wanted to treat right, or something to that effect. "That was a little different."

"No, it wasn't. It's just the same." She strode right up to him and locked on his eyes in a formidable way, setting her hands on her hips. "I want to cook for you. As a woman wanting to do something nice for a good-looking guy."

Walt felt a rash of heat at his neck and his ears burned hot.

"I'd also like to return the favor to Noelle, too. She has no business working so hard around here, when she's got two jobs besides. Plus, she's got her writing! She's written short stories. Really, really good ones! Did you know that, Walt?"

He stood there spellbound, enjoying her ravishing rant, as she went on and on about how much he and Noelle had done for her, and how it was high time she gave a little something back. She was going to make pancakes, and waffles…breakfast burritos and a very nice frittata. Maybe, if he was good, a wonderful quiche… And, that was only for breakfast! For dinner they'd have all sorts of great stuff, including *arroz con pollo*, *plátanos*, and *piñón*. Not to mention *flan* and *tembleque* for dessert. Because, if Walt hadn't tried any Puerto Rican food yet, he was going to now… It was way past time!

Gloria gave a loud huff and he realized she was done.

"Well?" she challenged with mesmerizing dark eyes. "What do you say?"

Walt swallowed hard. "I'd say you've got yourself a deal."

"Great!" Gloria grinned broadly, then she picked up her hat and left the room.

"Wait! Where are you going?" Walt asked hoarsely. His head was still spinning from her beautiful culinary tirade. He hadn't even known a woman could talk that fast! Much less look positively charming while she was doing it.

"To hang up my hat and coat!" she called back.

Gloria had only been gone a second, when she leaned back through the door. "I can also clean my own bathroom. Just treat me like family!"

Walt chuckled in amazement, as he absorbed the wonder of this magnificent woman. Gloria Chavez sure was something.

Something good.

Chapter Twenty-One

A short time later, Gloria sat beside Walt on the sofa in the library enjoying his company. He'd draped his arm casually around her shoulders as they sipped their scotch and watched the dancing flames of the fire, while romantic candlelight filled the room. They'd been talking over this and that, and telling each other funny stories about their college days.

Walt had wanted to know about Savannah's baby shower, but Gloria had glossed over it, not wanting to mention Savannah telling all those women that Gloria had kissed Walt. Everyone was ecstatic about it, particularly Lou. Lou only showed a moment's hesitation when she'd furrowed her brow and asked Gloria how her boyfriend might take it. Then, Gloria had to tell *another* lie by claiming that she and that boyfriend had broken up. This caused Savannah to stare at her in shock and say, *You're not telling me anything lately! Gosh!*

"Chocolate?" Walt reached over and took a bonbon off the silver tray on the end table beside him, holding it out in front of Gloria.

When she nodded, he lifted a piece of candy and brought it to her mouth, which she opened like an obedient baby bird. Gloria took a tiny nibble and groaned at its richness. "Oh my word. That's fabulous! Where is it from?" He handed her the rest of the morsel and she took it, eating it happily.

Walt grinned handsomely. "Nutcracker Sweets."

Gloria laughed. "I might have guessed."

"I'm glad you had a good time at the party, but I'm sorry that it ended early."

Gloria gazed up at him with a saucy stare. "I'm not."

"To tell you the truth," Walt said huskily. "I'm not, either." His lips brushed over hers, as he gave her the softest, sexiest kiss. Gloria's pulse fluttered.

"How do you do that?" she asked with a breathless murmur.

"It's in my skill set," he growled sexily, kissing her again. This time, Gloria nearly dropped her glass.

"You've got quite a skill set."

Walt gave her one last chaste kiss with his warm and wonderful lips. "Thanks. So do you."

"Oh?" Gloria eyed him carefully and took a sip of scotch. "What's in my toolbox?"

"Just about everything a man could want." His gaze poured over her and Gloria's heart stilled. "You don't know how glad I am you're staying in Christmas Town for Christmas."

A smile trembled across her lips. "I'm glad I'm staying, too."

He lifted her free hand and kissed the back of it. "Thanks for saying you'd go out with me yesterday. I had a really wonderful time."

Gloria sighed happily. "Yeah, I did too."

"We should do something again sometime."

"I'd like that."

"Particularly since you'll be around a little longer."

"Yes."

"There aren't many restaurants in Christmas Town, but the ones that we have here are really good. Is there one in particular you'd fancy?"

"Well...I'd actually like to really try the Reindeer Pub. I hear their pizza's legendary."

Walt laughed heartily at this. "Yeah, that's true. Okay! The Reindeer Pub it is. You're on for a date on the night of your choosing."

"Tomorrow?"

Walt roared with good-humored laughter. "The lady moves fast."

"I'd say the gentleman does, too." Gloria clinked her glass to his, and Walt chuckled again.

"Cheers!" he said, smiling with his eyes.

Gloria blushed happily. "Cheers!"

After a bit, he asked her, "When is that puppet show of Savannah's you were going to help her with?"

"Next Wednesday."

"Anything I can do to help?"

"Come cheer us on."

"Sounds arduous, but I'll train up for it."

"How will you do that?" Gloria asked, giggling.

His gaze was sultry. "I'll spend lots of time looking at you."

"You're not supposed to look at me! But at the stage and at the puppets!"

"I'm very sorry, but—if you're in the room—that won't be happening."

She smiled wryly. "Have you always been this smooth?"

"Nuh-uh, you bring it out in me."

"I'm not sure I believe that."

"Well, believe it. It's true." He nuzzled her neck, and delighted shivers raced down her spine. Gloria threw back her head and gasped breathlessly. "Walt...you're going to make me drop my drink."

"Then, here. Let me set it aside."

Gloria playfully swatted his shoulder. "Stop being such a Romeo."

"Why? You don't like it?" He actually looked a little hurt.

The truth was she liked it too much, and Gloria wanted time. Time to get to know Walt on a serious level. "Tell me about yourself," she said conversationally.

"I already have."

"I want you to tell me more."

He paled slightly.

"Tell me what it was like growing up in Christmas Town?"

"Oh, that?" Walt's expression registered relief, and Gloria wondered why. "Yeah, ha-ha! Sure." So, he told her about himself and his brothers, and the mischief they used to make growing up in their parents' house and around town. He mentioned the beach trips with Savannah's family, and that Sandy and Nick's folks were good friends of his parents, who had visited their family often. And, that Nick's dad, Cole, and his dad, Buddy, were second cousins.

Walt spoke of long, snowy winters, drenched in wintry white; beautifully flowering springs with burgeoning buds and gardens; warm, hazy summers filled with limitless sunshine; and spectacularly colorful autumns, with blazing fall foliage framing the sky. There'd been sledding and skiing…riding bikes to the mountain trails beyond the train tracks…long hikes in the woods, and tubing on the river on hot, humid days. The more Walt spoke of his childhood, the more Christmas Town began to sound like a fairy-tale land.

"What wonderful memories!" Gloria said. "Christmas Town sounds like it was a wonderful place to grow up."

"It was." His blue eyes twinkled. "That's why I returned here after college. I knew it was where I wanted to raise my own family."

"Well, I can't blame you for that! It's really wonderful here."

"How about you and your childhood?"

"Well, there was definitely no snow," Gloria said with a melancholy laugh. "But we sure got plenty of sunshine in south Florida. And, heat. There was no shortage of that!"

"Did you always live there?"

"In the greater Miami area, yes. My parents came there from Puerto Rico before David and I were born. They were already married at the time."

"What do your parents do?"

He must have read her troubled expression, because he tightened his embrace. "Gloria? What's wrong?"

She briefly turned away, not wanting to face him while she confronted the painful memories. "My father was a medical doctor. A family medicine practitioner like your brother Kurt." Walt waited patiently, not commenting on the fact that she was referring to her parents in the past tense. "My mother was an opera singer."

"Professionally?"

"Yes."

"Wow, I'm impressed."

"I lost them both when I was fourteen."

Walt set down their drinks and wrapped his other arm around her. "I'm so, so sorry."

"David was ten and we went to live with my *tia* and *tio* then. Tio Alberto was in the Coast Guard and Titi Mon managed a small jewelry store. They were wonderful relatives. Together, they made a home for David and me."

She turned back to him and there was heat in her eyes, the horrific recollections searing through her. "There was a hurricane, one of the big ones. My parents were in their car, hurrying to get David and me from our school, and home to safety. They shouldn't have been on the road, but they'd been watching the weather reports carefully and believed they had time..." Gloria stopped talking, as her tongue went numb. Then the tears started pouring from her eyes.

"How awful that must have been." Walt hugged her up against him and held her close.

"Families get broken," she said, as her chin warbled. "All the time."

"They do," Walt said gently. "But, Gloria..." He waited until she met his eyes. "They also get mended." Walt stroked back her tears with his thumbs. "I want you to believe that, sweetheart."

She viewed him, teary-eyed. "But how can you say that after what happened to you?"

Walt cradled her cheeks in his palms and said tenderly, "I'm saying that because of what's happened to me. What started happening to me—the moment a gorgeous brunette from Miami arrived in Christmas Town." A warm smile graced his lips. "You've helped me believe again, Gloria, in Christmas magic and happy endings."

Gloria desperately wanted to believe, too. To trust that someone as warm and wonderful as Walt could truly care for her.

"Oh, but I do," he rasped, tenderly bringing his lips to hers. "I can't help myself, or stop this any more than I could stop a runaway train. Gloria Chavez, I'm falling in love with you."

Then he kissed her for such a wonderfully long time that Gloria finally found herself believing, as well. In miracles and new beginnings… And, in following her heart to see where it might lead. "Walt," she said, breathlessly, "I'm falling in love with you, too."

Then, at that inopportune moment, there was a loud *crash* in the kitchen.

Gloria and Walt hurried into the kitchen to find the freezer door wide open! Something had burst out of it and landed on the floor. And, that *something* was…huh? A carton of eggnog ice cream…? Gloria stared at the item agog. Its lid had popped off on one end and shimmering rainbow colors were shooting like darts across the black and white checkered floor. "What on earth?" Gloria's knees trembled and she grabbed the center island to steady herself.

Walk waved a protective arm in front of her. "Stay back! Don't touch it!"

Walt inched forward and gingerly pressed the toe of his shoe against the partially opened lid. It popped off completely and Gloria used a hand to shield her eyes from the glare. Bright colors exploded in the kitchen, filling every corner of the room, and each shimmering light ray danced with fine glittery particles that twirled around in the air, emitting reflections that looked like little sparks. "Walt?" Gloria's voice shook in terror. "What is it?"

He carefully crouched low, resting his elbows on his knees as he leaned forward, squinting all the while. Walt peered into the sideways-turned ice cream carton then addressed Gloria. "Your cookie!"

"What?" Gloria's head spun.

Walt reached for the lid of the ice cream carton, which was now by his foot. He examined it curiously then turned it over in his hands, before knocking on it with his knuckles. "Why, this isn't a real ice cream carton at all! It's made of wood!"

"I know!" Gloria cried in return. "It's one of Noelle's hidey-holes!"

Walt cast the lid aside, and stared back in the open carton. "Well, what do you know?" He cracked a grin at Gloria. "The legend's real."

"What legend?"

"There is definitely something going on with this cookie, and it looks mighty tasty, too."

"Walt, no!" Gloria couldn't believe Walt was thinking of eating it. It was clearly radioactive. Likely, even poisonous… "Stay away from it!"

But instead of withdrawing, he reached into the carton. "Come here, little fellow." Gloria watched with dismay as Walt picked up the cookie and examined it on his palm, surveying the pretty red icing heart and the message written in swirly letters. "'Forever yours'!" Walt grinned dopily. "How sweet is that?"

"Walt," Gloria said as steadily as she could. "I think you need to put it down."

"Put it down? No, why?" He looked perplexed.

"Because..." Gloria heaved a breath. "It might be dangerous."

"I can hardly see the danger in a cookie, Gloria." He walked over and shut the freezer door. "I've been eating them all my life." He thoughtfully eyed the refrigerator, gripping its handle. "Maybe we should have some milk with this?" He turned jovially toward Gloria. "How does that sound?"

Was he nuts? Gloria had to intervene. She let go of the counter and blitzed toward him like a linebacker aiming to sack a quarterback. "Walt, no!"

He clearly didn't understand what she was doing because he lunged forward, attempting to catch her. He missed, though, and Gloria's right shoulder slammed into his chest. So hard he nearly dropped the cookie. Unfortunately, he'd hung onto it. "Ow! What was that for?"

"Give me that cookie, Walt!"

"No!"

She reached for it, but he snatched it away, holding it high above his head, which was really unfair since he was so much taller than Gloria. He peered down at her curiously. "Why do you want it so badly, anyway?" The cookie was still glowing with some really weird light, ribboning out through Walt's clenched fingers as he held it in his hand.

"Because, it's mine!" Gloria said jumping up and trying to grab it. "Savannah gave it…to…me!" But every time she leapt up in the air, Walt frustratingly moved his hand in another direction.

"We can share it then."

"We don't need to share it, Walt. You and I were doing just fine without it."

He stared down at her, obviously convinced by her reasonable argument. "You're right. This cookie's superfluous."

Then he lowered it to his mouth and took a huge bite. "Mmm. Really, really good! You should try this, Gloria."

Gloria goggled at him in disbelief. She didn't even know who to contact for help. Should she dial 9-1-1? Call Kurt? The first thing she had to do was get that contaminated cookie away from Walt, before he sucked down the whole thing like a giant vacuum cleaner. Based on previous experience, Gloria didn't have long to make her move.

"Walt Christmas!" Gloria commanded as firmly as she could. "I want you to give me that Commitment Cookie now!"

He smiled warmly in Gloria's direction and his easy compliance stunned her. "All right. Here you are. Just don't eat it all. Be sure to save at least one more bite for me." His voice grew husky when he said, "That's one seriously delicious cookie."

Sweat swept Gloria's hairline as Walt placed the cookie in her outstretched hand. She was surprised that the cookie felt warm, like it had recently come out of the oven. And, it smelled great, too. Like delicious gingerbread and cinnamon and cloves. Gloria detected a hint of orange too. And oh, how she loved orange-flavored things! *But, no. I will not be tempted!*

"Man!" Walt raked a hand through his hair. "That was good!"

He looked over at Gloria like a lovesick puppy dog. "Cupids. Whoa."

Gloria gasped. *Drugs! There are drugs in the cookie! Oh, no!*

"Love is a drug, Gloria."

"What? Wait…" Gloria took a mental step back to ponder his comment. "Do you know what I'm thinking?"

Walt grinned happily. "Sometimes."

"Nooo…"

"But, don't worry. It's not consistent, or anything."

That was supposed to make her feel better?

Gloria drew in a deep breath. Okay. She was imagining things. "Was there something in the scotch?" she asked warily.

"What? No."

"In the bonbons, then?"

All of a sudden these weird thoughts started popping into Gloria's head.

Eat me. Eat me. Eat me.

And, each time she thought she heard that high squeaky voice, the cookie in her hand pulsed and glowed.

"Guess what!" Walt said cheerfully. "I'm also related to Santa Claus!"

Gloria's jaw dropped. "Are you drunk?"

"*No-ho-ho!*"

"Okay, let me just find a place to put this…" Gloria glanced around the kitchen for some kind of container. Or, *cage*. "Then I'm calling 9-1-1."

"9-1-1? Why?"

But that orange smell kept getting stronger. It was so, so citrusy and enticing. Gloria's gaze locked on the cookie. This had to be some kind of dream. Savannah was her dearest friend. Savannah wouldn't give her something to make her mentally unhinged. She stared up at Walt, the answer dawning. "Ohhh! This is all a big dream!" Gloria glanced around the kitchen, waiting for it to disappear so she could wake up in her bed, laughing off the entire episode.

Only the kitchen didn't disappear, so Gloria didn't laugh.

Walt watched her worriedly. "You don't have to eat the cookie if you don't want to. Why don't you give what's left back to me?"

Gloria didn't think she should do that. Dream or not, Walt seemed like he'd had plenty. He sauntered in her direction and held out his hand. "Come on, I'll take it."

"I don't think you should have any more."

"I'll save it for later."

"I wasn't born yesterday, you know."

Walt kept moving toward her, so she backed up a step. Then another one, and a third…until her lower back was against the center island and she had nowhere else to go.

Walt cocked one dark eyebrow. "Give me back the cookie, Gloria."

"No."

He grabbed for it, but Gloria was faster—popping the whole thing in her mouth. She didn't know why she'd done it. Base instinct, maybe. Besides, her mouth was the closest hidey-hole she'd had at hand.

Walt eyed her curiously. "I thought you didn't want it?"

"Mmm...ndnt..." Gloria mumbled between clenched teeth. Then, the most amazing thing happened. The cookie starting melting on her tongue. And...oh! *Oh, my! Wow...* Gloria gripped the counter behind her, feeling faint.

Walt viewed her with concern, as a whole rainbow of flavors dazzled Gloria's taste buds. This was fabulous, fabulous stuff! "Walt!" she cried enthusiastically. "I see what you mean! This is one seriously delicious cookie. I've never tried anything like it!"

"I know! And, I've made tons of cookies in my time." He paused thoughtfully. "And milk, too, actually."

Gloria had no clue what Walt was talking about. She only knew that he looked really, really handsome. Maybe even more handsome than she'd ever seen him looking before! So what if he thought he could read her mind, and that he was related to Santa Claus? This was all a nutty dream, anyhow. Gloria might as well enjoy it. She'd certainly enjoyed the other dreams she'd had about Walt. And, they'd all been *very* lurid. *Reeoww.*

"Gloria?" Walt asked worriedly. "Why are you looking at me like that?"

"Like what?"

"Like you're the mouse and I'm the cheese?"

Did he really have to mention mice right now? Seriously, how unromantic.

Walt's neck flushed red. "I...honestly didn't mean it that way."

Big red hearts seemed to be floating in the air—all around Walt's head. Oh! And there was another one, a straggler probably, down by his knees. They all had cute Valentine-type lettering on them that said: Love Me.

Gloria gripped Walt's face in her hands, giddy at the feel of his ultra masculine beard. "Of course I do!"

"Of course you do *what*?"

"Love you, you silly man!"

"Well, that's pretty great." Walt pulled her close and Gloria's heart beat harder. "Because I love you."

"Kiss me, Walt," she said in a throaty whisper, and Walt did.

Boy oh boy! It was one of his good ones! Gloria felt herself moving up...up...up in the air. Then, she realized he'd grabbed her by the waist and had hoisted her up onto the counter. Gosh, he was talented! And so virile, too! Manly to the max!

"Gloria," he said, wrapping his arms around her. "You drive me crazy."

"And, you're so insanely hot!" she yelped as he trailed kisses down her neck and nibbled at her ear. Gloria sighed and moaned, pulling him even nearer...until she could tell he was just as excited about the situation as she was.

"I haven't been with anyone in a long time," he said between ravenous kisses.

"Mmm. Mmm. Me either." He was devouring her and she was devouring him. Gloria didn't imagine they'd have any trouble remembering what to do from here. All she knew was she wanted him *even closer* than he was now. And, probably naked.

Gloria wrapped her legs around him and Walt groaned. "You're asking for trouble, woman."

"I hope I'm going to get it."

Walt gave a hungry growl. "Just tell me where."

"Back in my bedroom," Gloria said, panting.

Walt grinned sexily and Gloria's temperature skyrocketed.

Then he swept her off of the counter and into his arms.

Walt woke up the next morning with his arms around a beautiful woman. His heart beat double-time when he realized the woman was Gloria. What an amazing night they'd had. Wow. Phenomenal.

She stirred under the covers and Walt held her closer. He was spooning her from behind and there was nothing between them but skin. "Are you awake?" she asked groggily.

"Yes." He lightly kissed her shoulder and Gloria giggled.

"Your beard tickles."

"That's what you kept telling me last night."

Gloria playfully swatted his arm. "You bad boy."

"You told me I was awfully good."

"Well, I'm not telling you again. You'll get an ego problem."

"My problem's not my ego," he said, wiggling up against her. "It's lower."

Gloria gasped and rolled over to face him. "I can't believe how naughty you are," she said, clearly teasing. "For someone related to Santa Claus that's bound to be an issue."

"Gloria. About that—"

"Did you know you also said you could read my mind?" Her dark eyes sparkled. "How much scotch did we have?"

"Sweetheart, it wasn't the scotch."

"No?" Her eyebrows rose and it was all Walt could do not to think of making love to her all over again. Very. Very. Slowly.

"Gloria." He gently laid a hand on her cheek. "There are a few things I need to tell you."

"All right." She yawned cheerily. "But can we have some coffee first?"

"Coffee?"

"Oh! And maybe a little of that fab OJ you make, too?"

Walt warmly kissed her lips. "Anything your heart desires."

A short time later they snuggled in bed, sitting up against the headboard with pillows propped behind them. Walt was the world's most perfect man, in Gloria's eyes. Not only had he brought hot coffee and freshly squeezed orange juice, he'd prepared hot buttered croissants for her as well. Some of them were *chocolate*. Gloria was almost sorry Savannah hadn't hooked back up with Kurt sooner. If she had, then she would have suggested Gloria get together with Walt

298 A Glorious Christmas

much earlier. "The service here is excellent," she told Walt with a grin. "Five stars!"

Walt chuckled warmly and sipped from his coffee. "Most of the guests don't get this kind of breakfast-in-bed treatment."

"Let's hope not!" Gloria said. Then she giggled. "I'd be awfully jealous."

He patted her thigh through the thick blankets. "I know you would, sweetheart. And, no worries! You're the only VIP I'll cater to in this...extremely personal manner."

"Well, good!" Gloria set down her coffee mug, reveling in the beautiful morning. She'd been floating on air ever since waking up next to Walt. So many great things had happened in the span of just a few days. From Walt's superb surf-and-turf dinner, to that romantic sleigh ride... The intimate conversation between her and Walt when they talked about their childhoods... Then, ultimately, they had admitted their feelings for each other.

Then there'd been last night in bed! Walt packed a punch in the sack, and she was still on a hormone high from having experienced it. Gloria opted to focus on these happy thoughts, rather than ponder certain oddities that couldn't be explained. Like those weird occurrences in the kitchen.

Even though Walt said it was not the alcohol, Gloria couldn't think of any other explanation for some of those wacky things she'd thought she'd witnessed. Gloria was not a very big drinker, and she'd had two scotches on top of a glass of white wine at Savannah's shower. That certainly could have been enough to push her over the edge.

Walt reached out and warmly took her hand. "You're a very important person to me, Gloria. Maybe more special than you know."

Walt was always saying nice things, which it made it impossible not to love him. She shot him a sunny smile. But, for some reason, his expression was terribly serious.

"I probably should have told you last night. Before we…" He hung his head. "It would have been the gentlemanly thing to do."

Gloria's heart thundered. What on earth was he talking about?

"I guess I got carried away in the moment. I was so blasted happy when you said you loved me that I…maybe made the wrong choice."

Icy fear coursed through Gloria's veins. "Choice?" she asked weakly.

He gripped her hand tightly and didn't let up. "It should have been your decision, and not mine."

"What?"

"Whether or not you wanted to move forward in spite of the truth."

The truth? What is he, sick? Dying? Oh my goodness, no! Gloria sent him a sidelong glance. *A wanted criminal perhaps, hiding here under an assumed name? No! That doesn't make sense! Everybody knows him. Or…or, maybe they're just pretending, and Walt's in the Witness Protection Program, living here under an assumed name!*

He turned to address her squarely. "Darling, it's none of those things. Truly."

Gloria gaped at him. "What?"

His gaze resonated sincerity and his words were measured and calm. Even as absurd as they were. "Gloria. I can read your mind."

"You're psychic!" She cupped her mouth in shock. Then, after thinking momentarily, she quickly said, "But...that's okay! I'm sure plenty of people are. They just don't talk about it. And, reasonably so."

Walt seemed to be weighing his response. "That's not exactly it."

Gloria viewed him wide-eyed, and her heart hammered. "You're not going to repeat the Santa Claus bit."

"I know how hard it is to believe. Very few people do anymore."

"Walt? Is that what you think? That you're Santa Claus?" She scooted back a little, worried he'd hear her thinking: *He's out of his ever-loving mind!*

Walt stared at her sadly and Gloria clapped her hands over her temples. She wasn't sure how ESP was transmitted, but she figured it didn't hurt to be careful.

"You can put down your hands. It's not going to help."

When she eyed him doubtfully, he continued, "It's not all the time, anyway. Just sporadic, like I said."

Gloria slowly lowered her arms and gazed at him. "So, you can do this with everyone?"

"No. Only with you."

"Me? Why me?"

"Because you're special somehow. For me, like I am for you. We bring out certain abilities in each other."

"No. That's not true."

"You knew Olivia was with me."

"What?"

"And, it made you fighting mad. Somehow you sensed that she and I were doing something 'romantic' together. Isn't that right?"

"Yes, but…why would that happen, and how?"

"You and I were starting to become connected, and you psychically intuited a threat." He quirked a grin. "Although your intuition was a little off the mark."

"Nothing like that has ever happened to me before."

"You have other abilities, too."

"No, nuh-uh."

"When you arrived that day, and the mail blew around like crazy? You helped cause that correspondence storm."

"I did *not*."

"At first, I thought it was just me. But later, I came to realize that having you around magnified my skills."

"Your 'skill set.'" Gloria gasped. "What else is involved?" She couldn't believe that she was asking, but decided to go along with it for now, just to see what Walt would say. *I don't care if you heard that!*

Walt chuckled and shook his head. "I can put out fires and so can you."

"No, I can't…" Suddenly, Gloria remembered. "In the library?"

"I never said I was Santa Claus. I said we were related. The Christmas and Claus lines go way back. Distantly, we come from the same family tree, so we share common DNA."

Gloria listened raptly as he went on. This was all so incredible. But, maybe it was making sense. In a crazy Christmas family way.

"Certain abilities have been transmitted through those DNA markers."

"Who has these abilities? You? Kurt? Your parents?"

"Not my mom. I inherited them through my dad's side."

"Your girls, then? Noelle and Joy?"

"They'll likely develop skill sets, too, but they may not know about them yet. Except for in rare circumstances, these abilities tend to surface only under one condition." He waited to be sure he had her full attention. "In the face of true love."

"Oh!"

"Gloria." He was holding her hand so tightly it was starting to go numb. "The power you have over me is very, very strong. And, you almost found out too early."

"What do you mean?"

"You saw certain things you shouldn't have. It was right after you'd gotten here, and it would have freaked you out, so I…" He hesitated, sounding very uncomfortable about it. "Had to wipe your memory."

"You *wiped* my memory?" Gloria tugged her hand away and massaged it. "Like my mind was some kind of thumb drive? Oh! My! Gosh!" Fury rose up inside her, raising its beastly head. "You're unbelievable, Walt!" She sprang from the bed, taking the top quilt with her and wrapping it around her body. Gloria heatedly stormed toward the window then began pacing back and forth.

"I'm sorry. I apologize!"

She glared at him fiercely. "Well, apologies aren't enough! I want them back!"

"What?"

"My memories, Walt! I didn't give them to you willingly. You robbed me of them! You're a thief! A memory thief!"

Walt's face was a storm of emotions. "I don't know if I can do that."

"Well then, I don't know if I can believe you! Or any of your cockamamie stories!"

She stormed to the closet and took out her suitcase, setting it on the bed. Then, she went to the dresser and started yanking things out and shoving them in the suitcase.

Walt threw back the covers and climbed from the bed. He'd put on his boxers before going to make the coffee, and there were stinking reindeer all over them. Santa's relative! Ha! Gloria was so flaming mad she didn't know where she would go. She just knew she didn't want to stay here with Walt Christmas and his pack of holiday lies!

"I'm not lying," Walt looked like he'd been run over by a truck and that truck was her, but Gloria didn't care. Seriously? He'd wiped her memory? Of what? That was positively scary.

Walt's shoulders sagged. "All right," he said hoarsely. "I'll try."

Gloria stopped what she was doing, which was trying to fold her high-heeled fashion boots up in a way so they fit in her small suitcase. "What do you mean you'll try?"

Walt sighed heavily. "To give you back your memories. I need to warn you, though. I've never tried it before."

This seemed to unnerve her. "What if I don't like them?"

"What?"

"These memories that you return to me? What if they're ugly?"

"I was worried that you might think that...which was why I erased them in the first place. I was trying to protect you, Gloria. Thinking the exposure might be too much."

"Exposure to what?"

"Christmas magic!"

Gloria squared her shoulders, causing the quilt wrapped around her to slip. She yanked it back up and held it against her. "You listen to me, Walt. Nobody decides for me what I can handle or not, okay?" Next, she spoke a little more calmly, yet still firmly. "I'd like my memories back, please. If you can give them to me."

Walt sighed heavily. "Okay, then come sit beside me on the bed."

She did and he placed his palms on her temples.

"What are you...?"

"Shhh. Just close your eyes and think back..." One of his palms slid around to her forehead while the other cradled the back of her head. "Think back to that day in the library when you came home from shopping with Savannah."

"After seeing you at Jolly Bean Java?"

"Yes."

Gloria did and she was walking down the street, approaching the Christmas Inn. Then, she was coming in the door, and Walt was talking to someone. No! He was training a pet of some kind, maybe a dog.

"Now tell me what you see?" Walt urged softly.

"You're talking. Giving commands. I'm thinking maybe you've gotten a dog, or are fostering one."

"Go on."

"I'm going into the library to say that I'm back and—oh! Oh my!"

"What do you see, Gloria?" he whispered huskily.

"The letters! They're dancing! And standing and obeying your every command." She swallowed hard and tried to open her eyes.

"Keep your eyes closed for just another minute. What happens next?"

"I'm asking you about it, and you're making up some silly story about a projector in your desk and I know there's no projector because of what I saw—"

"With your own eyes?"

Gloria nodded in amazement. "Yes."

"And, then?"

"I'm asking you about it, wanting you to explain things... and you, oh! Oh!"

Her body sagged and Walt supported her with his arms, his palms still pressed to her head. "What's going on?"

"I'm looking in your eyes, and you're taking me far away to someplace beautiful. There's sun and sand and wind, and the sound of the ocean crashing nearby." Gloria swallowed hard. "And, it's not the first time. We've been there before."

Walt set his chin on her shoulder. "Yes."

He slowly lowered his hands and wrapped his arms around her, which was probably a good thing, because Gloria felt like she was about to pass out and tumble off the edge of the bed.

Gloria turned to Walt, searching his eyes. "Noelle came home then. She called us and we were back. That's when I passed out, wasn't it?"

"The experience was too much. I was afraid for you, Gloria, because I didn't know you then like I know you now. Now, I know how strong you are. I also know that you are right and I was wrong. It wasn't my call, and I'm sorry, even though apologies can never be enough."

"When I looked in your eyes and we were in another place, where was that?"

"Somewhere in our minds that the two of us wanted to go to be alone together. Our perfect mutual space."

"So you saw the same things?"

"Yes."

"And felt them, too?"

"I did."

"And when you kissed me in the mistletoe forest?"

"You rocketed me to the moon."

"Wow. This is heady stuff."

"I understand it's a lot to process."

Gloria thought long and hard about what Walt was telling her. "Right before I passed out in the library, I remember seeing something on the floor—and on my boots. Did I bring that back with us somehow?"

"Yes."

"But how was that possible?"

"It's rare but it happens, when the connection is very strong." He held her tighter. "Our connection, Gloria, is like a titanium bond."

"Wow, I had no idea."

Gloria didn't know what to think or feel. It was all so surreal, yet starting to make sense. But all she had were her own strange memories to rely on and Walt's word. If only she had physical proof. "What happened to that sand? The sand that I brought back?"

"I cleaned it up. It's in the wastebasket in the library."

"You haven't emptied it?"

"Not yet."

"Will you bring it to me?"

Walt studied her worriedly. "Are you sure you're okay for me to let you go?"

"Yes."

Walt slipped from the room and returned minutes later with the library wastebasket in his hands. He carted it over to Gloria and she peered down inside it. There wasn't much to see. Some crumpled-up sticky notes, a discarded real estate flyer, and another piece of junk mail. She lifted each carefully and peered down at the bottom of the wastebasket. Walt tipped it sideways to afford her a better view. Way down at the bottom, Gloria spotted some tiny taupe beads. She reached down and lightly touched them, pinching up a few grains between her thumb and forefinger. Then, she set the miniscule brown balls in her palm and carried them closer to the light. "It's sand," she said, in a breathy whisper.

Walt set down the wastebasket and went to hold her as Gloria's arms hung limply at her side. She stared up at him in awe. "You were telling the truth?"

His blue gaze washed over her as he cupped her chin in his hand. "Yes, my darling."

"So...you really aren't like other men."

"In some critical ways, no."

Walt stared down at her with longing, love, and, mostly, hope.

"Does that make a difference?"

"Yes."

He looked shattered, but then Gloria reached up and stroked his beard. "It only makes me love you more. You told me the truth, Walt. About yourself and your heritage, and that took courage. I also forgive you for wiping my memory. While I don't approve, I understand why you did it, and I accept your apology. I only have one more question for you."

When his brow rose, she asked him, "What happens now?"

A single tear glistened in his eye, a tear of gratitude. He lowered his mouth toward hers and Gloria sighed as he rasped, "Anything your heart desires."

Then, his lips met hers, and her doubts melted away.

Chapter Twenty-Two

The next several days passed in a happy blur for Gloria. She and Walt developed a new routine of taking turns with meal preparation and only letting Noelle help out occasionally, when she had something special she wanted to make, like one of Gloria's Puerto Rican dishes, which she had great fun learning about. Noelle teased that when she was done writing fiction, she was going to compile a cookbook, and include the delicious recipes Gloria had shared.

Walt and Gloria's bond kept getting deeper, too. They had excursions into town, thoroughly explored the studios in the Grand Hotel, and also took in the school art show hosted in the ballroom. The ballroom was an awesome space and Gloria could imagine it with music playing and people dancing at the annual Christmas Town Ball. Walt had invited her to go with him on the spot, and Gloria had readily agreed. She'd already packed a dress for the occasion and had a pair of shoes and a purse to match.

Savannah's belly grew larger every day, and Gloria had a standing date to visit her at four o'clock each afternoon for coffee—or, decaf in Savannah's case—

when they weren't planning to meet otherwise for lunch or to work on puppet show planning. By now, everyone in town knew that Gloria and Walt were an item, and all were warmly supportive of the pair. Even though Gloria maintained she was going back to Miami after Savannah's baby was born, people seemed to dismiss her plan as idle talk. "Oh, you'll decide to stay!" Liz had said, her dimples deepening. "Mark my words! Those Christmas men are awfully hard to resist!" Then she'd added with a giggle, "According to Savannah."

Gloria had worried initially about telling David she was seeing someone. She didn't know how he would take it, given that she was here on a temporary basis. But David had surprised her with his good humor and encouragement. He'd quipped that if Gloria had to go all the way to East Tennessee to find a decent man, then that was a sorry commentary on the state of eligible dudes in Miami. His sweet and funny assertion had made Gloria laugh and warmed her heart. She really did miss her brother a lot. She missed Gitana, too. And yet, there was just something so magical about being in Christmas Town. And, there was definitely a lot that was magical about Walt.

She'd lightly broached the topic of Christmas family abilities with Savannah, and Savannah had opened up about Kurt, but just a little bit, staying vague about the particulars. This was okay with Gloria, because Walt had asked her to keep information about his "skill set" in confidence, as well, and she was honoring his wishes. How could she not? When he'd been so forthcoming and wonderful to her? One thing that she and Savannah shared and agreed on was that they were both involved with dynamite kissers. They'd laughed and giggled over this for hours—to the point where Savannah told Gloria they'd better stop, lest they induce a bout of Braxton Hicks.

The puppet show came and went, and was a tremendous success. Walt arrived to offer his support, and just as he'd promised, his eyes never left Gloria the whole time he was there. Gloria smiled, thinking about how much she loved him, and how quickly things were moving along. She'd finished up her school duties by computer, while also preparing for Christmas in her spare time. She had gifts for Savannah, Kurt, and her new friends, and had picked out something special for Walt and Noelle. Not wanting to leave Joy out, Gloria had also purchased a present for her, and had mailed it all the way to Italy while she was sending packages to David. Now, here it was—Christmas Eve! And, tonight was the Christmas Town Ball!

Gloria had joined Walt and Noelle for the sweet family Christmas service at the Corner Church at five. The small stone church with the high white steeple had been packed to the gills with local citizens. Gloria met the town deputy, Victoria Cho, for the first time, along with her husband, Frank, and their darling son, Bobby. Jade had been there, too, and introduced her husband Wendell, as well as their precious boys, Alexander and Josiah. Sandy and Ben Winchester had been there as well, with their polite preteen daughter, Lily, and a set of beautiful—yet impish—toddler twins girls named Holly and Rose, who kept trying to stir up trouble by tossing toys from their diaper bag around during the service.

As Gloria exited the church, the kindly older minister had taken her hand, wishing her a merry

Christmas and urging her not to be a stranger in Christmas Town. She, Walt, and Noelle had returned to the inn to have a light snack, before getting ready for the ball. Gloria was extremely excited about attending the fancy party, especially as she'd have Walt on her arm. Most everyone in town was going, apparently, even very pregnant Savannah, who'd had to buy a special new dress for the occasion just last week.

Gloria twirled around, examining her reflection in the dresser mirror. The long, red ball gown with glittery sequins had a low V-neck with a sultry halter top, and hugged all her curves snugly. She had sparkly gold sandals and a matching handbag to go with it, and Liz's darling Commitment Cookie barrette was clipped to the right of her side part, with her dark tresses secured tightly in chignon above her nape. Long glimmering gold earrings with strands of tiny stars complemented the look.

Gloria sighed happily and sat on the bed hugging one of her pillows. It smelled deliciously of Walt because he slept here nearly every night, though they were carefully discreet about it. Both agreed it was fine for Noelle to know they were dating, but she didn't need evidence that they were sleeping together. So, Walt set his phone alarm for five each morning and stole quietly up to his family apartment, where he later showered and dressed for the day, as he normally would have otherwise.

Someone knocked on the door and Gloria looked up, pulled out of her reverie.

"Can I come in?" It was Noelle's voice.

"Of course!"

Noelle appeared, an absolute vision in midnight blue. Her short velvet dress had cap sleeves and a high turtleneck collar. Her golden hair was up in a messy pile on her head that looked stylishly tousled. She wore small pearl earrings and a single gold ear cuff. Her long legs were in sheer black tights and her feet were tucked into chunky shoes with square heels and big gold buckles. She looked like a model straight out of a fashion magazine.

"Wow, Noelle!" Gloria said, standing to observe her more fully. "You look stunning!"

"Thanks, Gloria!" She smiled sweetly, appearing and acting so grown-up that Gloria wanted to cry. While Noelle wasn't her daughter, they'd already formed a special bond. Noelle had confided to her earlier that Devon Slade had asked her to go with him to the ball, platonically. Although it wasn't a romantic date, she'd hesitated at first since Devon was Joy's former boyfriend. She'd talked to Gloria at length about it, and Gloria had urged her to have an open dialogue with her sister. She had, and Joy—"being Joy," according to Noelle—had told Noelle to go for it.

"I hope you have a great time at the ball tonight," Gloria said, grinning. "I'm sure we'll see you there."

Devon was picking Noelle up soon, and Walt and Gloria were going to ride over together a little later with Kurt and Savannah.

"Thanks, Gloria. I hope you and Dad have a great time, too." She beheld Gloria a long moment, before continuing further, "You've been really good for my dad. He's smiling again and singing in the shower."

Gloria giggled. "Singing in the shower?"

"Oh, yeah."

"What does he sing?"

Noelle's eyes twinkled brightly. "'Angels We Have Heard on High.'"

Gloria chuckled with delight. "Seriously?"

"Seriously."

Noelle surprised her with a warm hug, but the young woman's words moved Gloria even more. "Thanks for making Dad happy."

Heat prickled Gloria's eyes, and she didn't know what to say. All she could do was hug Noelle tighter.

The doorbell rang and the women broke apart. "That must be Devon," Gloria said, trying to conceal a sniff.

"Yeah, I guess so. Well! See you, Gloria!"

And then, Noelle was gone...causing Gloria to feel *so* conflicted. She loved David dearly and had helped look after him forever. Although he was now a grown man, they had no other kin in Florida, and Gloria would feel horrible about abandoning him in Miami. But, how could she ever leave Christmas Town, and Walt and his wonderful family? How?

A little while later, Walt rapped lightly at Gloria's open doorway. "I was wondering if you'd like a glass of wine, while we're waiting on—" He stopped talking when he saw her and his jaw dropped. "Wow! Just *wow*, Gloria. You're gorgeous."

Her eyes swept over his tuxedo shirt and bowtie. He'd left his jacket over the back of a chair in the library. "You look pretty dashing yourself!" She strode forward and gave his lips a quick peck. "Merry Christmas Eve, Walt."

"Nuh-uh," he said, his eyes sparkling. "You're not getting off that easily." Then he took her in his arms and gave her a proper kiss.

"Walt," she said, sighing. "You'll mess up my makeup and hair."

"Yeah." He cracked a grin, assessing her again from head to toe. "But, what a way to go."

She laughed and shook her finger. "Naughty, naughty."

"Who, me?" Walt threw open his arms. "I'm the original nice guy!"

"Don't I *know-ho-ho* it!"

He glowed at her admiringly. "Say, you're pretty good."

One hour later, Walt escorted Gloria up the steps to the Grand Hotel. Savannah and Kurt were ahead of them, with Savannah complaining relentlessly that her feet hurt in those shoes, and asking Kurt whether she looked fat in her dress. Gloria gave Kurt an A-plus for answering Savannah's inquiries the same way, every single time: by telling her she looked fabulous.

The moment Gloria entered the glittering ballroom, someone handed her a glass of champagne. Savannah asked the waiter for nonalcoholic bubbly and he went and retrieved some at once. There were so many friendly faces in the room, and the foursome went around greeting them all cordially. They saw Buddy and Lou, Jade and Wendell, and Olivia and Nick. Sandy and Ben said their hellos, and Hannah's husband, the handsome dark-haired sheriff, Carter Livingston, offered a firm handshake and warm smile. Though Gloria had previously met Olivia in Miami, this was her first time meeting Savannah's green-eyed big brother. It was her first time meeting Sandy's handsome dark-haired, dark-eyed brother Ben, too.

Gloria also spied Noelle chatting with Devon across the way, and the couple smiled and waved, seeming in good spirits as they talked with other young people their age. The only friend of Savannah's Gloria couldn't spot was Liz Martin. "Where's Liz tonight?" Gloria asked Savannah when they paused to pluck some wild mushroom and goat cheese crostini off an outstretched tray. The men had walked on ahead to visit with Ray, who was standing alone while his wife chatted with a woman in her twenties with short black hair.

Savannah took a nibble of food then waved her napkin. "Liz doesn't come to these things."

"No? Why not?"

"She says she can't." Savannah frowned sadly. "Not until she finds her true Prince Charming."

"Really?"

Savannah nodded. "Liz's words, not mine."

"But, she's so cute! I can't believe she's not seeing anyone."

"Liz has lots of gumption," Savannah said. "Tons going for her, too. Unfortunately, she doesn't always believe that."

"That's too bad. Good women are hard to find, and Liz seems so genuine."

"She is!" Savannah cocked her chin. "I wish that I could think up someone for her."

"When did you become such a matchmaker?" Gloria asked, giggling. "You didn't used to be this way."

"Since coming to Christmas Town, I suppose. The happiness here is contagious." Savannah lifted a shoulder. "I guess once you've known it for yourself, you want to share the love." She said this on a sigh, and Gloria could feel the warm tingles spilling off of her.

Walt returned to Gloria, looking scrumptious. "Well, what do you think?"

"I think this is a fantastic party."

He gazed down at her and grinned. "Would you care to dance?"

Gloria glanced toward the back of the room, where a string quartet was beginning to reassemble after an apparent break. Behind them, a large mural lined the wall. It was of an old-timey Mr. and Mrs. Claus dancing happily beside a lit Christmas tree. For the life of her, Gloria thought Mrs. Claus looked like an older version of Olivia. Gloria smiled when she saw it, wondering what the story was behind that painting. "I'd love to!"

When Walt took her in his arms, she asked him, "Who did the mural?"

"Sandy, of course!"

"I should have guessed that."

Gloria laughed merrily, feeling happy and light in Walt's strong arms, as the music began to play and he guided her effortlessly around the dance floor. "Thanks for bringing me to the ball," she said. "I feel like a fairy princess."

His appreciative gaze said everything. "You look like one, too."

"Oh, no!" A woman's shrill cry caused the music to come to a sudden stop. All eyes turned on Savannah, where she stood in Kurt's arms. They both looked down at the floor, and everyone else in the ballroom looked down with them.

A large puddle of water pooled at Savannah's feet.

"Okay!" Kurt said, rubbing his palms together with a pleased grin. "Looks like this is it!"

Savannah latched onto his arm and moaned. "Kurt, ohhhh!"

"I don't think that's Braxton Hicks," Walt said to Gloria.

"I'll grab my purse."

The four of them piled into Kurt's SUV, with Savannah whining loudly up front. "It's coming! Kurt! The baby's coming!"

Kurt shot a panicked look at his brother in the back seat.

"Right," Walt said, with immediate understanding. "Let's switch! I'll drive and you sit with Savannah back here."

They made it to the hospital on time and, six hours later, Savannah's eight-pound baby was born. According to the doctor, this was some kind of Christmas miracle, as first babies typically didn't come that fast. Kurt motioned Walt and Gloria into the birthing room, and when Gloria saw Savannah, joyful tears sprang from her eyes. She'd never seen Savannah looking so happy, or so beautiful.

"Here," Savannah said, holding the tiny bundle in Gloria's direction. "Want to hold her?"

Gloria took newborn Julia in her arms, saying how adorable she was.

"Look at those tiny fingers and toes!" Walt said in utter awe. "Time moves so fast." He draped his arm around Gloria's shoulder, and Savannah and Kurt didn't miss the interaction. "I'd forgotten that Noelle and Joy were ever that size."

"They were even smaller!" Kurt said. "Your twins were born early."

Walt reached across the bed and shook his brother's hand. "Congratulations, Dad!"

Kurt grinned proudly. "Thanks. It feels good."

The sun was just rising when Kurt dropped Walt and Gloria off at the Christmas Inn.

"Thanks so much for being there, guys." Kurt had morning stubble and he sounded hoarse, but he looked like a guy who'd just won the lottery. Walt supposed in many ways he had. Kurt had a loving wife and a beautiful new family. Walt gazed longingly at Gloria. *What more could a man want?*

"Many congratulations, Kurt." Gloria smiled his way. "And, merry Christmas."

"Merry Christmas, Gloria! To you too, bro!"

"Thanks!" Walt soundly patted Kurt's shoulder. "Now, go home and get some rest."

Gloria stepped out of her shoes the moment they walked through the front door. Walt supposed her feet must really be aching by now. She'd dressed for a glamorous gala, not a night of midwifery. Though Walt knew from the happy glow on Gloria's face that she wouldn't have missed being at the hospital for the world.

"We should probably get a little shut-eye before Christmas morning."

"It already is Christmas morning," Gloria said with a wan smile.

"Yeah, and given that…"

"It's all right," she said softly. "Why don't you go take a nap upstairs?"

Walt kissed Gloria "goodnight" and began to head into the kitchen and toward the back staircase. Then he noticed Gloria wasn't walking down the hall and directly toward her suite; she was heading into the library. He cautiously tiptoed after her and peered through the door from the living room just in time to see Gloria opening her small purse. Then, she withdrew a little slip of paper and tucked it reverently into Rose's stocking.

Chapter Twenty-Three

When Gloria awoke four hours later, she smelled bacon frying in the kitchen. She showered and dressed in a white turtleneck and jeans, and wore her more sensible brown leather boots. She pulled back the curtains to see it was gloriously snowing outside, and stood there a few moments to appreciate the steady barrage of pretty white flakes. Gloria couldn't think of a more perfect place to be on Christmas morning than in Christmas Town and at the lovely Christmas Inn. The handsome innkeeper here and his sweet daughter made the accommodations that much more special. Gloria was excited to give Walt and Noelle their gifts, and also participate in the tradition with Rose's stocking.

Walt had said she was welcome to join them when they tossed their private messages to Rose into the bonfire, and Gloria had taken that as her cue. She'd sent her own private message to Rose early this morning when they'd returned from the hospital. While Gloria didn't want to intrude on the family tradition, she felt there was so much she needed to say. Gloria was grateful to Rose for the lovely family she'd helped build, and also for the time she'd spent in loving her daughters and Walt. When Noelle had thanked Gloria for making Walt happy, the comment had touched her heart. Gloria understood then—on an even deeper level—the important contributions Rose had made in this house. Gloria also wanted to ask Rose's permission, as well as her forgiveness, for capturing Walt's heart.

When Gloria entered the kitchen a short time later, she found Walt standing at the stove. He'd just finished with the bacon and had started making scrambled eggs. The oven light was on and the tasty scent of cinnamon rolls filled the air. "Good morning," he said with a handsome smile. Walt wore jeans, hiking boots, and a red Christmas sweater. With that special twinkle in his deep blue eyes, Gloria had never seen him look more appealing.

She strolled over to where he stood and planted a kiss on his cheek—right on that hairy beard. "Good morning!" she said brightly. "Merry Christmas."

Gloria walked to the coffeepot and poured herself some coffee. Everything was more casual now and Gloria helped herself. "Did you sleep well?"

"Like a rock," Walt said with a chuckle. "How about you?"

"Very soundly, too." She smiled and took a seat on a stool by the center island, near where he was cooking at the stove. "Can I help you?"

"You can pour the orange juice in a bit." He grinned happily. "It's fresh-squeezed."

Gloria sighed contentedly, savoring her coffee. "Thank you, Walt. You're a prince." Gloria glanced around the kitchen then through the door into the dining room, and the other to the hall. "Where's Noelle? Still sleeping?"

Walt shook his head. "She's stoking the fire pit out back. I got it started a little while ago, and she's adding a few more logs."

"What time did you get up?"

"About an hour ago."

Walt finished making the scrambled eggs then transferred them to a warming dish, which he popped in the bottom section of the double oven. Gloria saw that the timer on the top oven had ten minutes left on it. "The cinnamon rolls will be out in a few."

"Oh Walt, they smell delicious."

"We'll have just enough time to go out back for a bit."

"Sounds good," Gloria said, knowing he was talking about the family tradition.

"If you'd like to refill your coffee, you can bring it along. I'll go grab Rose's stocking and our coats."

A few minutes later, they stood outside with Noelle around the blazing fire pit.

"Good morning, Noelle," Gloria said. "Merry Christmas!"

"Merry Christmas, Gloria." Noelle smiled softly. "I was so excited to hear about Savannah's baby. A little girl!"

"Yeah."

"She's a tiny nugget," Walt said. He gazed fondly at his daughter. "Just like you were."

"We're going to Skype later with Joy," Noelle told Gloria. "Do you want to join in?"

"Sure! That would be great." She felt so happy to be included. "I'd love to say hi to Joy."

"She wants to meet you, too," Noelle replied. "And, say merry Christmas."

Noelle stared expectantly at her dad and he passed her Rose's stocking. "Would you like to do the honors?" he asked.

"Sure." She accepted the stocking matter-of-factly, like she'd done this many times before. Then Noelle dipped her hand inside and pulled out some slips of paper. "Hey, there are four messages this time?"

Heat warmed Gloria's cheeks as she admitted shyly, "I put one in, too." She looked at the others with an embarrassed flush. "I hope that was all right?"

"Of course it's all right," Walt said soothingly. He wrapped a supportive arm around her shoulders. "Thank you for doing that."

"Yes, thanks," Noelle said. "That was really nice of you, Gloria." She balled the papers up in her fist and said, "We've been doing this for years."

"Ten, to be exact," Walt added.

"Yeah," Noelle agreed. "It's been a *long* family tradition." She shot a look at her dad, and some kind of silent communication passed between them. Noelle turned to Gloria and smiled. "Joy texted me her message yesterday, so I could put it in Mom's stocking for her."

"It's very touching how you all remember your mom this way."

Noelle nodded and glanced at her dad. "Ready?"

"Yes, go ahead."

Noelle opened her hand and tossed the four folded-up pieces of papers into the fire. They ignited spontaneously, crackling and instantly burning up. The three of them stood there in silence, pondering the flickering flames, until Walt uttered softly, "Goodbye, Rose."

The mood lightened when they went back indoors and had a cheery breakfast at the kitchen table, laughing over stories about the ball—and their mad dash to the hospital with Kurt and Savannah. Noelle filled them in on the fun that had occurred after they'd gone. Buddy and Lou had done a compelling jig, holding court on the dance floor, while others fell back to observe them twirling expertly around the ballroom. They'd secretly been taking ballroom dance lessons, and had stunned the crowd with their smooth moves. Everyone had been extremely impressed, and had applauded soundly.

Gloria giggled at the picture this painted in her mind. "I'm glad the ball was such a success."

"Most everyone goes," Walt said, and Gloria thought of poor Liz, sitting at home by herself, while all of her friends had fun. If David had been in town, Gloria might have asked him to escort Liz to the ball, just to give her a chance to get out and enjoy the good times. David was such a kindhearted man, Gloria was certain he would have said yes. Thinking of David made Gloria recall she'd scheduled a merry Christmas phone chat with him a little later that afternoon.

"It sure seemed like a full house," she commented.

"Yeah," Noelle said. "It was packed." The excitement still shone in her eyes from attending the event. It was the first formal dance she'd been to, besides high school proms, and Gloria could tell by the way Noelle talked about it that she'd had a very good time.

Walt finished eating his eggs and took a sip of coffee. "The best part about the Christmas Town Ball is that it benefits charity. The proceeds go to the Lena Winchester memorial fund, and toward the ongoing restoration of the town."

Gloria had seen the donation jar in the foyer when they'd entered the Grand Hotel and had noticed both Walt and Kurt tucking checks inside it. She guessed these additional funds were added to the monies raised from selling tickets.

"Not just to town restoration, Dad," Noelle said lightly. "To other good works, too. Like our new soup kitchen."

"Yes, that's true. It's only been in operation now a couple of years."

"Thanks to Lena!" Noelle said, mentioning Hannah's late great-grandmother, who first believed in bolstering the flagging spirits of the townspeople when she started her cookie shop near the end of World War I. When Hannah came to Christmas Town to follow in Lena's footsteps, all sorts of great improvements started happening for the town.

"Thanks to Lena!" Walt agreed, raising his coffee mug. He smiled pleasantly around the table, seeing the ladies had finished their breakfasts. "What do you say? Should we carry our coffees into the library? I believe Santa left a few presents under the tree."

Walt couldn't remember being this excited about Christmas in a long while. He felt like he had when his girls were small and he couldn't wait to see their eyes light up at the sight of their bulging stockings. He still loved it that Noelle and Joy got so excited about the trinkets he bought for them. And, they hadn't outgrown liking candy, although their tastes had gotten more sophisticated. Walt had mailed Joy's stocking gifts and a few other presents to her in Italy a few weeks before, and he had some extra special items picked out for Gloria.

Noelle held her stocking on her lap, as they sat by the fire, examining its contents: the little bobble-head reindeer, the funny snowman socks, and the petite package of exquisite goodies from Nutcracker Sweets.

"Thanks, Dad!" She was grinning as she unwrapped the small box that had also been in her stocking. She opened it, seeing it was a thin gold chain necklace that held a pretty teardrop pearl on a dangly pendant. "Gosh, it's beautiful," she said, goggling at the piece of jewelry. "Thank you."

He smiled at her, pleased by her reaction. "I thought it might match those earrings you have."

"Perfectly!" she said, rising to hug him around the neck.

Noelle handed him some packages, and he chuckled happily at his new snowflake-patterned tie and the nice new set of pens she'd gotten him. "Thanks, Noelle. I love these."

Walt handed a medium-size box to Gloria. "What's this?" she asked, holding it up.

"Something to remind you of our date to the puppet show."

Gloria giggled happily. "That wasn't a date, Walt."

He eyed her carefully. "Oh yes, it was."

Noelle stared back and forth between the two of them and grinned. "Go on," she encouraged Gloria cheerfully. "Open it."

Gloria did and found the most darling marionette puppet on strings inside. It had long, wavy dark hair, bright pink cheeks, and big brown eyes. The puppet's dress was a flowing white gown, and she had shimmery wings and wore a golden halo.

"It's an angel!" Gloria proclaimed with absolute delight, making her dance.

"Aww, Dad," Noelle said, acknowledging her father. "She's so cute!"

"She reminded me of you," Walt said to Gloria. "The instant I saw her."

"Well, I love her!" Gloria cradled the puppet to her chest like a doll. "Thank you." She rose and gave Walt a kiss on the cheek, and he smiled. "I'll hang her in my office back at school as my mascot."

This brought silence to the room.

"When do you have to go?" Noelle asked sadly.

"Well, I'd only planned to stay until after Savannah's baby was born, and her mother's coming to help out tomorrow. So, I'd say..." Gloria purposely avoided Walt's gaze, because it hurt her heart too much to look at him. "Sometime in the next couple of days."

"I wish you could stay through the New Year," Noelle said. "You probably don't have to be back at school until after the first, right?"

"That's true, but—"

"I agree with Noelle," Walt said warmly. "I think you should stay." When Gloria met his gaze, he added more emphatically, "I want you to stay, please."

Gloria's heart beat madly because that was what she wanted, as well. To spend more time in Christmas Town, and specifically with Noelle—and Walt. "I'd hate to be an imposition—"

"You won't!" both Walt and Noelle said almost in unison, and Gloria giggled.

"All right, you two. I'd love to." She smiled sweetly at them both. "But I'll need to double-check with David about him staying on a little longer to pet-sit."

They nodded at her reasonable caveat and Gloria got up and walked over to the Christmas tree. "Now, I have something for the two of you!" Gloria said brightly. She reached under the tree, and retrieved a package and an envelope. She gave the package to Noelle and handed the envelope to Walt.

Noelle opened her present first, turning the thick tome over in her hands to peruse its jacket copy. Her eyes sparkled as she read the book's title aloud: *Great Women Writers throughout Time.* "Gloria, how special."

"I hope you don't have it?"

"No, no. It looks so cool! I've heard of most of these people, and I've read some of their work. Are these mini-biographies?"

"Yes."

"Excellent!"

"Jade helped me find it for you." Gloria grinned cryptically. "First she had to look at the schedule to see when you weren't working, so I could come in."

Walt appeared very touched, as Noelle stood and hugged Gloria tightly.

"Now, your turn," Gloria said to Walt.

He eagerly opened his envelope and grinned from ear to ear. "What do you *know-ho-ho*? I've been subscribed to the 'Cookie of the Month Club'!"

Noelle rolled her eyes and smiled at Gloria. "What a *perfect* gift."

"Thank you, Gloria," Walt said. "I know I'll enjoy it."

He lifted a small oblong package off the end table beside him, handing it to Noelle. "Here's one more gift for you, daughter."

"But you already gave me the beautiful necklace."

He twinkled at her. "What's Christmas without a few surprises?"

Noelle excitedly removed the wrapping on her gift. "A new smartphone! *Yusss!*"

Walt roared with pleased laughter at Noelle's delighted reply, and Gloria laughed happily, too. Noelle gave her dad a big hug, and then hunted under the tree.

She passed a pretty red package to Gloria. "This one's from me and Joy," Noelle said. "I got it at Olivia's shop."

Walt winked at Gloria at the mention of Olivia's name and she giggled at their private joke.

"Why thanks, Noelle. How sweet! I wasn't expecting anything from you girls. I'll be sure to thank

Joy later, as well." Gloria shook the box and something rattled inside. "Hmm. Sounds mysterious."

Noelle watched expectantly as Gloria slid off the ribbon. Walt watched her closely, as well. "Okay…" Gloria said, pulling back the wrapping. "Let's see what's in…here?" She removed the lid of the box and then pried back the folded tissue paper. A totally gorgeous handmade Christmas stocking nestled inside. "Oh! Oh, my!" Gloria felt moisture building in her eyes. "It's wonderful." She turned to Noelle. "Thank you so much. I haven't had a Christmas stocking in years."

"We got one for Dad, too," Noelle said, twinkling at her father.

Walt appeared gobsmacked. "What? You did?"

Noelle beamed brightly. "Yes, Dad. We did." She gave both adults an impish smile. "They're matching."

"Oh, well." Walt leaned forward on the sofa and clasped his hands together. "How nice!"

Gloria viewed them both with confusion, before Noelle prodded her further. "Why don't you try it out?"

"Pardon?"

"Try hanging it up?"

"I don't… I'm not sure I understand?"

"Right over there, in that spot," Noelle said, pointing to where Rose's stocking had been.

"Oh no, I couldn't," Gloria said, feeling overwhelmed. "I mean… That's where your mom's stocking goes."

"Not anymore," Walt said and Gloria turned to him.

"What?"

"I agree with Noelle." His deep voice rumbled.
"I'd like to see how your stocking looks hanging there."

Gloria darted a glance at Noelle and then at Walt,
speaking tentatively. "You're sure?"

He gave her the softest, warmest smile.
"Absolutely."

Gloria gently lifted the stocking out of the tissue.
Oddly, it felt heavy, like there was something down
inside it. Gloria curiously held it up and detected a boxy
form down in its toe.

"Would anyone like some fresh coffee?" Noelle
asked from out of nowhere.

Gloria blinked at her, then stared back at her
stocking, transfixed.

"Coffee's a fine idea! Thanks for making it,
Noelle!"

When Noelle left the room, Gloria turned to Walt.
"Walt...?"

"Seems like Santa left a little something in your
stocking this year." His blue eyes sparkled and—for a
split second—Gloria felt faint. Could this really be
what she thought it was?

"Well?" he asked tenderly. "Don't you want to see
what it is?"

Gloria held her breath, her heart blooming with
hope and happiness, as she dug her hand down into the
stocking and extracted a small black velvet box.
"Walt?"

Instead of answering, he slid the coffee table
forward and out of the way and dropped down on his
knees beside the sofa. When he took Gloria's hand,
tears sprang to her eyes.

"Gloria Chavez, you're the most wonderful woman I know. From the first moment I laid eyes on you, I knew you were different, and boy was I right. Because of you, sweetheart—" He gave her a tender look. "I'm a changed man. My whole world makes sense again, but my world can't be complete without you."

He kissed the back of her hand and continued. "I love you, Gloria, and I want you to be my bride. I want us to live together and grow old together—right here in Christmas Town. If you have to go back to Miami to finish the year, I'll understand. Just don't make me wait too long before we can become husband and wife. Say you'll marry me in Christmas Town in springtime, when the first dogwoods bloom. Because the spring of our love is eternal."

Tears streamed down Gloria's cheeks, as she beheld him: this incredibly kind, loving, and thoughtful man, the man that she adored with all her heart. "Oh, Walt," she said, her voice trembling. "That was beautiful."

He steadied her chin in his hand and gave her a soft kiss. Then he motioned to the velvet ring box. Gloria opened it and was dazzled by a radiant diamond surrounded by pretty red rubies. She'd never seen an engagement ring as stunning as this one. The ornate gold setting appeared to be ages old.

"It was my great-grandmother's ring," he told her. "The one who first owned the Christmas Inn."

Gloria loved it, but she stared at him questioningly, a moment's hesitation in her heart.

"Rose never wore it," he said, intuiting her worry. "She wanted a simple solitaire. I didn't even own this ring until this year."

334 *A Glorious Christmas*

"This year? What do you mean?"

"My dad had it in his bank box. When I told him I was going to ask you to marry me, Dad thought you might like this family heirloom as your engagement ring, so he gave it to me. I was hoping your answer would be yes."

Gloria pursed her lips as another stream of tears poured down her cheeks. Walt tenderly wiped them away. "Darling," he said, asking her a second time. "Won't you say yes?"

"Yes! Yes! Oh yes, Walt." Gloria's heart leapt and her spirit jumped for joy.

"You won't mind leaving Miami? I know that was a concern for you?"

"We'll find a way to work it out," she answered, believing they would. Then, she fretted over her dog. She couldn't have the poor animal displaced a second time. "And, Gitana?"

"She can come live here."

"Really?"

"Everybody loves a Labrador. She'll be an asset to the inn."

Walt grinned and slid the ring on her finger. It was a little loose, but otherwise looked gorgeous. "We'll have it sized for you," he said. "So it fits just right."

"We fit just right," Gloria said, sniffing happily. "The two of us together, don't we? I mean, all of us do."

Walt's gaze washed over her and Gloria felt swept away. "We're becoming a new family."

"I like that idea," Gloria said. "Very much."

Walt kissed her firmly then got off his knees and joined her on the sofa.

"Now, tell me," he said, taking her hand that wore the pretty engagement ring in his. "Where would you like to go on our honeymoon?"

Gloria didn't have to think about it for more than a minute.

"Italy!" she said gleefully. "I'd like for us to go to see Joy in Florence. And, take Noelle with us."

Walt quirked a smile and then his grin broadened. "That can be arranged."

"Oh yeah?"

He pulled her close and took her in his arms. "Yeah."

"Can we visit Rome and Venice, too?"

Walt gave her the most dashing smile and Gloria felt the wind lift her hair, and warm sunshine on her face. Somewhere in the distance, gulls called, and far, far away, waves rhythmically pounded the shore.

"Anything your heart desires," he said, giving her a kiss.

The End

A Note from the Author

Thanks for reading *A Glorious Christmas.* I hope you enjoyed it. If you did, please help other people find this book.

1. This book is lendable, so send it to a friend who you think might like it so that she (or he) can discover me, too.

2. Write a review at the site where you purchased this book and at Goodreads.

3. Sign up for my newsletter so that you can learn about the next book as soon as it's available. Write to GinnyBairdRomance@gmail.com with "newsletter" in the subject heading.

4. Come like my Facebook page: https://www.facebook.com/GinnyBairdRomance

5. Follow me on Twitter: @GinnyBaird.

6. Visit my website for details on other books available at multiple outlets now: http://www.ginnybairdromance.com.

This Christmas won't you come home to Christmas Town? Keep up with the series by reading Liz and David's story next. An excerpt from A Corner Church Christmas (Christmas Town, Book 6) *follows.*

Come home this Christmas to...
CHRISTMAS TOWN, TENNESSEE
Where everyday dreams come true!

**New York Times and *USA Today* bestselling author
Ginny Baird continues her heartwarming holiday
series...**

A CORNER CHURCH CHRISTMAS
(Christmas Town, Book 6)

When good-looking David Chavez comes to Christmas
Town to serve as the local pastor, the last thing he
envisions is becoming attracted to one of his
parishioners. Pretty Liz Martin is talented at more than
handicrafts and caring for babies during her day job at a
nursery. Shy Liz is also adept at turning outgoing
David's head. Yet—after years of romantic
disappointments—Liz has given up on finding true
love. Then special seasonal cookies lend a hint of
holiday magic to happenings at the Corner Church, and
Liz starts to wonder...if she can dare to believe in
miracles and happy endings.

Prologue

It was a perfect spring day and church bells rang merrily, sending their happy tune winging over Christmas Town. The surrounding lawns were verdant green and the sky burned bright blue. Big, billowy clouds accompanied the sunshine, and every single dogwood tree was in bloom. Liz Martin stood with the crowd outside the small stone church with the high white steeple, wearing her pretty yellow floral-print bridesmaid dress and clutching her bridesmaid bouquet. Liz's curly brown hair was tied up in a loose knot and she'd applied a modest amount of makeup: a sweep of blusher on her cheeks and some mascara framing her golden brown eyes. Twenty minutes ago, her special friend Gloria Chavez had married Christmas Town innkeeper Walt Christmas.

Walt's pretty twin daughters, Noelle and Joy, stood on the far side of the entrance waiting for the bride and groom to emerge from the Corner Church. Both college-age girls were tall, willowy blondes with big blue eyes like their dad's. For a time, Noelle had worn glasses, but since she'd switched to contacts, Liz had trouble telling the girls apart.

After group photos in the chancel, Gloria and Walt had remained with the photographer for their couple's shots. Soon, they'd be off on their honeymoon to Italy! Walt had flown Joy home from her year abroad in Florence, so she could attend her father's nuptials, then the newlyweds and Noelle would return to Europe with Joy for their first family vacation together. Part of the time, Noelle would stay with her sister in Florence, while Gloria and Walt visited Venice separately. Liz suspected that's when the real honeymoon would begin.

"Beautiful service."

Liz looked up to see Gloria's great-looking younger brother standing beside her. He'd been in the wedding, too, and none of the ladies in the church had been able to keep their eyes off him. David Chavez was tall, dark, and definitely handsome, with swoon-worthy brown eyes and an obviously athletic frame. He was also ten years younger than Liz, and a minister.

"Yeah," Liz answered. "Gloria and Walt seem so happy."

"I suppose that's what happens when the right people find each other."

"That's what they say!" Liz's heart beat faster just standing next to the gorgeous guy. She hadn't dated in forever, and had practically forgotten how to behave around single men, especially really chatty ones.

Since Walt and Gloria were keeping things fairly low-key, they hadn't held a fancy rehearsal dinner. Walt's parents, Buddy and Louise, had hosted a nice meal at their house instead. The group had mostly consisted of the wedding party. Walt's dad, Buddy, was his best man, and Walt's two brothers, Ray and Kurt, had served as groomsmen, as had Gloria's brother,

David, and sheriff Carter Livingston, who was an old friend of the Christmas family.

Carter's sister and Kurt's wife, Savannah, had been Gloria's maid of honor, while Liz, Walt's two girls, and Ray's wife Meredith had rounded out the bridal party by serving as bridesmaids. Carter's wife, Hannah, had also attended the dinner, and she'd been a huge help to Lou in the kitchen. Unfortunately, David had missed the party due to work obligations in Miami. He'd arrived in Christmas Town late last night, after the rehearsal dinner had ended, but in time to make this morning's ceremony. He was staying at the Christmas Inn.

"I'm sorry I can't make the reception," David said, referring to the wedding celebration Gloria and Walt had scheduled for summertime. Since Walt's girls and Gloria, a teacher in Florida, had to get back to school after the end of next week, Walt and Gloria had opted to hold their nuptials now before a short wedding trip, then have a big barbecue-style event at River Run in June. Everyone in Christmas Town was invited.

Liz turned to David briefly, and then quickly looked away. Each time she caught his warm brown eyes on her she blushed. "Oh?"

"My church has a youth mission trip then, and I'm one of the adult chaperones. We've been planning it for nearly a year now, so it would be hard for me to back out."

"I see! Well gosh, that's too bad." Liz was sorry for Gloria, but selfishly she wondered if that wasn't better for her. David Chavez made her way more nervous than necessary, given that he was simply being friendly. Warm breezes blew and Liz picked up the scent of his cologne, all masculine and spicy, and her pulse pounded harder.

A big commotion stirred near the front of the church and Liz saw its front doors swing open. Gloria appeared in a spectacular white gown with Walt on her arm. They were a stunning couple and so well suited to each other. Liz loved it when relationships worked out. She was a real romantic at heart, even though she hadn't found her true Prince Charming.

"Jumping jelly beans!" she cried excitedly. "Here they come!"

David quirked a grin. "'Jumping jelly beans'?"

Liz's cheeks steamed. "Um, yeah. It's just a little expression." She turned toward the church as the wedding guests cheered. Walt and Gloria hurried down the stone steps while eco-friendly confetti—shaped like tiny white hearts—rained down on them.

"I'll want to give my sister a quick hug before she goes," David said.

"Of course." Liz wished to say her goodbyes to the departing couple, too.

"Well, David. It's been nice being in a wedding with you."

"You too, Liz."

His gaze roved over her, and Liz nearly tripped on her feet in the two-inch heels she wasn't used to wearing. "Have a safe trip back to Miami!"

"Thanks. Though, I'll be back in Christmas Town soon."

Naturally, that made sense, with his sister living here. While Gloria and Walt were doing a long-distance marriage initially, Gloria intended to move to Christmas

Town permanently at the end of her teaching semester. "I know Gloria and Walt will love having you visit."

"I won't just be visiting."

Liz's forehead rose as they waited in the congratulatory line that had already formed by the bridal couple. "What do you mean?"

"Haven't you heard? I'm taking over at the Corner Church when Pastor Wilson retires in December."

Liz nearly swallowed her tongue. "Is this a recent development?"

"Fairly recent. The Corner Church's search committee reached out to me about a month ago, but I only confirmed with Pastor Wilson this morning. It's an interim position, for a year. We've got a divinity student coming on board at the church where I'm an associate pastor in Miami, so the timing works out."

"How great!" Liz hated that her voice sounded squeaky and kind of like a cartoon character's. "I guess you'll be living at the parsonage?"

David shook his head. "Pastor Wilson will remain there until February, while he's making arrangements to move in with his daughter and her family in Maryland."

"So, where will you be staying, then?" Sweat beaded Liz's hairline as she anticipated David's answer. *Please say the Christmas Inn. Please, please, please.* There was only one other guest accommodation nearby: the rental unit right beside the townhome Liz occupied at Sisters' Row. Or rather, where she would be living again after the renovations there were completed this summer.

Liz had barely been able to handle participating in a wedding with David for a few *hours*. If he moved in next door to her, she'd be seeing him all the time. Liz felt *so* embarrassed by her secret attraction to David. She'd heard of women being cougars, but she'd never expected to become one herself. Not that this was going to be happening, not in the least. Because Liz was *never* going to let David know she found him interesting and alluring. She'd positively die first, and they'd have to bury her in that small cemetery on the far side of the hill at River Run.

Then another hopeful possibility occurred to Liz. Maybe one of the parishioners had offered to put David up? When she asked him about this, David chuckled warmly and Liz's insides turned to melting marshmallows, the kind that dissolve in hot cocoa. When it's really, really *hot.* "I'm far too independent for that," he said. "I like having my own space. I'll be renting a town house at Sisters' Row."

Sugar plum fairy! Liz's bridesmaid bouquet slipped in her slick hands. Fortunately, she caught it before dropping it completely, and held on tight.

"It's a very short walk from here," David went on to explain. "Right down North Main Street."

Liz nodded, feeling paralyzed, and David surveyed her worriedly as the line inched forward. "Hey, are you all right?"

"Yeah! I think I'm…still overwhelmed from the ceremony."

"I know what you mean." David shared an enigmatic smile and Liz wished he'd stop doing that. Taking her breath away at every turn. She glanced around, seeing Kurt Christmas conversing happily with Savannah. At least there was a doctor on the scene, in case Liz fainted or something. She surely hoped that wouldn't take place, but Liz couldn't say for certain.

The sun was beaming brighter and she was feeling lightheaded.

"Liz! David!" Gloria called out to them with open arms and a sunny grin. "You two come over here and give me a hug!"

Liz couldn't wait to do that and share her best wishes with Gloria and Walt. Then, she was going straight back to her brother's house, where she was living temporarily, and taking a very cold shower. Probably even washing her hair, too. And maybe, wringing out this dress.

A short time later, the happy couple drove off with Walt's girls in the SUV that they'd had waiting, and David turned to Liz.

"Well, Liz. It's been great meeting you. I guess we'll be seeing each other around?"

"Yeah, uh-huh!" was all she managed to say. But, on the inside, Liz's misbehaving heart was beating wildly.

~*~ End of Excerpt ~*~

A Corner Church Christmas

Made in the USA
Columbia, SC
08 October 2018